GIRLS OF YELLOW

GIRLS OF YELLOW

a novel by
OREST STELMACH

"Everyone is in favour of free speech. Hardly a day passes without its being extolled, but some people's idea of it is that they are free to say what they like, but if someone says anything back, that is an outrage."

SIR WINSTON CHURCHILL

Dhimmi – a person living in a region overrun by Muslim conquest who is accorded a protected status and allowed to retain his or her original faith.

.

CHAPTER 1

Major Sami Ali knew he'd been assigned the dhimmi's murder because he was the worst detective on the Budapest police force. And he understood exactly what his boss expected him to do—use minimal departmental resources to conduct a basic investigation, find no evidence of religious cleansing, and bury the case.

Ali knew such a weak effort rendered him a fraud and he didn't care. Pride didn't pay his daughter's tuition. His job was to follow orders and provide for his family. Also, his father had made him take an oath as a child to hate Christians and Jews for the rest of his life. He didn't give a damn about the dhimmis.

The body had been found at the Matthias Catholic Church, one of only three remaining Christian churches in the section of the city known as Dhimmi Town. Gothic spires decorated with gargoyles towered above a diamond-patterned roof, green and brown ceramic tiles glittering in the sun. Ismael, the crime scene technician, was kneeling beside the corpse near the altar when Ali arrived inside. His friend reminded Ali of a mongoose—unassuming at first glance, but pity the snake who dared to test his mettle.

"First comes Saturday," Ismael said.

"Then comes Sunday," Ali said.

The salutation had originated in the Middle East during the early twentieth century, long before the third world war, the collapse of governments and economies, and the migration of survivors toward people who shared the same faith.

First we'll take care of the Jews, who pray on Saturday, and then we'll take care of the Christians, who pray on Sunday.

The old prophecy had been fulfilled in Arabia. Then, after Muslims flooded Europe, Sharia law had been enacted throughout the continent. Only the dhimmis prevented the prophecy from being true in what was now known as Eurabia, too.

And now there were one fewer dhimmis.

Ali couldn't see the corpse. Ismael was hovering over it, blocking his view.

"What are we celebrating?" Ali said.

"Death by strangulation," Ismael said.

"What? No machete?"

"No blood. He strangled her with his hands."

"No blood. You've got to be kidding… Wait. Did you say *her*?"

"Bruising on both sides of the neck but no actual prints. He must have worn gloves."

"Signs of struggle?" Ali said.

"None that I can see."

Ismael stepped back to reveal a girl's corpse, a lithe figure with hair the color of sun-drenched wheat. "Look, A. She can't be more than fourteen or fifteen."

"Ish," Ali said. The first syllable of his friend's name was the only sound he could muster because the sight of the girl had taken him to the place he hoped to never revisit.

"What a waste," Ismael said.

Ali's childhood memories were secured in an impenetrable vault protected by imaginary barbed wire, steel walls, and padlocks. Whenever something or someone prodded the vault, its protective devices tightened. This time, however, its defenses disintegrated and the locks sprang open. Out streamed the vision he loathed so much it made him long for sudden death.

It was all in the past, Ali tried to tell himself, but no one could detect a lie more easily than a cop, even a lousy one. A similar-looking girl was lying before him. And she, too, was dead.

"The eyes," Ismael said. He reached over and lifted the dead girl's eyelids. "You see the eyes?"

They looked like aquamarine jewels.

Of course Ali had noticed the eyes, as surely as he'd noticed the girl's oval face, alabaster skin, and golden locks. It wasn't their beauty that shocked Ali and Ismael, but rather their presence in their sockets, because the typical religious cleansing involved their removal. *Lower your head*—submit to Islam—*lest your eyes be snatched.*

Ismael nodded for Ali to come closer, then glanced in both directions to make sure the other two technicians taking pictures of the church interior couldn't hear him.

"She wasn't killed here," Ismael said. "She was brought here after the fact."

"How can you be sure?"

Ismail lowered his voice further. "Because there was a witness."

Ali lost his breath. "A witness?" There were never any witnesses in Dhimmi Town, at least none brave or stupid enough to come forward.

"The caretaker who called it in. He was here when the killer brought in the body. Point of entry, front door. Point of exit, front door."

"He saw the killer?"

"He was taken to headquarters to give his statement and for his own protection. But I don't think it's his protection your boss will be worried about. Especially not with the world leaders in town for that conference. Think about it. The heads of all four kingdoms—the Buddhists, Hindus, Christians and us—all in the same place. Can't have religious cleansing when the religions are trying to find a way to get along, can you?"

Ali heard the question and understood Ismael's point. His boss wanted the case buried quickly. But that mattered less to Ali than Ismael's previous implication, that the higher-ups would do everything necessary to make sure the witness was silenced. To Ali's own amazement, something compelled him right there and then to do everything in his power to make sure the witness was heard.

But was he too late?

Ali told Ismael he'd be in touch and rushed out of the church. As he ran toward his car, the call to prayer sounded. It was the second such call of the day which meant it was just past noon. The sound of the Muezzin's mellifluous voice always slowed Ali's pulse, drained him of angst and sorrow, and lifted his spirits. The thought of not stopping whatever he was doing to contemplate the substance of his Islamic beliefs five times a day was unthinkable.

Yet that's exactly what he considered doing the moment the initial call sounded. The image of the dead girl from his youth gripped him so tightly that he wanted—no, he needed —to begin a thorough investigation of this girl's murder immediately. One death bore no relation to the other. More than twenty-five years had past since the first girl had died. The victims merely resembled each other.

Ali realized this but it made no difference to him. To say that he'd failed the first girl was a gross understatement. He couldn't contemplate repeating the mistake. Did he even have the skills to solve a murder? Ali wasn't sure himself. The other cops called him the Dhimmi Lover precisely because he had no love for them. It was a joke well-known throughout the force. What would they say if the worst detective in Eurabia started acting like a real police? The Dhimmi Lover actually trying to solve the murder of a dhimmi? They'd all get a laugh out of that one.

When the second call came for prayer to begin, Ali didn't stop to face Mecca. Instead, he climbed in his car, hammered the gas pedal and raced toward the station. Never before had he thought of the streets of Dhimmi Town as his own. Who in his right mind would want them?

But they were his, he realized, whether he liked them or not, just as surely as he was among the few Muslims not prostrating themselves before Allah in the capital city of the central region of the Eurabian Caliphate.

Ali hoped like hell no one recognized him behind the wheel.

CHAPTER 2

When Elise De Jong arrived in Budapest a week ago, the call to prayer was a giant pain in the ass. The first call came before daybreak at five o'clock in the morning, right when she was trying to squeeze out her last hour of sleep before rising to get ready for work. Fat chance of that happening with a man whining in Arabic over a loudspeaker. But much to her shock, within a week she changed her mind. The man delivering the prayer was obviously a performer of the highest order, and what she initially considered to be whining became a hypnotic song that woke her up briefly and then lulled her into two more hours of delicious sleep.

After maintaining pretenses and praying with the rest of the city after noon, Elise pedaled furiously to Ottoman Health Network's offices. Women weren't allowed to drive cars in Eurabia. Even worse, no woman under the age of forty-five was allowed to go anywhere without a male escort. Driving was considered an inducement to low morals, while appearing in public unescorted at a child-bearing age was considered to be a sexual provocation. The woman's religion wasn't relevant. Sharia—Islamic law that prescribed religious and civil duties and penalties for disobedience—applied equally to dhimmis and Muslims. Elise was ten years too young to be out alone, and with her unblemished skin she looked even younger. As a result, she wore a *burqa,* the most concealing of all the Islamic coverings for women that included a mesh screen over her eyes.

Elise had done her research last night after work, when she'd tailed Dr. Rudolph Qattan to the Southern part of Pest, which was located east of the Danube. There she discovered a labyrinth of shops catering to those in need of things that were not supposed to be available in an Islamic state. Rubbish gathered at gutters as though neither state nor shopkeeper wanted to be accountable for them. The Saudis owned the stores, the Filipinos brewed the moonshine, the Pakistanis distributed the drugs, and Lebanese-Syrians trafficked in Far Eastern pornography called "Super Films." Arabians loitered on the sidewalks, not a single European face among them. At least that's what it seemed like on the outer rim of the maze of sin.

In fact, the deeper one ventured into the labyrinth, the lighter the skin became. The Middle East had portrayed Western women as sexually obsessed deviants for centuries. The disinformation had worked. First-timers to the inner maze were shocked to learn that the women were in it for the cash, not the sex. Italian and Greek girls from Western Eurabia beckoned from green-lit doorways, and when the lights turned red, the Southern Pest's most exotic sexual offerings revealed themselves—the Scandinavians. In fact, they were mostly Eastern European women masquerading as Scandinavians, but their clients either didn't know or didn't care. Many Muslim men paid a week's wages to have sex with a Swedish woman—or a reasonable body double—preferably with a cross dangling from her neck. Wearing a cross in public was a crime punishable by death, thus the prostitute's wearing it heightened the man's sense of power and pleasure. An hour with a cross-wearing, Christian goddess was the most expensive offering on Southern Pest's menu of forbidden indulgences, and lines stretched long for the best performers.

Qattan didn't lead her to the row of seamy doorways populated by the willing, white amazons of Western Eurabia. He led her *beyond* that place, where he engaged in an indulgence so immoral and forbidden that it would have taken a court less than sixty seconds to produce a guilty verdict. Elise photographed him going in and out of the unmarked door and later returned and interrogated the owner. One flash of her genuine-looking police credentials was all it took to win his complete cooperation. He told her everything she needed to know, escorted her into the back room, and let her take pictures of the goods in question. When the owner asked her what would happen to him and his business, Elise told him she would give him a pass for his cooperation with her investigation into the customer in question. He sobbed with gratitude.

Elise entered Ottoman Health offices after arriving by bicycle and found the waiting area looking like a hospital emergency room. A seventeen-year-old had arrived with her face slashed from ear to mouth, her eye sockets bashed in, and a knife protruding from the right side of her chest. Doctors and office personnel were shouting instructions to each other and scrambling to administer first-aid while the girl lay on the floor in shock.

It turned out she had escaped her attacker and run to her doctor's office because he was the only man she trusted, and she feared her assailant would find and kill her if she went to the hospital. Her assailant was her fifteen year-old brother, who'd tried to murder her with his parents' blessing to punish her for being raped a week earlier. The family had even planned a feast for this evening to celebrate its cleansing from the shame their daughter had brought upon them by being defiled against her will.

Muslims, Elise thought. What a savage people.

Qattan was a handsome man in his mid-forties with a square jaw and a neatly trimmed beard that matched his brown hair. He might have been the former lead singer of an Islamic boy band if such an enterprise hadn't been punishable by death. He was one of the doctors who treated the girl. He didn't throw her out of the building for breaking the law by showing up without a male escort, which she had done. He put her health first, and for this he earned Elise's respect.

Unfortunately for him, she was still going to ruin his life. She wished she could achieve her personal objective without making him suffer, but there was no other way. He was her last hope.

"*As-Salaam-Alikum*," Elise said, before sitting down in his office. The traditional greeting from one Muslim to another meant *peace be unto you.*

"*Wa-Alaikum-Salaam*," Qattan said. *And unto you peace.* He flashed an uncertain smile. "It's always a pleasure to meet a new patient. Who was it again that referred you to us?"

"Fate."

"I don't understand."

"It's a Hindu concept."

"I beg your pardon?"

"Last night. In the Southern Pest. We almost met in the store deepest in the maze. The one where weak men go to purchase the kind of depravity that brings eternal shame, that ruins them and their families."

"Who are you?"

Elise opened a leather wallet that featured a badge on one side and an ID on the other. The ID was embossed with the seal of the Eurabian Caliphate. Along with the badge, it identified Elise as Kawlah Ahmed, senior officer of the Commission for the Promotion of Virtue and Prevention of Vice, also known as the morality police.

The badge was real. The ID, with her picture laminated beside the seal, was a quality forgery.

Elise snapped the wallet closed and slipped it back into her pocket.

"Happy St. Valentine's Day," she said.

Qattan's lower lip began to tremble. "Oh, no."

"You bought thirty-six red roses, three teddy bears, and three heart-shaped boxes stuffed with chocolates made in the country formerly know as Belgium for your three wives. By doing so, you conspired with the shopkeeper to celebrate the life of a Christian saint and a holiday that encourages immoral relations between men and women."

"Oh, Allah."

"The punishment for promoting Christianity is death." Elise remained silent for a moment to allow the gravity of his situation to set in. "Let this be a lesson to you in your final days as a physician. A man needs virtue when he wants it the least."

Qattan nodded.

"However, in your case," Elise said, "there may be a chance for redemption."

His eyes lit up. "Redemption?"

"A concept that all the Abrahamic religions share. Christians, Muslims and Jews alike."

"Excuse me?"

"Yes, well, we'll see about that. I need your complete cooperation, Doctor, regarding a matter of great importance to the Caliphate."

"You have it."

"When was this office founded?"

"It predates my arrival. Two of my senior partners opened it. It's going on ... twelve, thirteen ... no. Fourteen years ago."

"That's consistent with our records," Elise said. "And as part of the services you offer to your most valued clients, you provide a full medical examination of any slaves acquired from conquered territories."

"That's correct."

"For instance, if a female slave is acquired, the proper uterine examination is made to determine if any pregnancy exists that would preclude sexual activity with the her male acquirer."

"Of course," Qattan said. "In strict accordance with Eurabian law."

"Or, if an infant or a child were acquired, a basic assessment of overall health—"

"Whatever you may think of my personal integrity, I can assure you that where our professional standards are concerned …"

"I have no doubt. Your office has a pristine reputation. I need the records of all female slaves examined during a certain time period, the results of those examinations, and the known names and addresses of all the females in question."

Elise handed him a note with the relevant years listed.

This was the moment when a calm man might realize Elise's inquiry didn't make sense, because the Eurabian Caliphate had access to all medical records of all its citizens. An officer of the Commission for the Promotion of Virtue and Prevention of Vice didn't need Qattan or any doctor to get the records Elise had just requested. She merely had to go through her superior. But few men remained calm when they faced the death penalty for a crime they knew they'd committed, or had the balls to follow through with any conclusions that might endanger them if they were wrong.

"Those records are protected by doctor-patient confidentiality," Qattan said. "In this case, there's dual protection, with the slaves in question, and with their owners."

"Based on that, I take it you've changed your mind, the Commission should seek help elsewhere, and I should proceed with your prosecution?"

Elise stood up to leave.

Qattan jumped to his feet. "No, please don't go. I'm sorry. Force of habit. Our patients. We're so protective of them. Please forgive me. Please."

Qattan sat back down, turned to his computer and worked on it for a minute.

"Where would you like me to send the results?" he said.

"I need a hard copy."

He pressed a button on his keyboard. "Done."

He wheeled toward Elise and gave her a blank look as though asking what else he could do for her.

"Where are the pages that you printed for me?" she said.

Qattan's eyebrows shot up for a split second, and then a look of confidence slowly spread across his face. As if that weren't bad enough, it was accompanied by a certain smug sense of male superiority that a woman was more likely than a man to detect.

Under other circumstances, Elise might have welcomed that look because it would have obliterated any guilt she harbored for ruining the man's life. But these circumstances had just turned dire. Qattan appeared to have experienced an epiphany of some kind. She'd given herself away somehow—unknowingly and unbelievably—and now it was he who was going to try to ruin her life.

"Wouldn't it have been easier for you to print this at your own computer?" Qattan said. "I'm sure the Commission has access to all Eurabian state files. Am I wrong?"

"You're not wrong. You're impertinent. And I'm starting to think I misjudged you. Perhaps you don't deserve—"

"Perhaps you'd like to remove your *burqa* and make yourself more comfortable. I'm not your relative but I am a physician and this is a private office so there's no need to concern yourself with matters of morality. I see many a female face every day. I even see a dhimmi now and then. Sort of, pro bono work."

A hot flash seized Elise.

Qattan intertwined his fingers and placed them on his desk. His countenance relaxed, his gaze bordering on condescension. "You're from Egypt, yes?"

"I learned Arabic in Egypt," she said, "but I'm not from Egypt."

"Where then?" Qattan narrowed his eyes and studied her. "Amsterdam? London?"

These days Elise lived in Montevideo, in the country formerly known as Uruguay. And she was no more the morality police than Qattan was the singer of that non-existent boy band. Qattan realized this now, but he couldn't know if Elise had a back-up plan. They sat frozen in their seats, eyes fixed on each other with stone faces.

"How did I give myself away?" Elise said.

"In Arabic, we include the pronoun in relative clauses. In English, you omit it. In English, you would say, 'where are the pages that you printed for me?' But in Arabic we say…"

"'Where are the pages that you printed *them* for me?'"

Qattan nodded with genuine-looking admiration. "Your language is truly excellent. I've never heard a non-native Arabian speak it better." He lifted a gun out of nowhere and pointed it at Elise. "Is that ID real? If I call the Commission of Promotion of Virtue and Prevention of Vice, will they even know your name?"

The gun startled Elise. She hadn't seen it coming. Perhaps it had been enclosed in a casing beneath his desk for emergency purposes. After all, a doctor never knew when a local lunatic would appear in disguise to deliver some frontier-style justice to a health care professional who'd treated a rape and near murder victim even though she'd arrived unescorted by a man in violation of Sharia.

"The Commission will most surely know my name," Elise said, "but you'll just be putting yourself in unnecessary danger."

"Really?" Qattan grinned, the invulnerable pillar of the medical community once again. "How so?"

"Nothing has changed. You're still guilty of promoting Christianity. And my friend from Cairo—who swears he loves me more than life itself—will deliver the pictures personally to the General of the Eurabian police if I die or disappear. And they'll be supplemented by a very willing shopkeeper's testimony in exchange for leniency."

"I don't believe you," Qattan said. "There are no such pictures."

Elise stood up, pulled an envelope from a pocket, removed copies of the pictures and tossed them onto his desk. Qattan turned increasingly darker shades of red as he rifled through them with his free hand.

"Fine," he said. "Maybe you took pictures."

"Maybe? Maybe you need a new ophthalmologist."

"But there's no such lover. You're bluffing about that part. Wait, don't tell me. You're going to suggest that I can't take that chance. That the smart move is to just go along with you."

"You caught up. Finally."

Qattan swore at her. He called her a bitch, a whore, and a prostitute.

Redundant bastard, she thought.

Then he aimed the gun at Elise's chest, pursed his lips, and tensed his shoulders.

A surge of euphoria shot through Elise. If he killed her, all her pain would be gone. There would be no need for her to suffer any more. The world was fucked and there was nothing she could do about. She had no one and nothing and no real reason to live. And then she pictured her sister as she imagined her today, healthy, curious and misguided in the hands of some wretched Muslim couple with medieval Islamic minds who'd bought her to be their slave.

Jesus, Elise thought, please don't take me yet.

Qattan lowered his gun, walked over to a closet and retrieved the papers he'd printed. When he approached Elise, his expression remained remarkably calm.

"They were just chocolates and trinkets," he said.

"You're preaching to the unconverted," Elise said.

She took the papers and left.

Having conducted her personal business during her lunch hour, Elise rode her bicycle back to the parliament building located along the Danube River. Before entering, she hid the badge that had been stolen from a morality policewoman named Kawlah Ahmed in the country formerly known as Portugal by a Christian spy. In its place she brandished her official credentials for the Intertheocratic Conference that accurately identified her as a translator and member of the delegation from Christendom.

But, of course, her real objective in Budapest, like the personal one which she'd just pursued, involved far more than translating Arabic into Spanish.

CHAPTER 3

Ali rushed to the holding cells at the central police station. His boss had every incentive to make the dhimmi witness disappear as quickly as possible if they wanted to suppress news of the murder during the Intertheocratic Conference. But it was just one murder, and a dhimmi child at that. Ali understood that the Caliph—Eurabia's religious and civic leader—wanted to portray a glorious picture of a pure Islamic society. But why did one murder matter so much?

Jalal, the desk sergeant in charge of the holding cells, enjoyed a forbidden sandwich and a fine lager, now and then. No one knew this besides Ali, who'd spotted him disguised as a Cuban-looking stonemason in Dhimmi Town one evening pounding pork sausage as though the apocalypse were imminent. He wasn't the only cop with a taste for *haram*—the forbidden—but he was the only one that mattered to Ali right now.

"I want to see the dhimmi from Matthias," Ali said. "The one that arrived this morning, probably within the hour."

Jalal frowned. "The who, the what, and the where?"

"Don't even start with me, Jalal," Ali said. "I have enough dirt on you to... I want to see him. I want to see him now. Let me in and give him to me."

"Sorry, Ali. Strict orders from Zaman." Zaman was Ali's boss. "No one can see the witness."

"I'm not no one. I'm the lead investigator on the case."

Jalal burst out laughing. "The great Dhimmi Lover on the case, right? That's pretty funny."

"Do I look like I'm laughing to you?"

No one doubted Ali's ability with his fists or his willingness to use them if provoked.

Jalal swallowed air. "Look, Zaman said that if I let anyone into that holding cell he'd have me digging ditches in Transylvania by the end of the week."

"Do they have pork in Transylvania?"

"Your threats won't work, Ali. Say what you want, do as you must. I'll get forty lashes and lose rank if you rat on me. But if I let you in I'll lose my job or worse."

"Then give me something, Jalal. You've got to give me something."

Jalal breathed hard as he contemplated a solution. Then he leaned over the front desk and whispered into Ali's ear. "The dhimmi didn't look good when he came in. He looked hard-up. Like he hadn't eaten in a long time. Zaman took pity on him and ordered a meal for him after he processed him."

Ali hurried to his office and called the kitchen. The cook was a disgraced Hungarian chef from a top Dubai restaurant who'd been caught dipping into a bottle of the owner's Chateau Petrus. The owner replenished his stock and continued serving the forbidden nectar to the Muslim elite who came to town to pretend they weren't Muslims. The chef ended up cooking for dhimmi prisoners in Budapest.

He would know that it was Ali who was calling him because the appropriate extension would appear on his phone's display. This was essential because Ali needed the cook to speak first before they conversed. Sharia precluded a Muslim from initiating a greeting with a dhimmi. Knowing this, the cook sometimes picked up and didn't say a word on purpose just to drive Ali mad. He did this because they were friends.

"Major," the cook said, without hesitation.

"Florence," Ali said. "I need a favor."

"I cook to serve."

"Not that kind of favor. A bigger favor."

"Why do I get the feeling this is the kind of favor that could earn me forty lashes?"

"And a bottle of that Tuscan wine you love so much."

"That's not necessary. A favor is a favor. What do you need?"

"There's a witness in the holding cells," Ali said. "They brought him in this morning. He would have come in dehydrated, probably hungry, too."

"A call came in about an hour ago for a dhimmi tray. They said to make sure he got dessert, so I added some sour cherries. Since they insisted on dessert, I figured either he was a valuable asset or this was his last meal."

"This is for your ears only. Get the large trolley prepared. The one where a flexible man can hide himself if he curls into a ball. I'll be right down."

"Too late," Florence said.

"What?"

"It was a rush order."

"Why?"

Florence didn't answer.

"What have you heard, my friend?"

Florence remained mute.

"We're not having this conversation," Ali said. "Now tell me, in the name of all that is holy in your religion and mine. What have you heard?"

Florence sighed. "When they took his picture and ran it through the system, it came back with a match. The dhimmi witness is a convicted terrorist. He was awaiting execution when he escaped prison."

Ali cursed Zaman. The odds this random witness was truly a convicted terrorist were too low to contemplate. He was a caretaker at a dhimmi church who'd seen a murder at a time when the government didn't want any murders taking place. And to silence him forever, Zaman had fabricated crimes in the man's past. It was clear to Ali Zaman was doing whatever was necessary to eliminate the witness immediately. And if Zaman was comfortable planting such false information, there was no telling what he would do when he found out that Ali was actually investigating the murder.

"So they fed him quickly because what," Ali said, "they scheduled him for an afternoon court appearance? Imminent threat to the safety of the Eurabian Caliphate?"

"He was already convicted, remember?"

Ali swore under his breath. "They're executing him now."

Florence's silence confirmed Ali's conclusion.

"Where?" Ali said.

"Heroes' Square."

"What method?"

"The *Khazouk*."

Ali pictured an innocent old man being impaled. He cringed and ended the call.

He ran to his car and raced to the execution site. On his way, he drove past three burned-down churches. The fires were officially deemed to have been caused by faulty electrical wiring, but most likely had been arson. None of them could be rebuilt because the Dhimmi Contract forbid the repair, reconstruction or construction of any church. This was just one of many humiliating restrictions to which the dhimmi submitted in exchange for the privilege of continuing to live in his own home and receiving the government's protection. The exact terms of the Dhimmi Contract were first established in the Pact of Umar, an ancient treaty negotiated by Muslim conquerors and Christian subjects that listed the rights and obligations of dhimmis in Muslim lands. The Pact of Umar later had become part of Islamic law.

The throng was already growing at Heroes Square. The dhimmis in the crowd were recognizable by the yellow belts they were required to wear by law. Businesses had to let their employees attend executions so that the population was constantly reminded of the penalty for disobeying the Caliph. Although no formal announcements were ever made that one was imminent, word always spread. It never ceased to amaze Ali how quickly and large the crowds grew. Some people came to be shocked, others sought to convince themselves their circumstances could be much worse, and a few showed up simply to pay their respects to a fellow human being. But they always came.

Today's capital punishment was no run-of-the-mill kind. Today they were coming in droves.

Ali parked beside the former Museum of Fine Arts to the left of the square. Twin colonnades flanked an empty space in the middle of Budapest's largest gathering place. The Millennium Monument had once stood in the square, erected to commemorate the one-thousand year history of the Magyars, who'd migrated from the Ural Mountains to first populate Hungary. A statue of the Christian Archangel Gabriel had stood atop the monument, holding the holy crown and double cross of Christianity. Within a month of Sharia becoming the national rule of law, the monument had been destroyed . For good measure, the statues of other kings and key historical figures that had stood upon the colonnades also had been destroyed.

Ali edged his way through the crowd to the front of the Square. An emaciated man lay naked on his stomach between the two colonnades where the Christian monument had once stood. A three-meter by three-meter square of gravel sat exposed amidst the granite promenade beside the dhimmi witness. His hands were tied behind his back. Gray hair covered his head, back and legs. The man's calves looked no thicker than Ali's wrists.

At least fifty policemen guarded the execution site. Another dozen were vaulted high in the air in tree-topping cranes, in compartments normally occupied by chainsaw-wielding laborers. They bore rifles with high-powered scopes and scanned the execution site in search of a terrorist threat from a local dhimmi, or a militant Hindu, Buddhist, or Christian insurgent.

Three executioners dressed in black stood to the dhimmi's right. They wore hoods that rendered only their eyes visible. One of them tended to a fire. A three-meter long iron stake lay smoldering atop the flames. A second executioner examined a hammer, while a third mixed a vat of lubricant. Zaman flanked the dhimmi to his left, supervising the construction of another rung on his ladder to success.

Ali hadn't contemplated that he'd have to get past his boss to interview the witness before his sentence was carried out. Informing Zaman that he was actually investigating the dhimmi girl's murder was the equivalent of admitting to his wife that he was risking a charge of insubordination because he felt guilty about something that had happened twenty-five years ago. It was unimaginable.

And yet Ali found himself marching toward his boss. What propelled him forward? He wondered. Was it his commitment to his mission, or the knowledge that he held a political advantage so powerful that Zaman wouldn't dare stop him?

Zaman looked like a schoolboy, the top-of-the-class teacher's pet, a trait that endeared him to his superiors but made him a rat-shit, ass-kisser in the eyes of his subordinates. Still, there was no denying that Zaman was an unstoppable political rocket ship on track to land on the Caliph's personal staff. If Islam really was the businessman's religion because it didn't stand in the way of a man's ambition, here was a most pious man.

When Zaman's eyes landed on him, they widened. "Ali," he said.

"Captain Zaman."

"Are you lost?"

"No."

"Then what are you doing here?"

"My job."

"Your job? What job?" Zaman stepped forward and put his palm on Ali's forehead. "Do you have a fever?"

If he'd imagined the scene earlier, Ali would have fantasized about taking Zaman's hand from his head and glaring at him, standing up to him like a real man. But now, in the heat of battle, he couldn't even look his superior in the eye. Authority needed to be respected. If there was one thing Islam had taught him it was to submit to the higher power. And yet, a heretofore unknown force propelled Ali to form fresh words and soldier on.

"No," Ali said, 'I don't have a fever. I've decided to do this murder right and I want to talk to the witness before you execute him."

"I thought we had an understanding when I assigned you this case that you were going to handle it like all the others. Was I wrong?"

Ali's face flushed. "That was ... that was before I heard there was a witness and I ... I felt a duty to interview him before you killed him."

Zaman laughed. "Wait. Did you just say you felt a duty?"

Ali looked away, unable to hold Zaman's eyes.

"Now, listen here, you imbecile. Your duty is to follow my orders, not any sudden pangs of sympathy for a dhimmi because she happens to be a girl. And watch your mouth when you speak to me. I'm not killing this scum terrorist. He was found guilty in a court of law. A judge handed down the sentence. I'm just here to make sure the sentence is executed properly."

"Right," Ali said, surprised to hear sarcasm rolling off his own lips. "I'm going to interview the witness now, Captain, and I would recommend you not get in my way." Ali summoned his courage and looked Zaman in the eyes. "Or there're going to be consequences."

Ali had one and only one political connection but it was a powerful one. Zaman reported to Ali's father-in-law—the army general on the Caliph's personal staff. Ali had never used the General's name on the job before because he was always trying like hell to be accountable, even though everyone knew he'd never have earned his stripes on his own merit. But Ali wasn't concerned about appearances today.

Zaman appraised Ali with a measure of surprise—if not newfound respect—and tempered his voice. "I'll have to report your insubordination during my weekly briefing. But until that report makes its way through the system, have at the terrorist, Dhimmi Lover." Zaman raised his arm for Ali to pass to see the witness.

Ali stepped up to the emaciated man lying on his stomach. "Roll him onto his back," Ali said.

Two of the executioners grabbed the prisoner by the shoulders and the legs and turned him over.

Ali was immediately taken aback. The dhimmi cut a different figure up close and chest up. A thin but noticeable slab of muscle covered his pectoral region, and a row of abdominal muscles defined his midsection. His thighs and calves looked like ropes of steel. Even his sunken jaw appeared the product of labor and diet as opposed to age or oppression. Up close, the dhimmi looked wiry, not emaciated.

But the man's build wasn't the reason Ali found himself questioning his assumption that Zaman had planted evidence to frame him. The dhimmi wore two tattoos. Both of them were faded from stretch marks on the skin suggesting they'd been acquired decades ago. They appeared on the sides of his left and right shoulders. The tattoo on the left shoulder featured a circular dome of a Christian church. The tattoo on the right shoulder consisted of two men riding a single horse.

Ali recognized the tattoos from a course on religious body art that was part of mandatory continuing education for all Eurabian police offers. The dome of the Christian church was called The Dome of the Rock, and the church was the Church of the Holy Sepulchre, also known as the Church of the Resurrection in Jerusalem. The men riding the horse represented the Poor Fellow-Soldiers of Christ and the Temple of Solomon.

The Poor Fellow-Soldiers of Christ and the Temple of Solomon were a Christian military organization formed in the twelfth century and endorsed by the Roman Catholic Church and the Pope himself. They were created to fight the Islamic heroes who had conquered the Holy Lands. In fact, Muslim scholars understood that the organization was a copy of the Shia Islamic sect of

Assassins. The Poor Fellow-Soldiers of Christ and the Temple of Solomon eventually came to be known by an abbreviated name. They came to be known as the Knights Templar.

The Knights Templar had comprised the most skilled fighting units during the Crusades against Muslims that had lasted close to four hundred years. Blessed by a Pope who wanted to unite a Catholic Church to expand his political power, the Crusades became a four hundred-year war perpetuated by greed and hatred. A French king eventually destroyed the Knights Templar to free himself from the debts he owed them, by having them arrested and tortured into signing false confessions of heresy. This resulted in many of the Knights being burned at the stake.

Christians, Ali thought. What filthy, savage, and murderous dogs.

Zaman walked over to Ali and handed him a computer tablet.

"He's sanctioned to kill by the Pope of Rome," Zaman said, "from the Vatican-in-Exile in the country formerly known as Uruguay. He was a cop in Vienna before Eurabia annexed the country formerly known as Austria, then suspected in a bombing in Amsterdam before he was convicted of blowing up a government building in Paris. A class of twenty-seven children from an Islamic school for high-achievers was touring the city legislature building that day. They all died in the blast. Three months later he was one of three prisoners to escape from Paris' Le Sante prison the day before his execution."

Ali studied the tablet. All the information appeared in the database before him. If Zaman's accounts were true, it would explain why the judges had facilitated such a quick execution. The man had escaped once before and justice was overdue. The question was whether the information in the database was true or if Zaman had made it all up.

Ali handed the tablet back to his boss and dropped to one knee.

The dhimmi witness' eyes were closed. His lips were moving but the sound coming from his mouth was barely audible. He looked focused, not happy or sad, eager or fearful—merely intense.

Ali leaned forward and lowered his ear. He'd learned rudimentary English and German in school and his language skills had only improved with the growth of Eurabia. When he got close enough to feel the dhimmi witness' breath on his ear, Ali discerned English words. They poured forth with the unmistakable rhythm and cadence of prayer.

> "… the hurts we absorb from one another, forgive us.
> In times of temptation and test, strengthen us.
> From trials too great to endure, spare us.
> From the grip of all that is evil, free us.
> For you reign in the glory of the power
> that is love, now and forever—"

The dhimmi witness's eyes popped open. When he saw Ali's face, the calm that had enveloped him vanished. Sweat gathered on his upper lip. He looked like he was trying to swallow but couldn't. Still he didn't ask for water. Instead he focused on Ali.

"Are you a cleric?" the dhimmi witness said.

"No. I'm a cop."

"Then I forgive you."

"For what?"

"All the crimes of your people."

An urge to strangle the arrogant Christian scum gripped Ali so ferociously he forgot his objective, until the tattoos caught his attention and reminded him why he was there.

"Speak to me of the last crime you saw," Ali said.

"Why should I waste my breath?"

"Justice."

"For Christians?"

"For the girl."

"By whose hand?" the dhimmi witness said.

"Mine."

"No cop has such power in this land."

"No land has such power over a real cop," Ali said.

"And you are a real cop?"

"That remains to be seen. What did you see?"

The dhimmi witness looked up into the clouds. His voice crackled with emotion. "Man came in. Dressed in robes. Head covered. Only a slit for eyes. He was carrying a young girl. A dead girl wrapped in a wool blanket."

"What color were his eyes?"

"Don't know. Too dark."

"Height, weight?"

"Average."

"Did he say anything?"

Ali heard Zaman's voice over his shoulder. He knew he had to hurry.

"Give me something," Ali said. "Give me anything that might help me find him."

The dhimmi witness took a breath. "He knew the priest by name."

"What?" Ali couldn't believe what he'd just heard. "He knew the priest?"

"I don't know if he knew the priest. I said he knew the priest's name. "

Even that was a revelation because priest names were kept secret for their own protection.

"How do you know he knew the priest's name?" Ali said. "What did he say? What did he say?"

"There was a tin in the blanket beside the deal girl's body. There were five gold dinars in it. He said, 'Give this to Father Peter. For his troubles.'"

Ali heard Zaman's footsteps behind him.

"What language did he speak?" Ali said. "What did his voice sound like?"

"He spoke perfect Arabic," the dhimmi witness said. "Like all the filthy Arabs in this place."

Zaman cast a shadow over Ali.

"Enough already," Zaman said. "The people want justice. It's time for this terrorist to suffer the way the families of those he killed have suffered."

The dhimmi witness began praying in earnest.

"My soul is protected by the armour of faith,
my body is protected by the armour of steel.
I fear neither demons nor men ..."

Ali turned and started to talk away.

Zaman blocked his path. "What did he say?"

"He said he forgives me."

"For what?"

"For being a Muslim," Ali said.

"Terrorist scum. What else did he say?"

"He said his body is protected by the armour of steel."

"Oh, really?" Zaman chuckled. "We'll see about that, won't we?"

Ali hurried past Zaman to avoid more questions and get away from the spectacle before it started.

Within a few minutes the dhimmi witness would be rolled onto his back. One of the executioners would lubricate his anus, while a second would take the red-hot steel rod and insert it into the dhimmi witness' rectum. The third executioner would then drive the rod through the convicted terrorist's body with his hammer. The executioner who would wield the hammer was such an expert in the *Khazouk* that he would make sure the rod avoided the heart and all other vital organs. The rod would emerge either through the shoulder, or, on an exceptional day, out of the dhimmi witness' mouth. The burning steel would cauterize the wound and minimize the bleeding in its wake, thus prolonging the dhimmi witness' life for as long as two days.

Once the process was complete, the three executioners would lift the rod and hammer it into the exposed gravel in the promenade beneath the place where the Christian Archangel Gabriel's monument had once stood, leaving the dhimmi witness to suffer a slow and grueling death while facing the residents of Eurabia in Heroes' Square.

The *Khazouk* had been a favorite form of execution during the rule of the Ottoman Empire, whose leaders thought its brutality would deter spies and insurgents. Ali suspected the reason the *Khazouk* was back in vogue had little to do with spies and insurgents this time, and everything to do with fear. The Caliphs of Eurabia and the men who helped them govern wanted to leave no doubt in people's minds just how cruel their leaders could be if anyone dared question them.

Ali didn't dwell on the issue, though. Such matters were beyond his calling. He was just a cop—or a General's son-in-law pretending to be one—and the witness who'd spoken with the killer had offered an unlikely clue. The killer was an Arabian who knew the priest's identity, which suggested the priest might know the murderer himself. The lead was so valuable that Ali was certain he would think of nothing else all day.

But as he hurried to his car and the crowd roared behind him, Ali knew right away he'd lied to himself just as surely as a hot flash had passed deep through his bowels.

There had been no body armour to save the Christian terrorist today.

CHAPTER 4

Only one name on Qattan's list of female slaves mattered to Elise. The doctor's records revealed that the man who'd acquired the girl in question was a prominent banker by the name of Faraz.

Elise found his townhouse in the early afternoon, tucked on a quiet side street near the cliffs of Buda. Surrounded by the Danube and valleys, Buda had served as a natural fortress for the ruling elite for centuries. Under Hungarian rule, members of the working class of Pest had aspired to live among Buda's upper class. *Buda is a life vision*, they had said. Younger residents of Buda had often teased their friends in Pest to carry their passports and come visit them, as though the former were rock stars living in a separate country.

Thus, it was no surprise that most of the current residents of Buda appeared to be Arabians, and only the workers who tended to the restaurants, operated the funicular, cleaned homes and provided other menial services looked like native Hungarians. The few dhimmis who still lived in Buda now wore their passports for all to see just like their counterparts from Pest. The ubiquitous yellow belt worn by the dhimmi was no life vision. In Buda, as in Pest, it was reality.

Buda was home to a restaurant named after the artist Jean Miro. Located diagonally across the street from the banker's home, it served as a sanctuary from which Elise could observe comings and goings with some discretion. She ordered a tall bottle of still water, drank slowly, and pretended to work on her computer. Every time the door to the banker's apartment opened she held her breath, but no children emerged. Instead, the banker's three wives took turns leaving their home. One of them left without an escort while a driver took the other two to their destinations. That arrangement suggested that the first wife was the eldest and the only one over the age of forty-five.

The two wives who were driven to their destinations returned in the late afternoon with three and four children in their cars respectively. Once again Elise's heart fluttered, but none of the kids could have been the little sister she'd never known, sold to an Arabian couple as a slave at birth. Five of the children were boys and two were girls. The ages weren't a match for Elise's sister. The younger children were toddlers. The others were older teenagers.

Elise had been in the hospital room with her mother, watched as the nurse lifted the baby from her arms and told her not to worry, that her little girl would be fed, cared for, and cherished as a valuable servant for the rest of her life. Islamic law forbid the abuse of slaves and the Caliphate took it seriously. The nurse had made no promise that the girl would be educated, however, and Elise realized her emotions had gotten the better of her. The thought of one of the banker's wives shepherding a slave back and forth to school with their children probably was wishful thinking.

Her sister was fourteen years old by now, capable of having been trained to do all sorts of menial work. Elise guessed that she'd been working in the house all day. Qattan's records indicated that her Arabian name was Safa, but her true given name was Valerie.

To Elise, she would always be Valerie. Valerie the brave.

The banker didn't keep banker's hours, which was to be expected because the business of banking was more complex under Sharia. The collection of interest on money loaned was considered immoral and was strictly forbidden. Instead of issuing a mortgage, a bank bought property and resold it the buyer at a profit. Instead of giving a business loan, a bank entered into a joint venture with the company that paid down the bank's investment with profit. As a result of these laws, the Sharia banker was more of an entrepreneur. On this given day, this banker worked accordingly.

He didn't get home until eight forty-five.

This left Elise with an unpleasant decision. She could knock on the door but the late hour would cast her arrival as suspicious. Alternatively, she could wait until the next morning and arrive at an equally early hour before the banker left for work. This might also raise suspicions. The third option, attempting to achieve her objective with only the wives at home, had been a non-starter. The wives' reactions to Elise's assertions, threats, and demands might be completely irrational if they were as attached to Valerie as Elise was to the idea of her existence.

Elise opted for the speedy solution. She was a spy in enemy territory who could be discovered at any moment. Also, the banker was home but she couldn't be certain he didn't have an early appointment.

Thus, at nine o'clock she rang the doorbell. Elise had dressed in a *niqab* instead of a *burqa*, which kept her mouth covered but revealed her eyes, thus reducing the risk that the banker would insist she remove her entire veil during their interview. One of the wives who had been driven by an escort opened the door with a frown. She had a plain round face with unremarkable features except for the one the banker's oldest wife could never attain again. This wife had the taut and supple skin of a younger woman.

Elise flashed her badge and requested to speak to the man of the house. The banker came to the door still dressed in a charcoal suit with padded shoulders that compensated for his pear-shaped lines. Patches of hair covered the side of his shining head and his eyes were pinched with anger.

"What is the meaning of this?" he said.

"That depends on you, Mr. Faraz," Elise said.

He took one look at Elise and her badge and sneered.

"The religious police. A bunch of former criminals who memorized the Quran to reduce their jail sentences and got the only jobs they could when they were released—tormenting good citizens for stupid transgressions. An old woman removes her *burqa* because she's suffocating under the sun and you beat her. You should be ashamed of yourselves. What are you doing at my home?"

"Tormenting a citizen, naturally."

Faraz blinked three times as though he couldn't believe what he'd just heard. "Do you know who I am? Do you know who my business partners are? Answer my question you insolent bitch or I'll have you under the whip tomorrow morning."

"It'll be difficult for you to have me under the whip tomorrow morning if it's busy lashing your back two hundred times in front of the parliament building where all your government partners will be able to see you for the degenerate sinner that you are."

Faraz blinked three more times. "Remember my face, woman. Let it be the one you think of when you take your last breath. I'm going to make some phone calls tonight and then we'll see what happens to you tomorrow."

He peered in to study Elise's ID but she closed her wallet before he could read her name.

"You have a slave by the name of Safa?" Elise said. "A child you acquired through your connections with your business partners?"

Faraz hesitated, no doubt digesting the realization that the religious police hadn't arrived at his home to discuss a minor issue. Consternation replaced some—but not all—of the outrage in his expression.

"What about her?" he said.

"How old is the girl?"

Faraz turned and shouted the same question toward a room deeper inside the house.

"Fourteen," one of the wives shouted back.

Elise said, "Is she present in your home right now?"

"She's part of our family," Faraz said. "Of course she's here."

Elise smiled on the inside. Three years of relentless research and pursuit of false leads were finally about to be rewarded. Only wood and wallboard stood between her and Valerie now.

"Then please let me into your home. I must speak with her immediately."

"Lick my ass," Faraz said, and started to close the door.

"Prostituting your slave is a crime against Allah."

Faraz pulled the door back open. Lines sprang on his greasy forehead. He seemed as genuinely horrified as he was surprised at the bogus accusation.

"Justice must be served," Elise said.

"How dare you make such an accusation?"

"Justice will be served."

"This is outrageous. What is your proof? Where is your evidence?"

"You can cooperate and submit to an interview here, in your home, right now, or be hauled out of your office tomorrow and explain yourself to a prosecutor whose deficiency in sleep will be exceeded only by his lack of patience."

Faraz flung the door open and squared himself, fists balled. "You think I'm going to let you leave my sight when you've made such a libelous statement? Your mother's vagina," he said. Arabic insults typically referred to one's family or sex. "Get in here and explain yourself, now."

"That doesn't sound very welcoming, sir. It's been a long, hot day filled with awful speak of reprehensible behavior. A glass of water and an understanding tone would be appreciated."

Faraz took a deep breath, closed his eyes, and exhaled slowly. Then he contorted his expression into something that might have amounted to a smile among condemned men.

"May I see your credentials again so that I may address you properly?" he said.

Elise complied with his wish.

Faraz leaned forward and scrunched his eyes. "Kawlah Ahmed. That is your name?"

Elise didn't bother answering. She just stared at him like the morally judgmental, Arabian bitch-goddess she was pretending to be, wondering if she needed to be worried about being discovered. If Faraz were to call one of his friends and have them verify her identity, Elise would likely survive the test. Her name was in the computer database and she bore a distant resemblance to the real Kawlah. Elise knew she would fail a more careful rigorous investigation that included deep background or biometric checks, but those were not tests she needed to worry about in the banker's home tonight.

Five minutes later she was seated in Faraz's study drinking tea. Book collections in burgundy and green leather bindings lined paneled shelves made of walnut. All of the names on the bindings were in the city's native language.

"You speak Hungarian?" Elise said.

"I speak whatever language is necessary to make money. You have your beverage, you're being treated with more hospitality than you or your kind deserve. Now tell me about these lies someone has been spreading about me before I get upset and slit your throat where you sit."

"I'll conduct the interview, Mr. Faraz. Thank you very much. And if your responses please me, then I perhaps I'll answer one of your questions. Describe the details of Safa's adoption."

"We did nothing wrong. It's a Muslim's right to share in the spoils of war. As the great Saudi cleric, Sheik Saleh Al-Fawzan, once said, 'slavery is part of jihad and jihad will remain as long as there is Islam.' All our arrangements were entirely lawful."

"I didn't say they weren't."

"The Deputy Minister of Defense is a friend of mine. He helped us make arrangements with the Department of Slave Procurement to acquire a raw specimen."

"A specimen?"

"A child at birth. Someone without life experience, emotional attachments or knowledge of any religion other than Islam. A girl whom we could mold to become a serving dependent. We paid a little extra to buy the mother's full cooperation. It's preferable to acquiring a baby without the mother's cooperation. Less risk of latent emotional scarring."

Serving dependent. As the phrase echoed in Elise's head, she pictured Faraz scolding, slapping and locking Valerie in a closet for not completely removing the stains in his underwear.

"What stipulations did you make about the specimen?" Elise said.

"Just the basic ones. That the mother be under the age of twenty-five to reduce the probability of birth defects and that she be in good health with no evidence of a destructive lifestyle."

Elise suppressed a laugh. If Faraz had been told that Valerie's mother had led a clean lifestyle, he'd been duped by his own people.

"And, of course," Faraz said, "that the father be dead."

Elise might have tried to imagine what Valerie's father looked like when he was alive but there was no way of knowing who he was. Valerie's mother had been an addict who'd traded her body for drugs. There had been so many men, she wouldn't have recognized their faces if she saw them.

"Why was it essential for the father to be dead?" she said.

"So that the child was a legitimate spoil of war," Faraz said. "Does the religious police not know the law?"

"The acquisition of international war booty is not my specialty. Once the Department of Slave Procurement completed its examination of the specimen—"

"She was transported here, to a doctor in Budapest, for the second mandatory medical examination. That's a local requirement, a prerequisite to obtaining permission for the slave to be domiciled in Eurabia."

"And that doctor was Rudolph Qattan of the Ottoman Health Network?" Elise said.

"I detest being asked questions by people who already know the answer, especially when it's by a woman."

"Why does it bother you so much when it's a woman asking the question?"

"Because she could be busy doing what she was meant to do, darning my socks, preparing dinner, or sewing a dress for one of my wives."

"How lucky for your wives to be married to a man so thoughtful."

Faraz took her seriously and shrugged. "I am their husband."

"Our records show that you returned to Doctor Qattan for annual visits until the specimen turned six."

"As I said, my wives and I have done everything according to the law."

"And that's all you've done, where Safa's—where the specimen's health is concerned?"

"Of course that's not all we've done. She gets fed, she has shelter, she is cared for. I told you, she serves at our wishes but she's part of our family."

"And yet you haven't taken her to see her physician for over six years."

"Further proof she's in excellent health. There's been no need for her to visit Qattan."

"Or," Elise said, "there's been a need not to visit him so that he might not detect any obvious physical signs of sexual abuse."

Faraz fumed. "The only abuse in this home is the unrelenting flow of insults and libelous accusations pouring from your satanic lips."

"Then show me the evidence."

Faraz frowned.

"The specimen," Elise said. "Let me see how healthy she is with my own eyes. Let her speak for herself.

"That's an excellent idea. Wait here." He stood up and left the room.

Logic rendered any celebration premature. Elise's biggest challenge remained. Faraz would never allow her to leave his home with his slave no matter what kind of authority Elise asserted or what spurious proof of abuse she provided. In fact,

Valerie herself would probably fight to stay in the only home she knew.

Elise's thoughts were interrupted by the hushed sound of voices. One of them belonged to a young girl. She spoke perfect Arabic and replied in the affirmative with the extreme deference of a human who belonged to another and didn't know to question the morality of such ownership. As the footsteps grew louder, Elise touched her hair to make sure it was in place, forgetting that it was tucked under her *niqab*. When two shadows appeared in the doorway and one of them belonged to a young girl, Elise held her breath.

An African girl stepped into the room with Faraz. Her hazel eyes were set in a perfectly oval face, and even though many pretty girls' looks faded as they matured, there was no doubt this girl was destined to be a beauty.

But she was not Valerie. For even though her mother had slept with men of various creeds and races, the skin of the daughter who had been ripped from her at birth had been as white as her mother's.

"Who is this girl?" Elise said.

"This is Safa," Faraz said.

Faraz's slave bowed her head as though they were living in medieval times, when Islamic warriors had routinely sent conquered Christians as slaves to their homelands.

"Do you take me for a complete fool?" Elise said.

"What are you talking about?" Faraz said.

"This is not Safa. This is not the girl you acquired twelve years ago."

"But of course it is. Our slave is standing here in front of you and still you don't believe me? You confound me, woman. I don't understand why you're here, let alone so late in the night, but believe me, I'm going to find out. Get out of my house."

A string tugged on the back Elise's eyes. She hadn't cried in forever. Despite the sensation, she wondered if her body really could create tears.

Elise's voice took on an apologetic note of its own accord. "There must be some misunderstanding. The Safa in our records has blonde hair. Blonde hair, do you hear me? White skin and blonde hair. The records say you adopted a girl like that."

Faraz's eyes flickered. He paused for a beat, then stood and whispered into his slave's ear. The girl left the room.

"I understand now," Faraz said, in the voice of the accommodating banker, not the enraged parent. "This really is a misunderstanding." He sat down again and sighed. "You meant *that* Safa."

"*That* Safa?" Elise could hear the disbelief in her own voice. "There's more than one Safa?"

"I'm afraid so. But the first one …" Faraz stumbled to find words. "The first one turned out to be a poor fit for our family."

"How so?"

Faraz shrugged. For the first time, he took his eyes off Elise and looked down as he spoke. "She had a combative nature. Very stubborn and unreceptive to my wives' orders. Once she turned … eight, I think it was … we opted to replace her with a new specimen."

"But Qattan …" Elise said, struggling to hide her disappointment. "There are no records of him conducting the necessary tests on this second specimen as he did on the first one."

"There was no need. We purchased her from a woman in the country formerly known as Spain. The woman's husband had died when Christian terrorists bombed his mosque and she was returning to live with her parents. Her plans to raise a family had been destroyed so she had no need for a slave. And my wives loved the name —"

"And what of the first Safa?"

"She was blessed to have been accepted into a religious slave training school of the highest moral caliber. To my knowledge, she's still there, benefitting from an education in Islam and all the skills a young slave girl needs to serve her masters."

"And who runs this wonderful training school?"

Faraz beamed. "The most wise and holy man by the name of Imam Salim."

Elise felt her gut ripped out. Salim was the most radical cleric in Eurabia, arguing openly for Islam's manifest destiny and Arabia's need to conquer additional Hindu and Buddhist lands by whatever means necessary. That said, he was a deeply religious and respected man who would surely provide quality care for his students. There was solace in that, Elise thought, wasn't there?

"I've told you all I know," Faraz said. "Why don't you knock on the Imam's door and try to visit with him tonight to verify my story? Morality doesn't sleep right?" Faraz glanced at his watch and shook his head in disgust. "See how that goes for you."

Elise bowed her head, muttered an apology and hurried out of the house, the tormentor fleeing the tormented.

CHAPTER 5

Ali returned home and engaged in his favorite therapy to relieve stress and relax his mind.

He had sex with his slave.

He called home ahead of time and instructed his wife, Sabida, to prepare his bed and their slave for him. Sabida laid out his favorite robe in the bathroom and informed the slave of his desire. After his shower, Ali found the slave waiting for him in the bed, wrapped in fresh linens, bathed and smelling of rose perfume. Ali didn't waste time on foreplay. This was not a romantic or emotional encounter. He wanted sex, she was legally bound to fulfill his desires, and they both acted accordingly.

Ali and Sabida had bought their slave legally through the Department of Slave Procurement from the country formerly known as Denmark. The slave's father had been a Danish accountant and her mother a hairdresser. After the father was executed for his involvement with the Danish national resistance, the mother was deported for being the spouse of a convicted terrorist. Meanwhile, the twenty year-old daughter was claimed as war booty by the Ministry of Defense and assigned to a training facility for slaves in Arabia. When she was put up for auction a year-later, Ali's father-in-law used his political connections to acquire her as an anniversary gift.

When Ali first saw her he was immediately aroused. This was less a function of her sleek figure, its exquisite proportions and her fresh face, and more the contrast between her overt beauty and the extreme shyness with which she carried herself. It was this sweetness that drew Sabida's approval, though Ali had no doubt that his wife could sense the magnitude of his attraction.

From their first sexual experience, Ali had no issue with the girl's submission. She was a slave and there was nothing she could do about her plight in life. Her only choices were to make her life miserable by adopting an adversarial stance with her owners, or improve it by being performing her duties enthusiastically. At first the girl pursued the latter path by yielding to Ali's every wish. Then, after she grew to understand a man's base sexual desires, she began to anticipate Ali's wants and stimulate him beyond his expectations. Eventually, Ali lost any semblance of inhibition that may have constrained him initially. He fulfilled all his fantasies without any shame.

All this was not only legal but healthy, Ali thought. Slavery was permitted according to the Quran and the Hadith, the holy sayings of the Prophet Mohammad. Ali had never cheated on his wife. In fact, he'd never entertained the prospect, not even once. He didn't favor prostitutes, indulge in *haram* pornographic images, or let his conduct toward Allah, his family, or his job suffer because he was sexually unfulfilled.

Ali thoroughly exhausted himself over the course of forty-five minutes. Afterwards, he took another shower, dressed, and retired to his favorite chair in the living room. Sabida brought him his customary glass of apple juice immediately. They never spoke of his sexual relationship with their slave, but Ali often detected a note of resentment when Sabida first saw him after one of his romps. Sometimes it was conveyed in her tone of voice, other times with a glance.

Today she put his apple juice on the coffee table in front of the sofa instead of on the one by his chair, forcing him to stand up to get it. Ali didn't grumble. It was only natural for a woman to momentarily resent her husband for having had sex with another woman, even if it was lawful and holy. Humans were jealous and possessive by nature. Sabida's great virtue was that her resentment never festered. She knew her husband's love for her exceeded his lust for his slave immeasurably, or at least so he thought. To discuss the topic with Sabida was such an awkward proposition that it was unthinkable.

She sat down on the sofa opposite him while he sipped his juice.

"How are you, my beloved?" she said.

"Refreshed, famished, never better," Ali said.

"You're home early today. Is everything all right at work?"

Ali stared into space, images of the dead dhimmi girls—both of them—flashing in his mind.

"No," he said. "Everything is not all right at work."

"I'm so sorry to hear that."

Ali leaned forward, reached out and gripped her hand. "Eyes to my soul, don't be sorry. There's nothing to be sorry about. I'm a policeman. By definition, everything is never all right at work."

"But something is different this time, isn't it?"

"Nonsense."

"No. It's not nonsense. I can tell. A wife can always tell."

Ali regarded her with amazement. It had taken her only a minute to realize that something was bothering him.

"Don't be so surprised," Sabida said. "You telegraph your emotions, in the living room and the bedroom."

Ali let go of his wife's hand. "I thought you stopped listening at the door a long time ago."

"That's my point. I didn't need to. The neighbors called and asked if you could turn down the volume a bit."

"They did?"

Sabida rolled her eyes. "No, my beloved. But you do understand what I'm telling you, don't you?"

Ali blushed, realizing he'd been a fool. He hated when she reminded him how much smarter she was, but realized that he was to blame for constantly blundering into her verbal traps. Now he understood what she was saying. He'd been noisy and self-indulgent. In fact, he'd pounded their poor slave without any regard for her welfare.

"Don't worry about her," Sabida said, reading his mind. "She's a slave. *She'll* be fine."

"And you, eyes to my soul. You're not fine?"

"I am what you are. I stand behind you, in front of you, and above all else, beside you with every choice you make, every action you take. I live for us, Sami. Not for myself, and not for you. For you, our daughter and me, and you know that."

He did know that. These were not merely words. They were the truth. But what he didn't know was what she was really talking about. And he was too damn tired, hungry and frustrated with his case to speak in code.

"If something is bothering you, wife, speak or go get me my dinner."

A commotion at the front door interrupted them, and a moment later their daughter bounded into the living room. Her uncle—Sabida's brother—also popped his head in. He exchanged quick pleasantries, reminded Ali that it was his turn to pick up the children after school tomorrow, and left as quickly as he arrived.

"Papa!"

Ali's daughter, Kinza, tossed her knapsack to the ground and jumped onto Ali's lap.

"*Ya Baba*," Ali said, a typical endearment used by fathers to their daughters, as though to say 'your father is talking—listen to him.'

He hugged Kinza tightly. The smell of her hair made him forget his troubles. It was a mix of sweat and her jasmine, sandalwood and aloe shampoo. For Ali, it was the scent of joy.

"What did you learn to cook today?" Sabida said.

"Manakeesh," Kinza said.

Ali moaned.

"Ah," Sabida said. "Papa love him some manakeesh." Arabia's pizza consisted of a round bread sprinkled with cheese, ground meat or herbs.

Ali grinned and nodded, and all three of them laughed.

Then Ali pulled back, looked into his daughter's eyes and said, "But what did you really learn?"

Kinza answered with a glint of pride in her eyes. "I learned the Pythagorean Theorem. The square of the hypotenuse—the side opposite the right angle—is equal to the sum of the squares of the other two sides of a right triangle."

Sabida clapped.

"Good news," Ali said. "You have your mother's brain."

"And I learned about gene theory."

"There is a theory on blue jeans?" Ali said.

Kinza punched him playfully in the chest. "No, not blue jean theory. Gene therapy."

"Really?" Ali said. "And what is gene theory?"

"It says that genes are located on chromosomes and consist of DNA. It says that traits are inherited through gene transmission from parents and grandparents."

"Bad news," Ali said. "You're smarter than your father."

"Is genetics the reason you share a bed with a slave, Papa?" Kinza said. "Is that what your father and his father used to do? Is that why you like it?"

"Okay," Ali said, blood rushing to his face. "It's time for you to wash up, prepare for prayers …" He glanced at Sabida for help. "… or do something, isn't it?"

Sabida whisked Kinza to her room. As his daughter skipped away, Ali wondered what future awaited her. Arabian parents coveted education for their daughters, but most expected them to shun careers to become wives, mothers and homemakers. Women who insisted on pursuing careers had to get permission from their husbands before they could apply for a job. Although Islam frowned on a woman working outside the home, it tolerated her occupying jobs that were seen as less desirable for men, such as cleaning homes, assisting in health care facilities, and serving food at restaurants.

But some women insisted on greater opportunities. In big cities such as Budapest, it was now possible for a woman to become an architect, a lawyer or a member of the diplomatic corps. It took perseverance, thick skin, and relentless ambition. Ali and Sabida were raising their daughter with the expectation that she would be one of those exceptions, a woman who would fulfill her potential regardless of the obstacles created by the men who controlled society.

Kinza's science lesson distracted Ali from whatever it was that Sabida had been trying to tell him. When his wife reappeared he hoped she'd walk right past him to the kitchen, but that was wishful thinking. Instead, she marched straight into the living room, stood before him and put her hands on her hips.

"Our social standing in the community doesn't matter to me," she said.

Ali still had no idea what she was talking about.

"And luxury doesn't matter to me either. I don't need to drive a Tesla. I don't need vacations in Morocco, and I don't need a slave. I can clean my own home. But we need a minimum of income to maintain a decent standard of living."

Ali continued to stare at her dumbfounded.

"What is wrong with my income?" he said. "Since I was promoted, we're saving money every month."

"Exactly. Since you were promoted. And if you were demoted ..."

"Why would I get demoted?"

"Or if you ... if you were dismissed from the national police ..."

"Dismissed?" Ali detected the shock in his own voice.

"How would we get by then?"

"Why would I be dismissed?"

Sabida's eyes welled. "I love you with all heart, my beloved, but I don't want to end up living in the countryside with uneducated people. And I don't want our daughter to end up marrying one of them and living a life beneath her potential. I draw the line there."

Ali took a moment to digest what she'd said.

"You didn't answer my question," he said. "Why would I be dismissed?"

Sabida's gaze fell to the floor. "You know why."

Ali let his voice rise. "No. I don't. You seem to know more about my career than I do. Why don't you tell me?"

Sabida took a deep breath. He could sense she was searching for the courage to speak with him about matters that didn't concern her, namely his profession and his obligation to provide for his family.

"You're a good man," she said. "Such a good man. When you saw the dead dhimmi girl you thought of your own daughter. I know you did. And you decided that you'd do the right thing, the noble thing, and find her killer. Because you'd want someone to do the same for you if the killer had taken your own daughter's life. But Father says that's not your job…"

Ali stood up. "You spoke with your father about my job?"

"I didn't call him. He called me. He asked if we were having marital problems. If I was treating you properly. If you were feeling ill. He said he didn't believe you were capable of showing such disrespect toward him after all that he'd done for us so there had to be a reason, and that as your wife I should know the reason —"

"How dare you humiliate me this way?" Ali said.

His wife should have terminated the conversation the minute her father broached the topic of her husband's job. That she continued conversing about him, the man of the house, was a massive insult to Ali's masculinity. She might as well have shown up at headquarters and laughed in his face.

"Father said you must cease and desist, or the next call won't be from him."

"Oh, no? Who will it be from?"

"No one," Sabida said. Her voice trembled. "If you don't cease and desist looking into the dhimmi girl's murder, there won't be another phone call."

Ali grabbed his car keys and wallet and stormed out of the house. He drove to a place that he loathed with his entire being, except for those times when fury or hopelessness consumed him, which seemed to be happening more frequently as he aged. While sex with his slave was his favorite form of therapy, smoking cannabis was the most effective one. Smoking tobacco from a hookah was *haram*, but the police turned a blind eye to the few bars that had popped up in Dhimmi Town. No one cared if the dhimmis ruined their health. Nor did they care if the dhimmis reduced their brainpower by smoking cannabis from the same device in the same places.

After his emasculation at his wife's hands, Ali craved the cannabis high even more than he'd wanted his slave's body earlier. He needed to shut his brain down and get some relief. It didn't take much for him to feel stressed out, he realized. Maybe that was why he'd never cared if he actually worked his cases until now. Perhaps deep down he knew that not only was he not smartest detective in the room, he wasn't the mentally toughest one, either. This thought, in turn, filled him with self-loathing and even more anxiety.

As the dhimmi hostess escorted him to the men's lounge, a man in a robe crossed his path in the lobby and brushed his shoulder. Ali glared at him, and when the person responded in kind Ali was shocked to see that she was a woman in a *niqab*. Only her eyes were visible.

They radiated such ferocity that Ali did a double take to see them again but by then the woman was gone.

CHAPTER 6

The next day, Elise labored through the morning session of the Intertheocratic Conference with a debilitating case of cottonmouth. She couldn't remember much about the prior night. The stress of her dual agenda had finally gotten to her, and she'd succumbed to the temptations of the hookah. She'd cursed herself upon waking up this morning, as she always did after straying from her sobriety.

She'd also developed a terrible toothache, at least in her imagination. Elise found that she performed her best work when she truly convinced herself that her fiction was reality. So when she arrived at the dentist's office, she would have passed a polygraph test if asked if her tooth was really killing her. In fact, she was there to see the dentist for personal and professional reasons, neither of which had anything to do with her teeth.

The dentist was also the local agent who controlled all of Christendom's assets in Central Eurabia.

Three of the six patients in the waiting room were Arabians even though the dentist who owned the establishment was a foreigner. This meant the dentist was no dhimmi, because the patients would have considered his hands too filthy for their mouths, even if it was covered by a sanitary glove.

"I need to see the dentist," Elise said to a grumpy Arabian receptionist. "I'm having unbearable pain. I think I need a root canal."

The receptionist offered no sympathy. "Are you a patient here?"

"No."

"Then we can't help you."

Elise flashed her ID. "It's difficult to promote virtue and prevent vice when one's tooth hurts."

The receptionist looked nervous and conflicted, as though she didn't relish disappointing her bosses or the morality police.

"Tell Doctor Darby I'm here," Elise said, "and that a friend of mine in the Caliph's office recommended him."

The receptionist called someone on the phone. Another employee came out, this one in aqua-colored scrubs. Elise repeated her story. The employee escorted Elise to the treatment area, where the dentists were tending to patients in a row of open bays. The employee told Elise to remove her *niqab*, take a seat in the dentist's chair, and wait for Darby. Elise did as the woman requested, letting her mahogany-colored hair fall to her shoulders. She'd dyed her blonde locks to attract less attention before arriving in Budapest—BP, as it was known locally in the English language.

A fit man with thinning salt and pepper hair and a gray beard walked in a few minutes later. He stood a head taller than Elise, moved deliberately and began measuring her immediately.

"I'm Doctor Darby," he said, as he lowered her seatback to a prone position. Darby spoke Arabic but with a hideous English accent. "I understand you're experiencing some discomfort."

"That's a gross understatement," Elise said.

"I'm so sorry to hear that. Which tooth?"

Elise met his eyes and held them for a long beat. Then she pressed her right index finger firmly to her nose.

"This one," she said.

Darby's eyes flickered. "I see." He lowered the headlight attached to a metallic crown around his head. "Let's have a closer look. Open wide, please."

Elise played along and let Darby examine her teeth. An employee popped her head in and asked him a question. Their verbal exchange allowed Elise to focus on the sounds beyond her seat. The chatter of dentists, hygienists and patients could be heard from adjacent bays. This left no doubt in Elise's mind that her voice would carry, too, unless she was careful.

Darby poked her teeth with his instrument. "Does this hurt?"

"No."

He poked again. "How about this?"

"No," Elise said.

He examined another tooth.

"And this?"

Elise gave a sharp yelp even though she'd felt no pain. Or had she? That was the tooth she'd convinced herself was hurting, but now she wasn't sure if she'd made it up or if it was true.

"I can see why that hurts," Darby said. "One of your teeth has cracked. We're going to have to take an X-ray to see what's going on underneath."

A man's voice sounded from the entry to the room—Elise hadn't even realized someone was standing there. "Shall I, Doctor?"

"No, thank you," Darby said. "I'll do it myself. This is a new patient and it'll give us a chance to get better acquainted."

"As you wish, sir."

Darby left and returned with a lead apron. He raised Elise's seatback and placed the apron on her chest. Then he leaned in, made the sign of the cross with his right hand and whispered in English.

"In this sign …" His voice trailed off in a manner that suggested he was waiting for Elise to finish the sentence.

Elise rolled her eyes but kept her voice low. "Oh, for God's sake. You know who I am. I'm with the delegation from Christendom. On special assignment for the Cardinal, here to establish the authenticity of a priceless treasure and acquire it if it checks out. You've been expecting me. You knew what I'd look like before I got here."

"Protocol," Darby said, with a strong note of disapproval. He repeated the sign of the cross. "In this sign …"

Elise sighed. "Thou shall conquer."

Darby gave her a quick nod and grunted with satisfaction.

"When do I meet the man in the wheelchair?" she said.

"Tonight. At his apartment."

"His apartment?" The cliché that a spy conducted her business in dark alleys had its origins in reality for obvious reasons.

"He hasn't left his home for twelve years," Darby said. "You'll understand when you meet him."

Darby brought his lips to within an inch of Elise's ear and whispered the address to her.

Elise committed it to memory.

"What do you know about him?" Elise said.

"He buys and sells. Mostly arts and antiquities."

"Can he be trusted?"

"Of course not. No one in Nazi Germany could be trusted, no one in the Soviet Union could be trusted, and no one in Eurabia can be trusted. We live in a land of fear and paranoia."

"You say that with such authority. As though you have no doubt."

Darby shrugged. "That's because I have none. I'm an Englishman. I *am* an authority. I hail from a society superior to the Islamic state, and that is the Western one. Where all human beings had inalienable rights, regardless of religion, race, or gender."

"So says the former colonialist."

"Notice I didn't say the Islamic religion. Muhammad preached for thirteen years in Mecca and converted a grand total of one hundred fifty Arabs to Islam. The part of the Quran that corresponds to that time period reads like religion. Then he moved to Medina, became a warlord, embraced violence, and converted ten thousand Arabs a year for nine years. The part of the Quran that corresponds to that time period reads like politics. Did you know that fifty-one percent of the sacred Islamic texts consist of instruction on how to deal with non-believers?"

"Last I looked, all the major religions became political movements..."

"A pity Muslims never got their house in order. A pity we succumbed to political correctness and didn't admit that ours was a better way of life. One third of all Arab men and half of all Arab women are illiterate. In two generations, the same will be said of us. That's the thing about the leaders of Arabia—they love their subjects ignorant. If only Western liberals could have seen past their self-loathing and understood what needed to be done back when they had the power to do it."

"And what was that?"

"'Slay the idolators wherever you find them, and take them captive and besiege them, and prepare for them each ambush.'"

Elise recognized the words. They weren't from the Bible.

"When did you renounce your prior religion?" she said.

The local spymaster could only function effectively if he was fully integrated into society, hiding in plain sight. In Eurabia, that meant submitting to Islam. That's why he had Muslim patients in his waiting room.

"Three months after Sharia law was enacted I formally bid Jesus and the Church of England a good day. And I must confess, praying five times a day has had a certain therapeutic benefit, though the Caliph wouldn't be pleased if he knew the content of those prayers."

"Speaking of prayer," Elise said. "I need assistance with a personal matter."

"The use of national resources for personal agenda is strictly forbidden. We could face trial and execution." Darby cleared his throat and raised his eyebrows. "What did you have in mind?"

"Extraction."

"How many?"

"One."

"Is the asset compliant?"

"She will be," Elise said.

"You mean she isn't yet?"

"She will be."

"How old is the asset?"

"Fourteen."

Darby pressed his lips together. Compassion flashed on his face. "And if she doesn't become compliant?"

"We extract anyways."

Darby thought about this for a moment before he spoke. "'The infidels should not think they can get away from us. Prepare against them any arms and weaponry you can muster so that you may terrorize them.'"

"I need another favor. An imam by the name of Salim runs a slave training school in BP."

"That beast," Darby said. "Even the Nazis and the Soviets believed in evolution as opposed to regression."

"I need access to one of the pupils. I presume the campus will have surveillance and security. But if they go off campus..."

"I'll see what I can learn. What number should I call?"

Elise whispered her mobile number into his ear.

"Do you need a prescription for the pain?"

Elise looked at him philosophically. "Is there such a thing?"

Darby considered her question. "Time machine?"

"That would work, but I'd only go back fourteen years."

"Then you wouldn't be leaving this place."

"It's not where you are," Elise said. "It's who you're with."

"Remember you said that the next time you hear the screams from Heroes Square."

Elise left the office.

The notion of a time machine sent her tumbling into the past. A deafening silence echoed in her ears. It accompanied the horrifying visual of Valerie's mother handing her baby to an Arabian nurse with total indifference to consummate the terms of her transaction. The terms consisted of trading a newborn child for money with which the mother could fuel her addictions.

CHAPTER 7

Ali fell asleep at the hookah bar. He returned home after five o'clock, took a shower, and drank some coffee that Sabida had prepared for him. When he saw her in the kitchen they ignored each other. She knew where he'd been. It was far from the first time. Such was their life. Tonight he would come home, they would pretend he'd never gone to the hookah bar, and they would resume raising their daughter as though nothing out of the ordinary had happened.

After breakfast, Ali went to the office early. The medical examiner's report on the dead dhimmi girl was waiting for him. She had a name now. She'd been identified by her fingerprints, which were found in the dhimmi database. All dhimmis were fingerprinted when they formally refused to submit to Islam.

Her name was Greta Gaspar.

Ali called Ismael to discuss the medical examiner's report. Ali knew he could depend on his friend's expertise. Ismael was the Caliphate's most respected crime scene investigator, who routinely traveled throughout Eurabia to conduct training seminars. Ali knew he also could depend on receiving a taste of Ismael's warped sense of humor, whether he was in the mood for it or not.

"Three guys walk into a bar," Ismael said. "A Catholic priest, a child molester, and a rapist. And that was just the first guy."

Ali couldn't even manage a chuckle. "I wonder what they say about us," he said.

"Who cares as long as they're saying it to the rearview mirror?"

"I'm looking at the autopsy report. Can't say as I've ever really read one before. It's like it's written in another language. I don't want to miss anything important, Ish, you know?"

"Cause of death was manual strangulation," Ismael said. "Just as I suspected. There was severe damage to the neck, throat and larynx. The toxicology report was clean."

"Other signs of trauma?"

"None."

"She wasn't assaulted in any other way?" Ali said.

"If anything, it's the contrary."

"What do you mean, the contrary?"

"The killer ... he cared about her," Ismael said.

"The hell you say."

"Her hair was washed, her nails cut, and her body was anointed with oil."

Ali pictured the killer rubbing oil on the corpse of the girl he'd just killed and wondered about his motive for doing so.

"The oil is a surprise," Ali said.

"You think that's a surprise? Are you lying down?"

"No."

"Neither did she. Her hymen was still intact. And there were no traces of semen anywhere on her body."

The absence of rape significantly reduced the odds that Greta's murder had been an act of religious cleansing. Theoretically, Zaman and the General should have been pleased about this development. The murder seemed to be the type of crime that could have occurred in any theocracy, or any society for that matter. But Ali had a feeling his bosses wouldn't be pleased no matter what he discovered. For some reason, they just wanted the case buried.

"You going to keep at it?" Ismael said.

"Keep at what?"

Ali recalled the last time he'd seen the girl who'd resembled Greta so many years ago, hanging from a drain pipe in the basement of her home.

"The murder, A. Are you going to keep investigating this murder? Because maybe … maybe it would be best to let it go."

"I'm sure it would," Ali said.

"A cop in Eurabia's got to know when to let it go."

"No one knows better when to let go than me. They don't call me the Dhimmi Lover for nothing."

Ali hung up and looked up Greta's parents in the dhimmi database. Then he drove to their barbershop in Dhimmi Town. It was located on the ground floor of a two-story brick building that looked like it had survived all three world wars. Eight battered and bruised barber chairs faced a mirrored wall. A teenager swept gray hair into a dustpan off a cracked tile floor while six mustachioed barbers tended to a bunch of old dhimmi customers. The display case at the front desk featured artisan chocolates and Hungarian shepherd axes, potassium iodide pills, and paperback copies of the Quran translated into Hungarian.

The chocolate might provide a dhimmi with enough energy to sink the axe into a Muslim cop's head, at least in his imagination, but the translation of the Quran was useless, Ali thought. Without the rhythm and rhyme of the original Arabic, without the passionate melody that accompanied the words, a person couldn't comprehend their majesty. That was why most dhimmis—and even Muslims who weren't fluent in Arabic—couldn't truly understand the glory of Islam.

A haggard woman in a gray pantsuit approached him at the front desk. Even though the years hadn't been kind to her skin, Ali spied the resemblance to Greta Gaspar immediately. There was no mistaking the symmetry of the face, the spacing between the eyes, or the delicacy of the lips.

"You want a shave?" Greta's mother said, in broken Arabic.

"I'm looking for Mr. and Mrs. Gaspar."

The woman's expression softened. "Is this about Greta? You have news of her killer?"

"No," an unoccupied barber said, seething behind her. "I guarantee you he's not here to tell us who killed our daughter. No one will ever tell us who killed our daughter."

Greta's father looked rawboned and battle-tested, especially because he was missing his left ear. His gruff exterior combined with the gleaming scissors in his right hand gave Ali pause. He glanced at the stoic customers in their fifties and sixties seated in the barber chairs, crew cuts and heavily lined faces on all of them. If elements of the Hungarian resistance didn't frequent this establishment, then the Caliph wasn't an Arab.

"Are you her parents?" Ali said, flashing his credentials.

The couple didn't speak, perhaps because they understood that Ali already knew the answer. The dhimmi database contained the picture of every Eurabian citizen who had refused to submit to Islam. The pictures were updated annually, and yet this couple looked like they'd aged six years in the last twelve months.

"I'm the officer investigating her case," Ali said.

"Is that a joke?" the father said.

"Heinrich," the mother said.

"What?" the father said. "The cops don't give a damn about crime in Dhimmi Town. Why should we believe they care about our Greta?" He turned to Ali. "What's this really about? What do you want?"

"This is about Greta. And all I really want is to ask you some questions about her."

The mother lifted her eyebrows while the father fumed. That informed Ali who was more likely to be honest with a Muslim cop.

The father took three steps to his barber's chair and motioned for Ali to sit down.

The other barbers continued tending to their customers as though nothing out of the ordinary was happening.

"Is there some place more private?" Ali said.

"No one is listening," the father said. "They all have their own problems and they've heard enough lies from your kind."

"My kind?" Ali said. "What kind is that?"

The mother slipped between them.

"Have a seat officer," she said, before glaring at her husband.

"Major," Ali said. "Major Ali."

The mother nodded. In fact, she did more than nod, she actually bowed her head a few inches. Ali appreciated her good manners, something that didn't come easily to the dhimmis. But then again, if he were being systematically forced out his own country, he might not be the portrait of congeniality either.

The father stepped aside and motioned to his chair again, this time waving with his scissors. "Have a seat, Major."

Ali eyed the scissors and chuckled. "I don't think so."

"I said, have a seat Major. A customer comes by, sees a man who looks like a cop standing in my shop, maybe he decides he doesn't need that haircut so badly after all. Maybe he finds another place where he can get one."

"The dhimmi tax, Major," the mother said. "It's killing us."

People who didn't submit to Islam were forced to pay a dhimmi tax. The percentage tax escalated annually to encourage the dhimmi to submit or leave. Only a dhimmi with increasing cashflow could survive in Eurabia and those types of success stories were scarce.

"You want to talk?" the father said. "I only talk to customers."

Ali considered the situation. "I'll pay you for a haircut but I don't want you to touch my hair. And I want you to put the scissors down and stand where I can see you."

The father shook his head. "We don't take charity here. We work for our living. You pay? You get served. Pick a service."

"I didn't realize there was a menu," Ali said. "What are my choices?"

Ali listened as the mother rattled off a variety of shaves, shampoos and haircuts. With each choice he feared he was going to have to drag these dhimmis to the station and convince the mother to cooperate apart from her husband. But then the mother concluded reciting the menu with a magical word.

Massage.

Ali sat down in the chair. The mother washed her hands. The father stood at an angle to the mirror, leaving enough room for Ali to see the mother work the knots out of his shoulders. The father continued to hold the scissors in his hand, but Ali decided not to make a big deal out of it. If he demanded the man drop his weapon, his request might be interpreted as a sign of weakness. Better to retain his dignity, Ali thought, and take the risk the father charged him. Worst case, Ali guessed he could deflect an attempt to stab him in the heart. After all, Ali was trained in self-defense while the father was trained only to cut hair, wasn't he?

"Let me start by saying I'm sorry for your loss," Ali said. "I have a daughter myself. She's a few years younger than … She's eleven. So while I can't say I understand what you're going through…"

"No, you can't," the father said. "Get on with it, Major."

Ali glanced at the mirror and made eye contact with the mother. "When did you first notice that Greta was missing?" he said.

"The day before…the day before…" The mother's voice cracked, and she had to take a breath to compose herself.

"Less than twenty-four hours before her body was found at the church," the father said.

"And where did you see her last?" Ali said.

"At Central Market," she said. "We went there to buy groceries. I gave her some money to buy a *Balaton*. She went off in the direction of the candy store and we never saw her again."

Balaton was a chocolate bar with wafers and cocoa cream.

"Did you notify the police?" Ali said.

"They told us we had to wait twenty-four hours before a report could be filed," the father said.

Ali questioned them about the trip to Central Market and whether they remembered anything suspicious, but their answers yielded nothing promising. Then he decided to switch topics.

"Tell me a little about Greta," he said. "What was she like? Was she serious or fun-loving?" Ali said.

"All the children in dhimmi town are serious," the father said. "Your kind give them no choice."

"That's not true," the mother said, "and you know it. That's what made Greta special. She wasn't serious. She loved to play. When she was little, she played spaceship with the other girls in the neighborhood. She made up names for everyone and pretended to be the captain of a ship taking them to faraway lands.

She was so sweet. She saw the best in people, even when there was none to see."

"Meaning she was trusting," Ali said.

"No one in Dhimmi Town trusts your kind," the father said. "Not even the children."

"But did Greta trust your kind?" Ali said.

The father blinked hard three times. "Oh, I see where this is going. You're trying to pin her murder on a dhimmi, aren't you? What, some stranger came to town and seduced her —"

"She wasn't violated in any way," Ali said.

The mother stopped kneading his shoulders. She stared at his reflection in the mirror.

Ali spoke softly and deliberately. "Greta's virtue remained intact until the end. No one seduced her—not a dhimmi or an Arab—at least not for that purpose. No one touched her in that way. No one violated her. No one."

The mother's eyes drew tears, while the father's expression softened just enough to convey relief.

"And if I were pinning Greta's murder on a dhimmi or a Muslim or an alien from Jupiter," Ali said, "I wouldn't bother coming here to speak with you, would I? I'd just do what it is you think Eurabian cops do."

A moment of silence passed among the three of them. Then the father nodded to the mother, and she resumed her massage.

"Greta was a sweet girl," the father said, "but she wasn't that smart."

"Heinrich," the mother said.

The father ignored her. "Street smart? Yes, always. She was our daughter, but not so much in school. Learning didn't come easy for her."

"Which was another reason we worried so much about her future," the mother said.

"Another?" Ali said.

The mother and father exchanged glances, and then the father stepped closer to Ali so that only the three of them could hear his voice.

Ali felt his muscles tense. He made sure the scissors remained within the confines of his peripheral vision.

"We're not going to survive here," the father said. "The dhimmi tax sees to that. We have a year left. Two at most, and then we'll have to pack up and move to Christendom."

"But life is very hard there," the mother said. "We have family in the countries formerly known as Argentina and Chile. There are too many refugees. Jobs are scarce. We have a trade, yes, but who'll be able to pay us? It's a life of poverty for Christians."

"I know of what you speak," Ali said. "All our kind know of what you speak. The Arab world knows the poverty that comes from being deemed a second-class citizen. What does this have to do with Greta?"

The mother lowered her gaze to Ali's trapezius and attacked the area between his shoulders with intensity. The initial pain of her assault gave way to release, and Ali could feel tension seeping from his body even as the father remained within striking distance.

"We had to make some tough choices for her," the father said. He sounded downbeat and embarrassed.

"For her," the mother said, "And for us. As parents, we had to put our daughter's health and survival above all else."

"All else," the father said. "No matter how painful it may have been from a ... from a religious perspective."

"Ah," Ali said, without thinking, as he realized what they were saying. They weren't the first to have sacrificed their daughter's Christianity to assure her a comfortable life, if not complete freedom. "You enrolled her in a slave training school."

The father hung his head but the mother continued working on Ali's neck.

"We did what was best for her," the mother said, "as opposed to what was best for our pride and ego. Isn't that right, Heinrich?"

The father didn't answer, but his pinched expression left no doubt that he still wasn't entirely comfortable with that decision.

"Which training school?" Ali said.

"Imam Salim's," the mother said.

Ali nodded, careful not to betray his negative bias. Salim was a man with an impeccable academic and religious pedigree and the standards in his school were undoubtedly of the highest order. But he was an old-school cleric who wanted to eradicate modern technology from the planet and return to the days of the caveman. His school wouldn't have been Ali's first, second or third choice. But at least the Gaspars could be certain their daughter had been fed, treated with the respect that a slave deserved by law, and provided all the health care that she needed.

"For how long was she enrolled?" Ali said.

"Nine months," the mother said. "She had three months to go before she would have been put up for acquisition."

"But she was with you when she disappeared," Ali said.

"We had her for the weekend," the mother said. "We got her one weekend a month."

Ali wished he could question someone at the school, but he wouldn't dare tread on Salim's ground. Salim was among the most powerful man in Eurabia. If Ali went anywhere near his school, one phone call from Salim could put such political pressure on the General that Ali's own father-in-law could become his enemy instead of his benefactor. Not only would Ali's investigation be over, his career might disintegrate, too.

"What did Greta think of the school?" Ali said.

The mother's expression brightened. "She actually liked it. That was the amazing thing."

"She liked it for now," the father said, "because she was a child and they hadn't taught her all her responsibilities yet."

Ali remembered his romp in bed with his slave yesterday and understood what the father meant, though by law no owner could have sex with his slave until she was of proper age. Admittedly, that was a tough law to enforce, and some slave owners had their own definition of proper age.

"What she loved most was that once she enrolled in the school, it became safe for her to make new friends," the mother said.

"What do you mean it became safe?" Ali said. "Was it dangerous for her to make friends before she entered the training school?"

"For a little girl," the mother said, "it was dangerous. Because she was taking the risk that as soon as she got close to someone, that friend might vanish overnight and never return. The dhimmi tax. It's forced so many families to leave, and every few months they'd take one of Greta's best friends with them —"

"To the point where she went out of her way not to make new friends," the father said.

"And she didn't have this problem at Imam Salim's school," Ali said, "because the girls were committed. They weren't going anywhere."

"There was a chance some future owner might move to another territory in Arabia," the father said, "but the odds were high they'd all be living in Eurabia if not Budapest when they were sold."

"How did she get along with her teachers?" Ali said.

"She didn't care for her religious studies so much," the mother said. "It was like schoolwork and she hated reading and committing things to memory. But she really took to the domestic care studies."

"Cleaning, cooking, especially knitting," the father said, voice etched with pride. "My girl was a worker."

"She had the potential to become a dressmaker," the mother said. "That would have been something, if the owner of a boutique had acquired her and made her a seamstress for life."

"She would have learned a craft," the father said. "It would have given her an identity above and beyond that of a slave."

Ali pictured Sabida learning that their daughter would be a slave who made dresses for Christian women the rest of her life and wondered which kitchen knife she would have chosen to slit her wrists at the prospect.

"Did she have any enemies in or outside of the training school?" Ali said. "Had anyone threatened her?"

The parents looked at each other and shook their heads.

"Was anything bothering her recently?" Ali said.

"No," the mother said. She was barely squeezing Ali's muscles. The conversation seemed to have sapped her of all her strength. "Quite the opposite."

"What do you mean, the opposite?"

"She was ecstatic," the father said.

Perhaps Salim was a miracle-worker after all, Ali thought, if he was helping young girls discover the bliss of Islam so quickly.

"She got her class rank," the mother said.

"Class rank?" Ali said. He'd never heard of such a thing at a religious slave training school.

"She was number two," the father said proudly. "Out of sixty-six."

"That's impressive," Ali said.

Perhaps the girl had found her true niche in domestic care, Ali thought, but he didn't dare say so for fear the parents would be insulted or think he was patronizing them.

When he met the father's eyes, however, Ali could tell by the way he tightened his lips that the man had read his face and could see exactly what he was thinking. The father put his scissors on the counter and blocked the mirror so that Ali could only see him.

"We just wanted our girl to survive," the father said.

"We wanted her to have a life," the mother said. "Is that so bad?"

Ali could detect the guilt in the parents' voices. Their guilt was a function of forsaking their daughter's soul in exchange for a more secure life on Earth, and for not being able to save her life. Ali was all too familiar with the latter, for he had arrived too late to save the girl who had resembled their Greta, and the red lips he'd kissed the day before had turned purple, and her porcelain skin had decayed into green and blue.

Ali pulled the smock off his body, handed it to the mother and stood up.

"Are you really investigating her murder?" the father said.

Ali removed his wallet from his pocket. "How much do I owe you?"

The mother circled around and stood beside her husband. Together they looked exhausted and wounded but not entirely defeated.

The father shook his head.

"Just do you job, Major," he said.

Ali hesitated, considered leaving them a gold dinar and then decided to treat the dhimmis with the dignity he would have appreciated if their roles were reversed.

"If I learn anything else that might interest you," Ali said, "I'll come visit you again."

"Sure you will," the father said.

Ali left the barber shop and returned to his car. He drove to the meeting place where he expected to learn the identity of the priest who belonged to Matthias Church with a renewed sense of self. Never had Ali felt so completely fulfilled. In addition to his wife and daughter, he now had a purpose in his professional life. Greta Gaspar had been an underdog, a minority with little hope whom society had deemed a second-class citizen. And then some son of-a-bitch had gone and killed her.

Islam was a religion rooted in support of the underdog even more than it was the religion of the businessman.

Ali pressed the gas pedal.

He was all business now.

CHAPTER 8

Elise got a call from Darby within two hours of leaving his offices. Imam Salim's slave training school was located in his personal compound next door to Buda Castle. The latter was a recreation of the palace that had been occupied by Hungarian kings and was now the Caliph's home. The Imam's residence was a Baroque masterpiece with ornate decoration, a style that had been encouraged by the Catholic Church to lend the Pope a regal aura. Salim's compound was fortress-like and impenetrable by an unannounced visitor, even one posing as the morality police.

While most of the school's classes were conducted on campus, some required field trips to provide the future slaves with access to the requisite equipment. Darby gave Elise the address of the Persian School of Dressmaking and told her that classes were conducted in the afternoon.

By the time Elise got his call it was almost two o'clock. She knew nothing about the school. She didn't know the layout or have a clue as to what awaited her inside. Plus, if her credentials were discovered to be fraudulent and she were revealed to be a spy, she'd fail on both her missions. She'd neither acquire the supposed treasure for Christendom nor save her sister from a life of slavery.

So Elise did what any self-respecting Christian woman would do.

She got on her bicycle and pedaled toward the school with all her might. She drove past a new mosque that had once been St. Stephen's Basilica dating back to the tenth century, and into the heart of Pest's commercial area. A sign for the Persian School of Dressmaking hung above a store that sold kitchen tools and personal accessories disguised as toys.

Elise secured her bicycle to a lamppost and walked up to the door. An intercom was attached to the brick wall beside it. Two names were emblazoned on placards above the intercom—REZA COUTURE and PERSIAN SCHOOL OF DRESSMAKING. Above the intercom hung a camera. No doubt it had captured her image when she'd looked up, though her *niqab* had hid all but her eyes.

Elise's instincts told her to leave because if she entered the school she had no leverage over anyone who might challenge her authority. And yet she couldn't stop herself any more than she could have slowed down en route on her bicycle.

She pressed the intercom button until a woman responded on the other end.

As she spoke the words she'd rehearsed during her bike ride, Elise released the intercom button in selected spots so that only part of her sentences could be heard on the other end, as though the system were broken.

"... appointment ... Persian School ..."

"I'm sorry, could you repeat that please?" the woman at the school said.

"...appointment ... Persian School ... Kawlah ..."

"There must be something wrong with the intercom—"

This time Elise spoke without lifting her finger from the intercom button. "Commission for the Promotion of Virtue and Prevention of Vice."

The door buzzed open.

Elise climbed the wooden stairs to the second floor. A sign above the door to the left welcomed visitors to Reza Couture, while the one to the right led to the Persian School of Dressmaking. Elise took a breath and entered the latter.

A plain girl in her late teens dressed in a *hijab* that left her face fully visible sat behind a desk in the lobby. The sound of young boys shouting and machines whirring could be heard from beyond the walls. The girl stared at Elise with uncertainty.

Before either of them could say a word, a bustling matron emerged from a door in the wall behind the receptionist. Skin hung loosely around her eyes and neck, and creases marred her expression. She wore a stylish charcoal business suit with a scarf wrapped around her head. She looked permanently stressed.

"I'm sorry to have kept you waiting," she said. It was the voice of the woman with whom Elise had spoken over the intercom. "I couldn't make out everything you said. Of course, the Commission for the Promotion of Virtue is always welcome. Did you say you had an appointment?"

"Actually," Elise said, "I said the opposite. I don't have an appointment but I have a very important matter I'd like to discuss with the school's owner."

The matron tensed. "My husband and I are the owners here. You can speak to me. What is this about?"

Elise glanced at the receptionist, who lowered her head as though she'd been eavesdropping. The matron motioned for the girl to leave. The receptionist bowed and disappeared into the back of the school through the same door the matron had used to enter.

"This is about opportunity," Elise said.

"What kind of opportunity?" the matron said.

"The financial kind," Elise said. "My cousin is a man of great importance. If I were to mention his name, you'd recognize it immediately. But for business purposes, it's essential that his identity remain confidential for now."

Elise's introduction, as expected, served only to deepen the lines in the matron's forehead.

"For a decade now, he's run one of the most successful slave training schools in greater Arabia," Elise said. "His pupils are regarded as the finest specimens who provide great service and pleasure to their masters. And now he's thinking about developing a chain of such schools—for the glory of Islam and the benefit of society at large. And to develop such a chain, he needs partners in key locations. Budapest is a key location, and your school and your work with Imam Salim's pupils comes highly recommended."

"You're acquainted with Imam Salim?"

"Well..."

"Why didn't you say so?" The matron beamed. "My name is Miss Mona. Let's discuss this wonderful opportunity in my office over a cup of tea. I have several ideas, yes, several ideas that I think you'd find very interesting."

The receptionist brought them tea and they spoke for half an hour. Elise fabricated a crude business plan, boasted of her imaginary cousin's social standing and entrepreneurial success, and deflected the conversation when Miss Mona probed his identity. Money and power were respected above all else in Eurabia. Elise could see Miss Mona counting her profit if she were to double, triple or quadruple the number of students in her school.

"My cousin is still in the preliminary stages of planning," Elise said, "but at some point I'd like to visit one of your classes, perhaps when the students from Imam Salim's school are here."

"That's a wonderful idea," Miss Mona said. "And as luck would have it, they're here right now. Come. Let me give you a tour of the classroom."

Elise shook off the nerves that came from the prospect of seeing Valerie for the first time in her life and followed Miss Mona into an open room the size of half a football field. Sixty-six girls between the ages of eleven and sixteen sat working at sewing machines, four to a table. They were crafting the same item of clothing they were wearing, simple black *hijabs*. Three schoolboys were running around the tables shouting at the girls to watch their technique or speed up their pace. They looked ridiculous. A woman, probably the teacher, stood on an elevated platform studying the classroom. She looked fierce.

"I didn't realize there were boys in your class, too," Elise said.

"There aren't," Miss Mona said. She arched her chin. "Those are my sons. They'll be teachers and supervisors some day."

Elise scanned the girls. From her angle, she could see only some of their faces. Elise expected to be hit by a lightning bolt of recognition when her eyes finally landed on those of her own flesh and blood. After all, the blood bond was forever. A sister would always recognize her own, even if she'd never seen her before, wouldn't she?

The classroom was a sartorial pigsty. Dust balls gathered in corners and grime covered the legs of the tables. The walls were lined with partially broken-down boxes and cloth remnants. The air smelled vaguely of oil, and Elise found herself sweating almost immediately. She looked around for vents or windows but found none.

"The specimens seem very focused," Elise said. "I'm impressed."

"We'd like to take credit for that but they come prepared. All credit goes to Imam Salim and the education he provides."

"I appreciate being able to see a class in session. There's no substitute for personal due diligence."

Miss Mona said something agreeable, but by then Elise wasn't listening. Approaching the middle of the room, she'd seen a quarter, a third and then half the girls' faces. As she circled the tables with Miss Mona beside her, the rest of the girls came into view. There was something familiar about one girl's nose, something else about another's mouth. But overall, neither of them struck a chord.

And then Elise saw her. Sitting at a table with ramrod posture, guiding material along the feed dog toward the needle with expert precision, foot firm on the pedal beside the bobbin compartment. Even before the girl looked up, Elise knew. She had no idea how she knew. She just did.

As Elise waited for the girl to raise her chin and reveal her eyes, she realized that Miss Mona was speaking to her with enthusiasm and excitement.

"And here is someone you know," Miss Mona said.

Elise couldn't believe Miss Mona's words. Her cover was blown, Elise thought. Miss Mona knew she was a spy, that she had a sister, and that she'd come for Valerie. It was absolutely impossible and yet it was obviously true. Elise couldn't begin to contemplate how she'd revealed herself but inferred she'd been a fool from the moment she'd arrived in BP.

"Here he is," Miss Mona said, looking beyond Elise.

Elise turned and saw a gaunt man with a white beard limping into the room from a backdoor. One bodyguard led the way, while two others trailed behind him.

Elise recognized the man from television, newspapers, and surveillance photographs.

He was Imam Salim.

CHAPTER 9

Chef Florence was the only dhimmi Ali considered a friend, and even that relationship was tainted by professional hierarchy. Still, Ali enjoyed his company more than that of any of his colleagues on the police force because Florence was never condescending toward him. Today, Ali would push the boundaries of their friendship. He wished he didn't have to, but he had no choice. This was the nature of real detective work, and probably one of the reasons Ali had never really taken to it until now. A man had to use every tool at his disposal to solve a crime and sometimes those tools were human beings.

Florence had taught Ali that a bowl of pasta was the equivalent of a dose anti-depressant medication. He said the food generated a chemical in the brain similar to the medicine. Since then, Ali had become addicted to pasta primavera. He'd convinced Sabida to add it to their dinner rotation by informing her that spaghetti was invented in Libya and brought to Sicily in 800 AD during the Arab conquests. According to some historians, that was, in fact, the truth.

Ali met Florence at their usual spot in Pest, three blocks away from the Danube River and the stately Gresham Palace. The place was called Café Kor and it served delicious Hungarian dishes, including a tasty veal risotto. The open dining room bustled with young Hungarian servers, all of them men. They regarded Ali with the warmth and respect that a regular customer deserved, but Ali knew their true feelings toward him were mixed, at best.

The Hungarians who didn't flee to Christendom had resisted Muslim conquest mightily. Previously, they had survived occupations by the Soviet Union, Nazi Germany, and the Islamic warriors who had comprised the Ottoman Empire in the sixteenth century. Ultimately, however, they had neither the numbers nor the nuclear weapons to prevail.

Florence was among those who stayed, after he returned from Dubai, despite his dhimmi status, out of pure love for their country. Ali joined him at a solitary table in the private loft where they always sat, out of sight and earshot of the other patrons. Ali ordered bottled water and the risotto. Florence opted for a cup of cheese soup and the goulash.

"Twenty times we've been here, and twenty times you've ordered the risotto," Florence said. "You know, I never told you this before. You may think it's delicious but it's not risotto."

"It isn't?"

"Most definitely not."

Ali was aghast. "What is it then?"

"It's just a plate of veal and rice masquerading as a sublime culinary invention. Risotto's an Italian dish made with a short grain rice like arborio—the best in the world. The ingredients are cooked to creamy perfection in a broth, which in this case, would have included the veal."

Ali shrugged. "Well, I guess I'm just another filthy Arab with poor taste."

"That's not fair, Major. I didn't say that. All I'm saying is what I'm saying, and that's just my opinion. Heck, we're in a Hungarian joint. The locals would agree with you, not with me."

"If you never told me this risotto was a fraud before, why are you telling me now?"

"Because I have a feeling this lunch is going to be about the truth."

"Why do you say that?"

Florence dropped his gaze for a moment before looking up again. "Because they're talking about you at the station, Major."

Ali shifted uncomfortably in his seat. "Oh, really? And what are they saying?"

"That you're not well," Florence said.

"What do they say is wrong with me?"

"They say you're suffering from amnesia. That you forgot who you are."

Ali chuckled because he didn't know what else to do. If everyone was talking about him, that meant Zaman was likely plotting his payback, which implied that Ali had little time before he was formally removed from the case.

"They say you woke up out of a coma thinking you really are the Dhimmi Lover," Florence said. "That this murder case has your mind all twisted."

"Well, we know that part's true. But as for loving dhimmis …."

"As long as the dhimmis are lying dead at the bottom of the ocean, right?"

"You've been talking to Ismael," Ali said, referring to his friend from CSI and his warped sense of humor.

They shared a laugh, or rather, something masquerading as one. Then a bead of sweat trickled out from Florence's hairline onto his forehead. In all the years they'd exchanged information—Ali might warn Florence that a truck of *haram* alcohol and tobacco products was going to be intercepted, while Florence might tell Ali where he could find a stolen police vehicle—Florence had never shown any signs of being nervous.

"I need the name of the priest that belongs to Saint Matthias," Ali said.

Florence remained stone-faced. "I like your choice of verbs. The priest who *belongs* to Saint Matthias."

Ali shrugged. "It's the truth, isn't it? It's not like he conducts services there on Sunday, or any other day for that matter."

Churches were, in fact, symbolic in their importance. Thugs targeted Christian priests for beatings and assassinations so the latter had taken to leading prayers and services in private residences, catacombs, and the wooded outskirts of major metropolitan areas throughout Eurabia. It was the only way the priests could preserve their anonymity, because the Dhimmi Contract gave all Muslims the legal right to demand entry into any dhimmi home, including churches. That right effectively exposed every priest who dared conduct a service in a real church.

Chef Florence shook his head. "What kind of Christian would I be ... what kind of man would I be if I betrayed the person who's a conduit to my personal God?"

"What kind of man will you be if you don't help me figure out who murdered Greta Gaspar?"

Shock sprang to Florence's face and his voice fell to a whisper. "Christ, Sami. You really are serious. You know her name."

"That's twice in ten seconds that you've used the word 'Christ' in public. I cut you slack because we're friends, Florence, but do you have to push me?"

"Won't happen again." Florence narrowed his eyes. "Why do you suddenly care, Major? What's this all about? What is it about this girl? "

"She was my first crush," Ali said. He'd rehearsed his answer in case the subject came up. Part of his story was true, the other part a complete fabrication. "First girl I ever kissed. She was ... I don't know ... fourteen or fifteen. I was sixteen. She was the housekeeper's daughter. My parents forbid me to see her. Her parents forbid her to see me. Her step-father was abusive. I was her protector until the one day I didn't get there in time and she took her own life."

Florence sat quietly for a moment. "I thought you'd tell me ... I just assumed that because you had a daughter ..."

"No," Ali said. "Greta Gaspar happens to be the spitting image of a girl from my past. That's why this case is so personal. I didn't do right by the first girl. I'm not going to let this one down, too."

Florence paused again. "I guess this is a lunch of truths."

"It is. What's the priest's name?"

Florence shook his head. "I can't help you, Major. I wish I could. Anything else. Anything ... But not this."

"Then you leave me no choice," Ali said.

Florence froze.

"Islam and Christianity," Ali said, "They have some things in common. They agree that your Jesus was a prophet and conceived in an immaculate way. Islam parts ways when it comes to him being the son of God, but both our religions agree that he was a man. As opposed to a woman. That there are men, and there are women."

Florence's face reddened.

"Your fellow Christians down below," Ali said, nodding at the stairs that led to the lower level, "they'll banish you from your holy communion, your church, and never look at you the same again. Meanwhile, some of my fellow Muslims will toss you from a roof and splatter your brains on the asphalt. All for being a homosexual. Which would you prefer?"

"I prefer neither," Florence said.

"That makes two of us, but that's not an option on the table."

"How did you know?"

"I'm a cop."

Florence continued staring at him in an inquiring manner.

"You have a tendency to look at men the way men look at women," Ali said. "All we're talking about is a second here and there, but it's noticeable. And at the risk of sounding conceited, I have to admit that I've felt your eyes all over me in the wrong places on a couple of occasions."

Florence shrugged. "I could pay you a compliment..."

Ali raised his hand. "Please, Florence. Please don't. It's none of my business what a man does with his own equipment. It's between you and your personal God. But keep me out of it."

They sat in silence.

"There's one dhimmi butcher left at Central Market," Florence finally said. "The priest is his daughter."

"The priest is a woman?" Ali couldn't hide his shock.

Florence shrugged.

"Since when does the Catholic Church ordain women as priests?"

"Since no man wants the job."

Florence told Ali that the priest had a day job and exactly where he could find her.

The waiter delivered their lunches. Florence eyed Ali's risotto with palpable disdain. Ali devoured three massive forkfuls, left some money on the table and thanked Florence with a quick nod of the head. The chef, in turn, flicked his eyebrows once in disappointment. Their friendship would never be the same, Ali thought. He knew he'd never look at a friend the same way if he'd been threatened by him.

After he left the restaurant, Ali climbed in his car and drove to the Chain Bridge to find the priestess so that he might hear her confession.

CHAPTER 10

Elise and Miss Mona bowed their heads as Imam Salim strolled toward them. Elise prepared to be peppered with questions. She repeated the fiction she'd concocted to justify her presence at the school over and over again. The truth was in the details. Elise had blinded Miss Mona with the vague promise of profit participation in an expanding franchise. Salim would insist on a name and force her to lie even more. The greater the lies, Elise knew, the greater her risk of exposure.

The best Elise could hope for was to escape the Persian School of Dressmaking without contradicting herself. Valerie was sitting at a table behind her—the girl with the perfect posture was most certainly her sister. If only Elise could wheel around and steal one more glance—

Salim arrived. He was sixty-three years old, but with his chaotic gray beard, weathered complexion and circular wire-rimmed glasses, he looked closer to eighty. Still, a palpable sense of calm emanated from the man. Each step he took spoke of an eerie self-assuredness. Here came the man least likely to promote violence in the world based on his carriage, Elise thought.

She took a deep breath and prepared for introductions and the incisive questions that would follow.

But Salim walked right past them.

"Where are my finest pupils?" His voice complimented his mien, gentle to the core, born to soothe, not aggravate. "Ah, there they are."

Elise breathed a sigh of relief. How could she have been so stupid? She was a woman. Miss Mona was a woman. Salim wouldn't stop to have a conversation with either of them because discussing business with women was beneath him. In his eyes, women were beneath him, period.

As she straightened, Elise noticed that all the girls had stood up and that Salim was aiming for the table where the girl with the perfect posture was now standing. Then the female teacher who had been presiding over class clapped her hands and the future slaves began falling in line.

Class was over. They were leaving.

Despair gripped Elise. The girl with the perfect posture was falling in line, too. Elise wouldn't get to see her face, not today, and possibly not ever, she thought.

And then Elise realized that Miss Mona was still bowing and what she should have known all along—that she was screwed. Two of the bodyguards continued onward with Salim, but the third one marched right up to Miss Mona. They exchanged the traditional Muslim greeting, and then the bodyguard glared at Elise with eyes as black as coal.

"Who is this woman?" he said.

"She's a friend," Miss Mona said. "A distinguished officer of the Commission of Promotion of Virtue and Prevention of Vice."

"The morality police? Here? Why?"

"She's not here in her capacity as an officer but as a private citizen. As an envoy, so to speak. An envoy for her even more distinguished cousin, isn't that right Miss Kawlah?"

"An envoy?" the bodyguard said. "On a diplomatic mission? To a dressmaking school?"

"Forgive my choice of words," Miss Mona said. "Not a diplomatic mission." She turned and smiled at Elise like the smart-money bitch that she was revealing herself to be. "A business mission."

"Business?" the bodyguard said. "Well, given I'm the Imam's business manager and all that goes on in this school is his concern, don't you think an introduction is in order?"

Elise cursed to herself. The man looked like a thug but probably had a degree in business, which meant her lies would have to sound like the truth.

Miss Mona made the introductions. The business manager's name was Moncef Zaid. Elise bowed appropriately, but she couldn't help but pay attention to the shuffling of children's feet behind her. The girl with the perfect posture was leaving and there was nothing Elise could do about it.

"What kind of business deal are you proposing?" Zaid said.

Miss Mona's lips moved, but Elise answered before she could speak. If one had to lie it was best to maintain complete control of one's side of the conversation to avoid further entanglements. Elise told him the same story she'd told the Miss Mona.

"And who is your cousin?" Zaid said.

"This is all very preliminary," Elise said. "I don't really have his permission to do anything other than explore the facility on his behalf."

"Actually," Zaid said, "you have no such permission and neither does he. If either of you had any proper manners, you would have discussed this with Imam Salim first given he's already in partnership with the school."

"I understand," Elise said. "Perhaps it's best I leave and pass on your comments to my cousin." She started toward the exit.

Zaid blocked her path. "You'll do no such thing."

Miss Mona stepped back, alarm registering on her face.

Then Zaid smiled. "Because Imam Salim is constantly on the lookout for new business opportunities that can expand his portfolio. And if the relationships that create such opportunities also enlarge his audience…. Come now, Miss Kawlah. If your cousin and Imam Salim share certain philosophies, perhaps this business opportunity has even greater possibilities?"

"You make a compelling argument," Elise said, wondering if the kids were all getting on a bus. How else could they travel to and from Salim's campus? Did they walk for an hour to get exercise? "I'll put it to my cousin."

"Excellent," Zaid said. He grabbed her by the arm just above the elbow, with sufficient force to leave a bruise. "And what is your cousin's name? You may have mentioned it, but during all this excitement…"

Elise knew she wouldn't get away without fabricating the lie she most wanted to avoid.

"My cousin's name is Imam Labib. He hails from the Maldives."

Such a man did, in fact, exist. Elise had memorized his bio just in case she needed it. She'd chosen Labib because he was stationed at the most remote region of greater Arabia and was relatively unknown. And he did, in fact, run a small but highly regarded slave training school. Last year, one of his slaves had been extracted from the capital, Malé, by a militant Buddhist uncle from Thailand. The story, recounted by a Christian spy who'd been operating in the Kingdom of Buddha at the time, had provided Elise with the final bit of inspiration she needed to begin her quest to find Valerie and save her from a life of slavery.

A condescending grin spread across Zaid's face. "The Maldives? I've heard of this place. What is the population there?"

Elise said, "I'm not exactly sure…"

"He has produced slaves that are among the most valued in greater Arabia? In the Maldives?"

"Greatness does not choose its birthplace," Elise said.

Zaid turned reflective. "Well said. You are very wise for a woman, which may bode well for this business proposition. Here's my business card. I'll expect your cousin's phone call by the end of the day."

"He may be on a pilgrimage," Elise said.

"By the end of the day," Zaid said. He turned to Miss Mona. "A word in private?"

"Of course." Miss Mona glanced at Elise victoriously. "Would you wait for me in the kitchenette?"

She pointed to a door along the same wall where the entrance was found.

Elise looked around for the girls but they were gone. She shuffled to the kitchen instead, contemplating what had just transpired.

Miss Mona had accomplished her goal. She'd minimized any risk of offending Imam Salim by informing his business manager of a possible new venture, discovered the mysterious cousin's true identity, and created the possibility of a three-way deal with Salim. Only a deft operator could survive as an entrepreneur in a society where women were considered undesirable business leaders because of the risk of anger management issues during their menstrual cycles.

As Elise approached the kitchenette, a dim light reflected off the tile floor beneath the scuffed and stained door. She tried to turn the knob but it didn't rotate, so she yanked on it instead.

The hollow door flew open and almost escaped her grasp. Elise caught it just in time before it crashed into the wall.

The girl with the perfect posture stood with her back to Elise, prematurely broad shoulders thrown back to form a straight line.

It was the girl's natural stance, not an affectation. Elise was certain of this because she shared the same genetic pre-disposition. She carried herself in an identical manner.

The girl turned. She was the spitting image of what Elise had seen in the mirror when she was the same age.

The girl was Valerie.

Elise had found her. She'd really found her.

Valerie held a cigarette in her left hand. An open can of Darjeeling tea rested on the counter. The door to the cabinet above the counter had been flung open. Elise guessed that Miss Mona hid the *haram* tobacco in a tea can and that the kids had somehow discovered it. Chatter and road noise sounded from Valerie's right. Elise spotted the open window above a table, no doubt her means of re-entry to commit the theft that could get her dismissed from school, arrested and jailed.

Alarm registered in Valerie's eyes.

Fury that Valerie was smoking cigarettes at age fourteen mixed with the sheer joy of seeing her sister. The combination rendered Elise stationary and mute. For the moment, Elise forgot about her job and her mission. Here before her stood a reason to live.

"Are you really the morality police?" Valerie said.

The sound of perfect Arabic words coming from her sister's mouth stunned Elise. She had expected Valerie to speak Arabic, of course, but a human being dreamed in her native language. In Elise's dreams, she and Valerie spoke English. This was the first moment where Elise's dreams had merged with reality. And in reality, they were going to speak Arabic.

"What makes you think I'm the morality police?" Elise said.

"I heard you introduced that way. In the classroom."

Elise folded her arms over chest. "That's right. I'm an officer with the Commission for the Promotion of Virtue."

Valerie's voice cracked. "And Prevention of Vice."

"Oh, yes," Elise said, in a tone that implied the cigarette thief was in big trouble. "Most definitely. What's your name?"

"My name ... is Safa."

"Safa," Elise said. "I'm going to remember that. My name is Miss Kawlah."

Valerie swallowed hard. "Are you ... are you going to arrest me?"

She sounded mortified, which pleased Elise. So did her sister's gumption, however misguided.

"That depends," Elise said.

"On what?"

Elise nodded at the tea can. "Is there another one of those in there for me?"

Valerie's jaw dropped. She thrust her hand into the tin and almost knocked it over to pull out another smoke. She offered the cigarette to Elise, fingers shaking, eyes wide open.

Elise stepped forward. She made sure not to touch Valerie's fingers to avoid creeping her out, though she desperately wanted to do so. Instead Elise, snatched the cigarette, sniffed it, and let it hang between the second and third fingers of her right hand. All the while, she never took her eyes off Valerie's.

"Do you do this every day?" Elise said.

Valerie pursed her lips.

"See you tomorrow then. Same time. Be here or you're in trouble. Now scram," Elise said, nodding toward the window.

Valerie hesitated for a second. Then she pocketed her cig and vaulted out the window all too gracefully, leaving no doubt that this was not the first smoke she'd pilfered.

Elise sealed the tin can and placed it back in the cupboard among the other teas. She hid the cigarette Valerie had given her in a pocket and took a seat beside the water cooler to wait for Miss Mona.

In another time and another place, if she'd had a lighter, she would have been smoking already, savoring the rush from the nicotine and the memory of what had just transpired.

CHAPTER 11

No man-made structure inspired Ali quite like Budapest's Chain Bridge. Its roadbed hung suspended over the Danube from iron chains connected to two stone pillars. At night the pillars were illuminated green and the gigantic steel bolts that secured the roadbed to the river pier glowed black beside them. When it was created in 1849, the bridge was considered one of the engineering marvels of the world and a source of great pride, not only within Hungary, but in all of Europe as well. It was the first permanent bridge to connect Buda to Pest, and as such, it symbolized a desire for closer relations between Eastern and Western Europe. Now it served as a metaphorical link between old Europe and the new Ottoman Empire.

When his car turned left onto the entrance to the bridge, Ali forced himself to look past the abutment. Lion-head capstones with the coat of arms of the country formerly known as Hungary had once greeted drivers and pedestrians. In his infinite desire to wipe out all traces of anything but Islam, the Caliph had ordered the capstones destroyed. In their places, the abutments on both sides of the bridge now featured slabs of granite painted red with the white star and crescent symbol of many of the successor states of the Ottoman Empire. The star and crescent also had become symbols of Islamism in the late twentieth century. Ali didn't understand why Caliphs felt compelled to destroy beautiful and historic things just because they'd been built by other people.

Ali parked his car beside a cruiser that belonged to the cop who was providing protection for the construction crew on the bridge. The bored veteran recognized Ali, saluted wearily, and nodded at the compact mobile home that served as construction headquarters.

"Heads up," he said. "The supervisor's a real bastard."

"Why's that?" Ali said.

"He's the Caliph's nephew, or cousin, or some such shit."

"Isn't everyone?"

"What," the veteran said, "a real bastard?"

Ali pointed at his colleague with appreciation as he walked away. There was a man who understood Eurabia, which is why they had him guarding a mobile home.

When he got to the door, Ali decided to announce himself in a manner that would resonate with an entitled man. He burst inside without knocking.

The supervisor, with no more than five whiskers that needed shaving, glared at Ali. "Who are you?" he said. "And why didn't you knock?"

"You have a man named Peter Noel working on the Bridge today?" Ali said.

According to Florence, the priest's name was Petra Noel but she lived incognito as a man to generate a second income and help her family pay the dhimmi tax and survive in Budapest.

"I have four men working on the bridge," the supervisor said. "And you didn't answer my question. Who are you and why didn't you knock? Didn't your mother teach you any manners?"

Ali flashed his ID. "I'm here investigating a major crime. Would you please tell Peter Noel to come down from the Bridge so that I can talk to him?"

"No," the supervisor said. "Can't do it."

"Why not?"

"He's still welding repairs to the iron saddles. That was supposed to be done over an hour ago. It would take ten minutes to get him down, another ten to get him up, plus whatever time it takes for you to question him. I can't fall behind schedule. It's out of the question."

"It'll only take me five minutes," Ali said.

"No, it won't. Even if you only speak to him for a second, the whole thing will take more than twenty minutes because we have to get him down and back up again." The supervisor measured Ali. "You're not too smart, are you?"

Ali had at least fifteen years on the kid but the punk couldn't have cared less. The cop providing protection outside hadn't been joking. The kid really was a bastard.

Ali laughed as he always did when they made fun of him at the station. "Nope. I'm not. They say my brain is in my fist." He raised his right hand and curled his massive fingers. "How about if my brain meets your brain so they can get to know each other better?"

The supervisor blanched.

"Look, I get it," Ali said. "You have a deadline. You're the man. It's all on you. You have a reputation for getting stuff done which is why you were given all this responsibility at such a young age."

The supervisor shrugged.

"But do you really want me to call the General and tell him you refused to cooperate on a matter of national security? Then what? Maybe you make your call and we see who's yanking on the bigger chain. If it's me, maybe my father-in-law will have mercy on you and not have you banished to Transylvania."

It was the moment of truth. If the supervisor was really connected to the Caliph, Ali might have made a catastrophic mistake. That's all it took in Eurabia. One wrong word from the wrong man.

"I'll compromise with you," the supervisor said. "I can't afford the time to bring him down, but I can send you up to talk to him."

Ali glanced at the scaffolding, his palms instantly sweaty, and then looked up at the top of the bridge. The men were so high up he couldn't see them.

"This is my best and final," the supervisor said. "Otherwise we reach for our phones, and may the man with the most pull win."

Evidently the little bastard was connected, Ali thought. Ali couldn't admit to his fear of heights because it would have been seen as a weakness and caused him great shame. His only choices were to face his fear or wait to speak to the priestess once she descended. But Ali couldn't afford the delay. The longer he waited the greater the opportunity for the killer to cover his tracks, create an alibi or disappear. That's why the first twenty-four hours were so critical to any murder investigation. At least that's what real murder police who closed cases and actually found the killers had told him.

Ali climbed on the scaffolding before he could convince himself to do otherwise and watched as the supervisor started the engine that would lift him up.

"Have a safe ride, Major," the supervisor said.

Ali hated all venues that exposed him to great heights—helicopters, planes, seven-foot ladders, even hills masquerading as mountains. Once, during police training, he'd run ten kilometers up Jabal Ram mountain in Jordan with his fellow cadets. When they arrived at the summit, their instructor told them to gather at the mountain ridge to see the valley below. Ali tried to hide behind some of the men but the instructor insisted they form a line along a strip of land barely wide enough for their feet. While the instructor compared the ground upon which they were standing to their integrity as future police officers—one false move led to a slippery slope and swift decline—Ali did all that he could to forestall a full-blown panic attack.

He kept his eyes level as he rode the scaffolding and focused on his breathing. The next five minutes seemed like twenty until the roadbed finally came into view directly before him, and for a moment the pounding in his heart subsided. But his relief was short lived because the scaffolding never stopped—he was only halfway to his destination. By the time the other two scaffoldings appeared overhead to the right, Ali was sweating profusely. He measured each breath to make sure the length of his exhalations matched those of his inhalations.

As his scaffolding continued to rise to the height of the other two, eight pairs of legs came into view. Three of the sets of legs were lined up in a row facing the fourth pair, as though the leader was issuing instructions. Ali stood on his tiptoes and craned his neck just enough to see that all four men had removed their hard hats, and the leader wasn't conducting a meeting. She was making the sign of a cross with her right hand before slipping a wafer into the open mouth before her. Then all four workers put their helmets back on and hurried back to work, three of them stepping over a railing and moving on to a parallel scaffolding.

Making the sign of the cross in public was enough to get a person's hand cut off. Practicing a Christian service in public, especially one that involved the priest sharing the so-called Holy

Sacrament with others, would surely result in the death penalty for all those involved.

This brazen breach of Sharia law distracted Ali from his anxious state. Images of shackling the priestess flitted in and out of his mind as the scaffolding came to a halt parallel to the other two. He would arrest the priestess after he extracted the information he needed, and call for back-up to take down her followers. The balls on this Christian, Ali thought, to disregard the law of her land. And it was her land because she paid the dhimmi tax and refused to leave it.

When the priestess laid eyes on Ali she did a double-take, no doubt shocked to see a man other than the supervisor approaching. Then she lifted her long legs and straddled the two scaffoldings to climb from hers to his.

A tremendous gust of wind blew Ali's scaffolding backward, away from the bridge. He took his eyes off the priestess and looked forward, grasping the handrail even tighter. The scaffolding swung back and crashed into the bridge before another gust of wind sent it flying even higher in reverse. The sequence repeated itself two more times, and by the fourth swing backward Ali could sense the fear in his belly, the clamps closing down on his lungs. He commanded himself not to panic, told himself that he refused to lose his composure, and as was inevitably the case when he desperately wished for something, the exact opposite occurred.

His breaths shortened. He envisioned himself fainting on the scaffolding and requiring assistance, the emergency medical technicians later recalling the incident to Zaman and a bunch of other cops, all of them laughing so hard they spit coffee and bits of baklava from their mouths. When black splotches began to mar his vision, Ali knew he was going down and that it was just a matter of time before he fainted.

And as the scaffolding swung wildly back and forth, he did what he detested more than anything, which was look for help from another human being. In this case there was only one person nearby, and she was moving toward him as though she were standing on flat land, strangely unaffected by the seesawing planks beneath her feet ...

The next thing Ali knew he was gazing at patches of white clouds rolling through a clear blue sky with the sun peaking out from behind them. He didn't understand how he could be gazing upward if he was standing on his feet, until he realized that he wasn't standing at all. He was lying down.

A hand touched his shoulder.

An androgynous face crisscrossed with premature age lines and sun damage peered down at him.

The priestess, Ali remembered. The priest was a woman because no man wanted the job.

"Are you all right?" she said, with a strange sense of joy that didn't reflect the circumstances.

Ali tried to scramble to his feet but his head swirled. The best he could do was sit up. His face burned from the humiliation of remaining in a subordinate physical position to a dhimmi. And not just a dhimmi. A dhimmi woman.

"Some water will help," the priestess said. A thermos materialized out of nowhere. "Here," she said, extending a long arm toward Ali's mouth. "Drink from my cup."

Ali turned away, disgusted by the thought of a cup that had touched the dhimmi's lips.

"Don't worry. I've been fasting. My lips haven't touched my thermos all day. It's the same one that I wash thoroughly every night with fine Eurabian water. Straight from the tap."

Ali drank from the thermos and then managed to stand up. His ego soothed by having done so without a dhimmi woman's help, he recalled his agenda.

"I know who you are," Ali said. "I knew even before I saw you giving your Holy Sacrament to the others."

The priestess hesitated but the joy never left her face. "There's no one but the faithful up here," she said.

"We don't share the same faith."

"Actually, we do. It's what binds us together more than any other couple in Eurabia."

Ali glared at her. "And what exactly is that?"

"Faith in scaffolding," the priestess said.

Ali chuckled. He hadn't been expecting humor, only sanctimonious Christian bullshit.

"I need your help," he said. "I'm investigating the murder of Greta Gaspar."

The priestess considered his statement before answering. "If you came all the way up here with your …" She appeared on the verge of mentioning Ali's fear of heights but then found a way to help him save face. "… questions, then you must be serious."

"The dhimmi witness said the killer handed him a tin to give to you," Ali said. "He said the tin contained money."

"For a funeral service."

"I don't care about the money. I'm interested in the man who gave you the money. How did he know your name?"

"I don't know," the priestess said. "I asked myself that same question when he gave me a tin the first time."

"The first time? He gave you another tin?"

The priestess nodded. "When the first girl was killed."

Ali grasped the handrail.

The first girl.

How could another girl have been killed earlier and he not know about it? He desperately wanted to ask the priestess everything she knew about the first girl but the humiliation of admitting he didn't know what was happening in his own department stopped him.

The priestess, however, saw right through him. She told him the girl's name, Hanna Kalmar, and the date her body was discovered, three weeks earlier.

Ali dispensed with his pride without any further thought. He wanted all the information she had and to hell with everything else.

"Do we … do the police know about the first tin?" he said.

"If you … if the police knew about that tin, that would mean they know about me. If that was the case, would I be standing up here now?"

The only question was whether she'd still be vertical at all, Ali thought.

"And you saw the killer that first time?" Ali said. "Yourself?"

"I saw him the way the caretaker saw him. Face and body covered, you couldn't even see his eyes. He spoke in perfect Arabic, handed me the tin and left."

"He said the money was for a funeral service?"

"He said it was for all my troubles. But I knew what he meant."

Ali tried to think of more questions to ask but none came to mind. His frustration almost boiled over. He wished he'd conducted a real investigation before. Twelve years on the force and he felt like a rookie.

"Is there anything else you know that could help me?" he said,

"It's unusual for a Eurabian cop to care about a dead dhimmi girl. Why is this girl so important to you?"

Ali opted for the truth in hopes it might encourage her to answer his question honestly. "She reminds me of someone I used to know."

"Someone from your childhood, no doubt," the priestess said. "Someone who's part of the trauma that's left its mark on you forever."

"What mark?"

The scaffolding swayed back and forth, and the priestess let his question slide to let him save face again. Instead of humiliating him by mentioning his panic attack, she merely smiled with compassion.

"The man … the killer," she said. "When he handed me the tin, he had a smell about him."

"A smell?" Ali said. He'd never heard a witness detect a smell, but then again, he hadn't met many cooperative witnesses in Eurabia.

"Yes."

"What kind of smell?"

"Curry," the priestess said.

"You're kidding me."

"Spicy curry made with peanut powder."

"How can you possibly know that?" Ali said. "What are you, an expert in curries?"

"There were once ten Indian restaurants in Budapest. Three have survived. Only one of them makes curry with peanut powder and mutton. They've been buying the mutton from the same butcher for fifteen years. That butcher is my father."

Ali studied her expression and could see that she was dead serious.

"What's the name of the restaurant?" he said.

"The Curry House. And that kind of curry? With peanut and mutton? It's not the most popular dish."

"Why's that?"

"It's an acquired taste," the priestess said.

"That might be helpful. Was there anything else about him? Anything else that made him seem different from other men?"

The priestess thought about the question for a moment. "There was this thing he did but I might be making too much of it."

"What thing?"

"After he gave me the tin and started walking away, he flicked his right wrist three times, like this."

The priestess turned her hand in a semi-circle as though to stretch it out. Then she brought her wrists together and held them out for him to cuff.

Ali turned away, powered up the scaffolding and hit the lever for it to begin its descent.

"You better get back to work," he said. "Your supervisor said you're behind schedule. Just remember that this is a nation, it has laws and they must be abided. If you don't like them, leave."

Ali wanted to ask her if she understood that men of her faith had told men of his faith that exact same thing for centuries, but that would have been self-indulgent. Instead, he watched as she vaulted gracefully to her own scaffolding and vanished out of sight.

He wasn't sure if he didn't arrest her because he was grateful, he liked her, or he was indifferent, and he didn't care. All he knew for certain was that the scaffolding couldn't move quickly enough for his liking.

He no longer had a murder to solve.

He had two murders to solve.

CHAPTER 12

Elise knew that Salim's business partner, Zaid, would be expecting a call from her fictional cousin this evening and that if he didn't get one he'd begin questioning her integrity immediately. Most likely he'd wonder about her professionalism or the level of influence she held with Imam Labib, the man she'd pretended was her relative. Zaid probably wouldn't suspect she was an imposter yet because there wasn't sufficient cause for him to do so. But he might place a call to Labib in the Maldives himself, nonetheless, if he were an extraordinarily enterprising young man.

Elise didn't dare ask Darby to use a local asset to fake a call from Labib. Darby was already risking plenty by offering to help with Valerie's extraction. Asking him for more help meant putting him at greater personal risk for a non-sanctioned operation and Elise's conscience wouldn't allow her to do that. Her only solution was to extract Valerie before Zaid or Miss Mona knew for certain that she was a fraud. Thankfully, her timetable was immediate, because as soon as she verified the treasure's authenticity and acquired it for Christendom, she'd be gone.

With her official mission firmly in mind, Elise rang the buzzer to one of the units in a broken-down multi-family house at six o'clock in the evening in a grim section of Dhimmi Town on the outskirts of Pest. Light shone from behind the curtains of the unit next door, and a man sat reading a newspaper in his living room. In contrast, the home that belonged to the man in the wheelchair appeared dark and empty.

When no one answered, Elise reached out to press the buzzer again but the door budged first. A middle-aged woman with a face full of tumors and sores appeared in the doorway. Elise had never seen a leper in person before and the sight rendered her mute. She had to clear her throat to find her voice.

"My name is Elise De Jong," she said in Arabic. She'd hidden her morality police ID in her hotel room. As far as she and the rest of the world were concerned, she was a diplomat from Christendom meeting with a highly reputable antique dealer to complete a legal, private transaction. "I have an appointment to see the owner."

The woman lifted her right arm to open the door further. A black metal hand with silver knuckles emerged from beneath her *hijab* instead of a human one. After creating a wider opening for Elise to enter, she pulled her *hijab* over the bionic hand with her other one. That one, too, had been severed at the wrist and replaced with the same state-of-the-art prosthetic.

Elise drew four conclusions from this as she entered the home. First, the man in the wheelchair made a comfortable living as a dealer in arts and antiquities to be able to afford such devices. Second, he cared about this woman very much. Third, she'd been a thief at one time. Hands were usually cut off as punishment for stealing. In her case, she appeared to have been caught and convicted not just twice, but *three* times. The right hand was cut off after a thief's first offense, the right foot was amputated after her second offense, and the left hand was removed only after a third offense. Elise's fourth conclusion followed—the woman had at least one prosthetic leg, too.

The bionic leper led Elise down a corridor. Dim lights flickered from around the corner. When the corridor veered left, candles ensconced on the walls came into view. It was darker than hell, Elise thought. As they moved onward, a sliver of light appeared in a doorway on the right toward the inside of the house. The bionic leper pushed it open and went in first. Elise followed her, the floor squeaking as she walked.

Paintings and maps filled the walls of the large room. The man in the wheelchair rolled toward her from the far corner. The warped wood floor buckled and creaked. Elise saw the man in the wheelchair and almost winced. Blisters and boils covered his face, his nose was an inch too long, and the tips of two front teeth protruded over a pair of lips that slanted downward at an angle.

"Don't be alarmed," he said in English, his voice hoarse. "I get medical treatment. I'm not contagious anymore."

"Oh, no," Elise said, so quickly and awkwardly as to confirm the depth of her shock. "I'm not worried about that."

"Don't mind my housekeeper, either," the man in the wheelchair said. "She's deaf and mute. Been with me for eighteen years. The three of us, we have much in common. The Christian, the handicapped and the man in the wheelchair. We're all lepers in Eurabia."

He laughed at his own joke, then raised his eyebrows for the bionic leper to leave.

She closed the door on her way out.

"Have a seat?" the man in the wheelchair said.

"Let's get down to business," Elise said. "I'm here to verify the merchandise."

"I told your man that's not realistic. For you to verify it, you'd have to see it. And once you see it, I'll have nothing to sell you."

"I don't understand," Elise said.

"You will once you buy it," the man in the wheelchair said. "And besides, my reputation speaks for itself or your people wouldn't have sent you."

"What exactly is it you're selling?"

"Something every citizen of every theocracy craves and every leader of every theocracy fears."

"You already told us that," Elise said. "And your reputation for authenticity in arts and antiquities is the reason I was sent. But now I'm here, and I need more."

The man wheeled himself over to a metal serving tray with three pots. "Coffee, tea, hot chocolate?" he said. "Please. I never get visitors, let alone someone like you. It would mean so much to me."

"I haven't had hot chocolate since forever," Elise said.

The man in the wheelchair smiled.

Elise almost vomited at the sight.

"I like you already," he said. "I like a person who can pause to enjoy the finer things in life under any circumstances. Do you want hot milk with that?"

"How else can you have it?"

"You could have just the melted chocolate. I use Belgian stuff. The chocolatier at Central Market is a friend of mine."

"I'll take mine fifty-fifty. How does that sound?"

"Like a diplomatic solution."

The man in the wheelchair poured melted Belgian chocolate from a sterling silver container into a porcelain cup and added steaming milk. After mixing it with a spoon, he brought it over to a side table beside a plush velvet chair.

He watched as Elise sat down, took a sip, and made a few noises that might have previously been heard only in her bedroom. This seemed to please the man in the wheelchair immensely because he exhaled with satisfaction, poured himself a clear liquid from a crystal decanter, and rolled to a halt in front of Elise.

"What I'm offering to sell you," he said, "is proof of God."

Elise burned her tongue on the hot chocolate. "Proof… *of God?*"

The man in the wheelchair let her words hang in the air for a few seconds.

"Tantalizing, isn't it?" he said. "And wonderful and terrifying and…"

"And hard to believe."

The man in the wheelchair shrugged. "If you'd rather I sold it to the Hindus or the Buddhists—"

"I didn't say that," Elise said. "I'm here to acquire the details of what you're selling. I've been sent to establish authenticity. So you see, I need proof."

His eyebrows shot up. "You want proof, of proof of God?"

"Yes."

"I love it." He laughed. "You're more provocative than my housekeeper's hands, but that I cannot give you."

"Let me put it this way. What exactly will we get for our money? Is it a picture? Pictures can be created. Is it a witness? Witnesses lie. Is it an artifact? Artifacts can be forged."

"It's none of those things," the man in the wheelchair said. "What I'm selling you is a set of numbers and my reputation for delivering what I promise."

"A set of numbers?" Elise said.

"An angular unit of measure, a prime meridian, and a datum. Those are the three numbers that form a geographic coordinate system. These coordinates will lead you to proof of God. So you see, I can't show them to you because you'd memorize them right away and then I'd have nothing to sell you."

"If that kind of proof exists," Elise said, "how did you get a hold of it?"

"I use scavengers to help me accumulate my inventory." The man in the wheelchair motioned toward the paintings on the walls. "The one who brought me this information has never let me down. He's a Ukrainian from the irradiated territory of Chornobyl. No one gets stuff like he does. No one. He sold me the information and vanished. He understands the magnitude of his discovery and the personal risks of having discovered it. So don't try to find him. Neither you, nor I, or anyone else will ever find him."

"Why are you selling this to us? Why not to the Hindus or Buddhists, or quite frankly, why not to the Caliphate?"

The man in the wheelchair reflected for a moment. "I'm an atheist. I don't discriminate for or against the religions. History says Jesus cured leprosy while Muhammad told people to run from us. I couldn't care less about history. What I do care about is modern medicine. What I do care about is civilization. I got my treatment at a dhimmi Christian hospital. The Christians saved me. Now I'll save them."

"Save them how?" Elise said. "Why is this proof of God necessarily going to save any religion?"

The man from the wheelchair raised his chin before he answered. His facial tumors stretched horizontally and the lips beneath his saber-teeth curled upward. He was smiling the smile of a man who'd reached the top of his profession. In his case, a dealer who'd acquired the most priceless treasure ever known to man.

"Because it consists of evidence that the dead have risen," he said. "And that all the dead who have risen belong to one and only one religion."

Elise pictured the hands of the dead thrusting up through solid ground as they returned to life from their graves. It was a preposterous idea. But so was a world where a woman couldn't drive a car. The reasons for Christendom's interest were clear now. Not only would such proof of God validate a single religion, it might also destroy the others.

That which every citizen of every theocracy craves and every leader of every theocracy fears.

"What can I assume about the religion in question if you're selling the proof to us?" Elise said.

"Oh, anything you like," the man in the wheelchair said. "Cemeteries are filled with people who make simplistic assumptions. I have no knowledge of the religion of the resurrected. I made certain the scavenger didn't tell me so that I didn't know."

Elise took another sip of the hot chocolate.

"So do we have a deal?" he said.

"I have to report to my superiors. But let's make an appointment for tomorrow night. Same time?"

"This time you'll bring the diamonds?"

"How will you deliver the goods?" Elise said.

"In the belly of a porcelain cat. It'll look like a Herend but this one will be much more valuable."

"Thanks for the hot chocolate," Elise said, as she stood up to leave. "It was … authentic."

CHAPTER 13

Ali returned to his car after he descended from the Chain Bridge and called Ismael.

"What's the flaw in the Christian ritual of baptism?" Ismael said.

Ali sighed.

"They don't hold them under water long enough," Ismael said.

Ali waited a beat. "Another girl was killed three weeks ago."

"What are you talking about?"

"Greta Gaspar was the second girl killed. Another girl was killed before her and I'm guessing it was the same way by the same guy."

"How do you know this?"

"It doesn't matter," Ali said. He didn't want to give up Petra Noel's name for fear Ismael would enter it into the dhimmi database and expose her. "Is there a record of another dead dhimmi girl? Her name was Hanna Kalmar. Did someone in your office work that case?"

Unspoken was what they both knew Ali to be asking. Had Ismael worked that case and not told him about it?

"Your sister's vagina," Ismael said. "I never heard anything about a Hanna Kalmar or any other dead dhimmi girl and nothing goes down in CSI without me knowing about it. But just to be safe, let me check the records."

Ali waited a minute before Ismael returned.

"Nope," Ismael said. "No record of a Hanna Kalmar or any other dhimmi girls except for Greta."

"Zaman," Ali said. "Now I understand why the murder of a single dhimmi mattered to him so much. Now I get why he put me on the case to get it whitewashed without an investigation."

"The Intertheocratic Conference. You can't show the rest of the theocracies how superior your culture is if you have a killer running around. And a killer of girls, no less."

"It makes a man wonder, Ish."

"What? What does it make you wonder?"

"It makes me wonder if there's more."

Ismael muttered some obscenities.

"Do me a favor and call Arabiapol," Ali said, in reference to the network of police departments throughout Islamic lands. "See if there's any unsolved murders of teenage girls in the last year. Especially in Eurabia. I'd make the call myself but—"

"Say no more. The last thing you need is for Zaman to find out that you're nosing around murders that don't even belong to us. What are you going to do next?"

"Get some curry for dinner."

"Curry?" Ismael said. "You hate curry."

"I'm trying new things, going where the leads take me."

"I think that's what detectives are supposed to do."

"Then it's no surprise it's a new thing for me."

Ali drove to the curry restaurant that the priestess had told him about. He knew from the dhimmi records that the restaurant was owned by Hindus. Parking spaces were hard to find so he had to settle for one three blocks away. When he got out of his car he had a clear view of the nearby *Szabadsag Hid*, the Liberty Bridge, which connected Pest to Buda over the Danube. Ali took a quick glance to make sure no one was about to jump. The bridge overlooked the slums of Dhimmi Town and was the venue of choice for suicidal dhimmi teens.

Then he marched toward the Curry House. Halfway to his destination, a waif in the prime of her life with haggard jade eyes and razor-sharp cheekbones hustled up to him with her hands cupped together. She begged him to buy whatever it was she was holding. Normally, Ali would have blazed past the beggar before she could finish pleading in broken Arabic. But beauty compromised even the strongest man's discipline, and Ali found himself unconsciously slowing down, his heart breaking as he imagined what this girl had looked like when her parents had been able to hold decent jobs.

The waif uncupped her hands to reveal a gold tooth. When she smiled to try to entice Ali to buy it, the gap between her candy corn teeth revealed the source of her loot. Ali hurried past her, cursing her parents for not leaving for Christendom where their own kind might take care of them.

But then a previously unfamiliar wave of sympathy washed over him and he found himself doubling back to the girl. He gave her enough coin for her to buy food for a week and left her staring at the dinars in her palm with complete and utter shock. Afterwards, Ali continued onward to the Curry House unsure if he should be proud of having helped a citizen whose rights he'd sworn to protect, or ashamed of having encouraged her to continue breaking the law by begging. What he did realize was that he'd made his own choice and acted on it, and this, like conducting a real police investigation, felt real and true.

The Curry House was no larger than a two-car garage. The smell of coriander, cumin, and paprika blew Ali away when he walked inside. The seating area was a barebones affair with folding tables and room for no more than twelve. The take-out business was booming, however, with the phone off the hook constantly and a line of six beside the door waiting for their dinners.

A young woman in her late teens or early twenties with dark circles under her eyes told him to sit anywhere he liked and brought him a menu. She was pleasant and polite but sounded so weary that Ali had to strain to hear her. He ordered a mint lemonade and the girl told him someone would come by to take his order shortly.

Ali looked around the restaurant. Take-out appeared to be the establishment's primary business. Only one other person was eating at a table. Ali could hear the pensioner chewing three tables away. The confines were tight, too, suggesting the staff might have overheard diner conversations.

Five minutes later, an older woman with a hunched back came by to take his order. She held a pencil and pad and had a maternal air about her. To Ali, that smelled like opportunity.

"I want to try a curry," Ali said, "but I'm not sure which one. I need a quick lesson."

"You want a lesson in curry?" she said. "That's like saying you want a lesson in language. It's all a matter of local custom and tradition. They make it different in the place they used to call Nepal than in Sri Lanka, and in the country that used to be known as India there are hundreds of kinds depending on where you are. Where do you want to go? Tell me where you want to be transported, and I'll tell you what curry you should get."

Ali considered the question. "I want to be transported to a safe place."

"Why? Are you in some sort of trouble?"

"I'm in trouble with my wife."

The hunchbacked woman's eyes lit up. She tucked her pencil behind her ear. "What have you done?"

"That's the thing. I haven't done anything."

"That's what they all say. But what have you really done?"

"Nothing. Really."

The hunchbacked woman shrugged. "Then maybe it's your karma. Actions have consequences. People are accountable for what they do and punishments are inevitable."

"Here?" Ali said. "In this world?"

"In our lifetime," she said.

"So if it's my karma that my marriage fall apart, that would imply that..."

"You brought mayhem and destruction to other relationships."

In the time it took him to blink, Ali was sixteen years old and back in the country formerly known as Turkey, struggling with his algebra homework. As was often the case, he wasn't home alone even though his parents worked. They always seemed to have visitors. This particular bunch was the most vile of all. They were filthy, ignorant and rude thugs. They prayed, watched television and made fun of him all day. Their rucksacks lined the wall of whatever room they happened to be occupying, never out of their sights. The bags were reinforced with rebar hidden in the canvas and could have supported schoolbooks made of steel. Ali hated them almost as much as he wished he were one of them at the time.

"Did you?" the hunchbacked woman said.

"Did I what?" Ali said, still distracted by his memories.

"Bring mayhem and destruction to other people's relationships."

Ali pushed the image of the rucksacks further from his mind.

"Of course I did," he said. "I'm a cop."

Disdain flashed in the hunchbacked woman's expression. She pulled her pencil from behind her ear. It shook in her hand as though she were dying to write his order and get away from him.

"You wanted a lesson in curry? You got one. What can I get you, officer?"

"Major," he said.

"What kind I get you, Major?"

"Information."

The hunchbacked woman looked around furtively before glancing at Ali with disgust. "I'm just a waitress. I don't know anything about anything."

"I'm looking for a man who either ate here or ordered take-out during the last two weeks. Possibly twice, or more."

"That narrows it down."

"I even have the dates." Ali pulled out his own notepad and gave her the dates when the two girls had been killed.

"How am I supposed to remember—"

"He ordered a particular dish. I'm told it's not that popular."

"I don't remember him," she said.

"I haven't even told you what the dish is."

"Trust me. After you tell me what it is, I still won't remember him. Now, do you want some curry or not? I have other customers I need to take care of."

Ali looked around the joint. Other than the man slurping the soup and the people waiting for takeout, it was empty.

"Listen," Ali whispered. "How many times has a detective—and a major at that—come in here in plainclothes and told you he's investigating the murder of a Christian girl and that he needs your help?"

The hunchbacked woman frowned but didn't say anything.

Ali was certain she knew about Greta Gaspar's death, as did everyone else in Dhimmi Town by now. She probably knew that another girl had been murdered before her, too.

"Greta was fourteen years old," Ali said. He nodded at the young woman at the counter who'd seated him. "Is that your daughter?"

The hunchbacked woman glanced at the young woman at the register in a possessive way.

"Look at me," Ali said. "I'm not threatening you and I'm not trying to be clever. I don't even know how to be clever. Some people would say that I'm not that smart. But I'm trying to do the right thing here. I'm trying to do my job."

The hunchbacked woman studied Ali. "Don't sell yourself short. When you tell someone you don't know how to be clever, you're being clever." She glanced at her daughter again. "What did he look like?"

"I don't have much detail there. He was of average height and weight, and probably wore a black robe that covered his head to keep his face concealed. He would have spoken perfect Arabic."

"Are you joking?" she said. "You just described half the men in this city. What did he order?"

"Spicy curry made with peanut powder and mutton."

The hunchbacked woman narrowed her eyes. "You're right. We don't get too many orders for that here. They make it in Maharashtra, in Malegaon, a former Islamic stronghold in the Kingdom of Hindu."

"Do you remember serving it recently?"

"No. And I sure would remember if I had. Let me ask the cook. He would have had to unfreeze some mutton. He'd remember, too."

The hunchbacked woman disappeared into the kitchen.

A boy delivered a glass of lemonade to his table and Ali drank some of it. Being honest left him thirstier than lying.

The woman returned less than a minute later with her daughter.

"Tell him what you saw," the hunchbacked woman.

The young woman appeared more likely to spit in Ali's eye.

"Tell him," the mother said.

"I served a man spicy curry with peanut and mutton," the young woman said. "Could have been on the same days you're talking about. Sounds right, but I don't really remember."

"Did you see his face?" Ali said.

The girl shook her head. "No. That's one of the reasons I remember him. His head was covered up and he kept his face down the entire time. But I saw her face."

"*Her* face?"

The young woman nodded. "He was with a woman. She ordered Arabic chicken curry with noodle rice."

Ali opened his notebook. "And you saw her face?"

"Well, sort of," the young woman said. "She was wearing a *niqab*."

"How old was she?"

"Old," the young woman said. She glanced at her mother and nodded with conviction. "Not like my mother. Like, real old."

"Like a grandmother?" Ali said.

"I wouldn't go that far," the young woman said.

Ali guessed the hunchbacked woman was in her mid-forties. To a woman as young as her daughter, someone in her fifties was really old.

"Did you get a look at her eyes?" he said.

"Yes."

"What did they look like?"

"Fat and old," the young woman said.

"Fat and old eyes. That's a new one."

"She had folds of fat and wrinkles under her eyes. And I got a look at the list she was showing him."

"What list?" Ali said.

"It was a list of girls. I remember because of the pictures and because of the heading at the top of the list. It said 'Girls of Yellow.'"

Ali wrote down the phrase in his notebook.

"There were pictures of girls on the page," the young woman said. "All the girls had numbers next to them. They all looked really young, like teens or something. I don't know. I can't tell those ages apart. But they were all girls of yellow."

"What do you mean, girls of yellow?"

"They were all very beautiful. And they all had blond hair."

Ali jotted that down, too.

"You've been very helpful," he said. "I'm so grateful to both of you. Is there anything else about the woman—or the man—that you can remember?"

"Just her garment bag," the young woman said. "I remember it because it had the name of a school printed on it."

Ali wanted to cry with joy. "What was the name of this school?"

"It was a dressmaking school," the young woman said. "It was the Persian School of Dressmaking."

CHAPTER 14

The hookah pulled Elise toward it like a living, breathing thing that targeted the weak, attached itself to their brains, and wouldn't let go.

The more she thought of it, the more she insisted that she wouldn't succumb to its temptation and put her professional and personal missions at risk, the more she knew, deep down, that she was going there and going there now, with no further adieu. And as she navigated the streets and sidewalks on her bicycle, the anticipation of the high, the numbness, and the sweet relief that would soon be hers filled her veins with a rush unlike any other, so much so that by the time she'd arrived at the hookah bar she would have chewed through a window and swallowed the glass to gain access to her medication of choice.

The place was to lounges as dive bars were to five-star hotel taverns, filled with vagrants, addicts, prostitutes, transients and any human being bent on personal destruction. Women and men entered through the same door, but once they paid they were escorted into separate facilities, mingling only in the lobby area. The room for women was an assortment of nooks and crannies where a person could sprawl on a dilapidated sofa retrieved from a junkyard and smoke and toke her way into oblivion.

Elise paid for a large order of cannabis and four hours of refuge. She told the fearsome Arabian manager behind the iron bars at the front desk to be sure to roust her when her time was up. She was a fool for entering a place where she could be mugged, robbed of her fake ID, and assaulted, but she wasn't a complete idiot. She was translating the Eurabian Minister's speech regarding the Caliphate's peaceful intentions at tomorrow morning's session of the Intertheocratic Conference. The Cardinal—also the Foreign Minister of Christendom—would be depending on her to capture the meaning of all the inflections, pauses and nuances of the Eurabian Minister's speech that comprised a true translation. Elise had no intention of letting him down.

After the first half hour of smoking weed, Elise was able to calm down. Being a member of Christendom's diplomatic corps and one of its finest translators only helped with her clandestine responsibilities as a spy. In addition to the requisite language skills—her gaffe with Qattan notwithstanding—she also benefited from being a delegation fixture. No one at immigration at any of the kingdoms' airports ever questioned the purpose of her visit when she crossed borders. No one had reason to suspect that she was actually a spy.

It was her duties in this role that she focused on once her medication of choice soothed her nerves. She replayed her meeting with the man in the wheelchair and felt good about her mission. She had reported the details of the meeting to her superiors in the hotel and received the go-ahead. She would acquire the diamonds at the hotel tomorrow afternoon and consummate the deal with the man in the wheelchair at the agreed-upon time.

After her second half hour at the hookah bar, Elise drifted to that glorious border of unconsciousness. Wasn't it great to be alive? she thought.

Two hours later, upon waking up from a brief nap, she wished she were dead. *Proof of God?* She laughed at the thought. If ever there were a waste of money, this would be it—paying for proof of something that didn't exist.

How could there be proof of God when there obviously was no such entity? What kind of God would allow a soulless woman to sit and watch her own sister be given away to a life of slavery and do nothing about it? For she, Elise De Jong, was the living embodiment of callous disregard for all that truly mattered in life—one's family. She hadn't wanted to compromise her life to take care of a sibling, hadn't wanted the financial burden, or the daily toil. It was so hard to function in this world. It was such a challenge to maintain the will to survive. She simply hadn't had it in her. How pathetic, Elise thought.

If God existed, he wouldn't have wasted his time creating such a miserable bitch as herself in the first place.

Elise rolled around the couch and flitted in and out of sleep for another hour, finally rising when her time was up. She gathered her things, vowing never to return and suffer through such misery again.

As she left the room, a barn-like door slid open in the wall that separated the sexes, and Elise caught a glimpse of several men. Among them was a man holed up in a private alcove. He looked fitter than all the others, in a button-downed shirt and charcoal dress pants accompanied by black combat boots. When his eyes met Elise's they appeared to be glowing, and as she left the building Elise wondered what such an interesting-looking man was doing in such a shithole.

CHAPTER 15

That evening after dinner, Ali accessed Eurabian business records via the Eurabian police database through his home computer and identified the owners of the Persian School of Dressmaking. Their names were Mona and Daniel Rahbar, ages fifty-seven and sixty-nine, of Budapest, Eurabia. They also owned a retail store called Reza Couture. Both businesses shared a space in Pest's commercial center.

Ali slept fitfully that night, shots of adrenaline waking him up intermittently, encouraging him to glance at his clock to see if the work day was upon him yet. When morning finally came, he left an hour earlier than usual and stopped at a Eurabian diner on the way to the station. It featured a traditional Arabic breakfast buffet, a massive table filled with small platters of delicious goodness. Ali always woke up famished after a night of indulgence at the hookah bar and this morning was no different. He dunked warm pita bread in fava bean and eggplant dips and scooped dollops of hummus, too. He chased them with warm sweet tea and even enjoyed a serving of *Kanafah*, a breakfast dessert that consisted of cheese pastry soaked in syrup. It too, dated back to the Ottoman Empire.

Ali ate and drank with unusual gusto and enthusiasm. Ismael had left him a text message in the middle of the night to meet him in the bowels of the station before the day shift began. That meant he'd discovered something pertinent to the murders via Arabiapol.

Ali found Ismael waiting for him in the station's sub-basement beside boxes of old police uniforms that had been worn before the most recent Muslim conquest of Budapest.

"What do you call seven dead dhimmi girls?" Ismael said.

Ali rolled his eyes. "You're relentless. I'll give you that."

Ismael, however, didn't give him the smug look that always preceded his religious barbs. Instead, he drew a straight line with lips.

"No, Sami," he said. "What do you call seven dead dhimmi girls?"

The words reverberated in Ali's head. "You found seven more?"

"You're not answering my question."

In fact, he wasn't even thinking about it. Ali was too busy picturing the killer at work, strangling dhimmi girls all over Eurabia ... and Ali had a beat on him. A woman had met him with some sort of list at the Curry House. And he knew where she worked.

"What do you call seven dead dhimmi girls?" Ismael said.

Ali focused on what his friend was saying and shook his head.

"Not a good start," Ismael said. "A bad ending. A bad ending for us, A. If the higher-ups wanted this case investigated, they would have been on it. But they don't. They don't want anyone to know there's a killer out there but now we do and that means this shit is going to end bad for us, A. Real bad."

"What did you find out?" Ali said.

"Seven dhimmi girls murdered in the last six months. And that excludes the two we have here. Copenhagen, Bruges, Nice, Amsterdam, Munich, Vienna, and Bern."

"Nine murders." Ali listened to his echo. "No two murders in the same city. Except Budapest."

"All cases closed almost immediately."

"Lack of evidence?"

"Look who's the detective."

"What do you know about the dead girls?" Ali said.

"All between the ages of thirteen and sixteen—"

"Eyeballs intact," Ali said. "And all of them had blond hair."

"How did you know about the hair?"

"Were all the bodies found in Christian churches?"

"No," Ismael said. "Two of them were brought to the Salvation Army. Which I looked up. It was originally known as the East London Christian Mission."

"Nice. Anyone see the killer? Any money left for the priest?"

"I didn't reach out to anyone local. I didn't dig that deep. I just ran it through the computer to start. I figured that if I start asking questions about cases that closed really fast before any real investigation took place … "

At first, the magnitude of Ismael's fear surprised Ali. They'd formed a bond because they were both crusty cynics who knew their place in a system that rewarded loyalty and those that shielded their superiors from accountability. But then Ali understood his friend's attitude all too well. Ali was the one experiencing an epiphany. He was the one pursuing the dhimmi girl's killer.

"You did the right thing, Ish," Ali said. "Now I need you to do one more thing for me."

Ismael stared at him with a blank face.

"Go back to work," Ali said. "Forget about all this, and stay away from me."

"The thing is, A, my search got flagged. Someone put a marker on all those murders."

"How do you know?" Ali said.

"I got a phone call."

Footsteps sounded from the direction of the stairwell. Ismael's eyes fell toward the floor as a man appeared.

"There he is," Zaman said, wearing his shit-eating grin. "The Dhimmi Lover, himself."

Ali cursed under his breath. His investigation was over. Now that Zaman had evidence that Ali had gone off on his own and discovered the other murders, even the General wouldn't be able to help his son-in-law. Ali had overstepped his bounds and acquired knowledge that was dangerous to one's career track, if not more.

"Who would have thought it would turn out to be true?" Zaman said, still smiling. "Is it not unbelievable? A crisis of conscience or some such mental illness for the guy least likely to give a shit about a dhimmi, the man whose father gave shelter to more soldiers than all of Pakistan back in the day."

Ali's face flushed. "What about the next girl, Captain? Does it bother you at all that it's just a matter of time before he kills again?"

"I have to use the toilet," Ismael said, and disappeared toward the stairs.

Zaman turned serious. "Actually, it troubles me more than you'll ever know. You think I became a cop because I don't care about the law—yes, even the laws for the protection of dhimmis? Unfortunately, sometimes the real world forces you to compromise your ideals for the greater good."

"And we can't have a serial killer running around Eurabia during the Intertheocratic Conference, can we?"

Zaman bared his teeth. "If you value your life, you'll never use that phrase again, and you won't make any inquiries into crimes committed outside of Budapest, either. If you do, no one will help you, that I promise you. Now follow me to my office. I want you to tell me everything you know about this murder—these murders—and how you learned it."

Zaman led him into the elevator. As they walked, Ali's mind went to the murders he'd known in his youth. Once again he saw the five boys who'd been staying with his family run into a temple wearing their rucksacks. A moment later the building blew up. Ali wasn't sure what made him happier back then, that the temple contained dead Jews or the corpses of the boys he'd hated so much. Now the thought of being happy that any human being had been blown up seemed wrong. Now that he was a parent, the thought of teaching a child to hate made him sick.

"Does it ever bother you?" Ali said.

"Does what bother me?" Zaman said.

"That they're in the process of becoming an endangered species, like the man-eating tigers in Bangladesh."

"Bangladesh?" Zaman frowned. "What the hell are you talking about?"

"The dhimmis. The fewer of them that are left, the more they deserve their rightful protection under the law, don't you think? Otherwise they'll become extinct and how can extinction of any living thing possibly be good?"

"That's something for our betters to worry about," Zaman said.

"Why's that?"

"Because they're rich and they don't have to worry about keeping their jobs."

"But don't you think every person is accountable for his actions in this life and the next?

Zaman looked genuinely concerned for his subordinate's mental health. "What's happened to you, Ali? Why won't you let go of this case?"

"If you have to ask that, then you won't understand. It's a calling."

"I thought Islam is our calling."

"It is. That's the thing. Islam and this murder investigation. They're one and the same."

"How's that exactly?"

"The dead girl was the scum of the Earth just like we all used to be. Not even her parents could provide for her—they gave her up for a life of slavery, a life of misery we Arabs can understand. Who if not a Muslim cop is going to seek justice for her? Who else is going to care for the ones that no one else cares about?"

"Ali," Zaman said, "you're scaring me."

Ali shrugged. This was the moment where a man might have answered, "That makes two of us." But that would have been a lie, Ali thought, because he wasn't frightened at all. And it was this realization, in fact, that scared the living shit out of him.

They arrived on the main floor and the elevator door opened. Zaman stepped out first and headed for his office, no doubt assuming Ali would follow. But Ali ignored him and marched straight to the front door and out the station.

The last thing Ali heard was Zaman repeating his name over and over again, each time successively louder, until the station door slammed shut and Ali couldn't hear anyone's voice but his own.

CHAPTER 16

Elise liked the Cardinal who delivered the speech on the need for religious enlightenment at the Intertheocratic Conference. He was reviled in certain Catholic circles for being too progressive. He embraced gays, birth control and female priests, and she admired him for being his own man. She also sympathized with him because his philosophy made him a target for assassination by haters within his religion as well as those outside it. Maybe this was why his speech on religious enlightenment ran forty-five minutes longer than planned. Perhaps he wanted to get his words in while he was still alive. But more likely, Elise thought, like all great orators, he simply loved the sound of his own voice.

As a result of his speech running so long, Elise didn't complete her translation duties until early afternoon. She skipped lunch, swapped her diplomatic ID for that of the morality police, and hopped onto her bicycle. By the time she arrived at the Persian School of Dressmaking, she was out of breath and the students from Imam Salim's training school were rising from their seats under the same teacher's supervision.

Elise stood beside Miss Mona, who'd welcomed her with a smile and brought her back into the classroom for her second visit. They watched as the students fell into formation and left. Elise found Valerie in the same seat as yesterday and made sure to steal only a glance for fear Miss Mona or the teacher would notice if she stared.

"The children worked on bridal dresses today," Miss Mona said. "That's our couture store's specialty, but the girls were working on entry level models that would appeal to the wife of a working class Eurabian."

"One has to learn to speak before one can sing," Elise said.

"Quite right."

"I couldn't help but notice that you refer to the children as … well … children."

"As opposed to?" Miss Mona said.

"I believe the proper Eurabian term for the young and indentured is 'specimen.'"

"I'm the mother of two boys and three girls." Miss Mona slipped her arm under the crook of Elise's elbow and gave her an affectionate squeeze. "Legally they may be specimens but to us they're children, are they not Miss Kawlah?"

Elise indulged in another glance at her sister before the girl left, and felt a tug at the corner of her eyes.

"Yes, ma'am," Elise said. "They most certainly are."

Miss Mona withdrew her arm and smiled again. "I'm so happy you returned today. I take it as a sign that you're genuinely interested in a potential partnership."

"Most definitely," Elise said. "I thought we could discuss curriculum, how you'd handle the demand on your teachers and resources, that sort of thing."

What Elise really needed to do was get to the kitchenette within the next five minutes because Valerie would be waiting for her.

"I would welcome such a discussion," Miss Mona said, her voice suddenly stern, "but I think it's a bit premature."

"Yes," Elise said robotically, before realizing what Miss Mona had just said. "Wait. Premature? Why is that?"

"Because you've been lying to me."

"What?" Elise focused on looking outraged and not betraying her surprise.

"And you lied to Mister Zaid, and when one lies to Mister Zaid, one is lying to Imam Salim. And that is not tolerated."

Elise raised her chin and added some pepper to her voice. "This is a serious accusation. What is it I presumably lied about?"

"Your family tree."

"I beg your pardon?"

"Mister Zaid called Imam Labib of the Maldives this morning. He has no plans to expand his training school into a franchise. He's never heard of the plan you proposed, and he's never heard of you. He has no cousin named Kawlah Ahmed."

A muscular man in a black leather jacket ambled toward them. Elise hadn't seen him enter the classroom so he must have been lurking behind a rack of clothing or one of the support beams that held up the roof. His eyes were as dark and as lifeless as his jacket, and Elise guessed the bodyguard's blood pressure would barely rise if he had to kill her.

"That is ridiculous," Elise said. When the lie was exposed, the only course of action was to deny the truth. "There must be some misunderstanding. Mister Zaid must have called the wrong Imam Labib."

Miss Mona started to speak but stopped and frowned instead. "Are there two of them?"

"Evidently."

Miss Mona considered this for a moment. "We'll get to the bottom of this when Mister Zaid gets here."

"We certainly will," Elise said. "Do you expect him soon?"

"Any minute."

Miss Mona glanced from Elise to the bodyguard and back to Elise. The sequence left no doubt that if Elise tried to leave, he would stop her.

Miss Mona said, "You'll wait here until then."

"And so shall you," Elise said.

Miss Mona wrinkled her brow, just enough to confirm Elise had cast doubt on whether Kawlah Ahmed had fabricated a story about a fictional cousin named Labid, or if there'd been a genuine misunderstanding.

"May I have a glass of water while I wait?" Elise said. "Don't trouble yourself. I know my way to the water cooler."

Elise bounded toward the kitchenette without waiting for an answer. She kept Miss Mona and the bodyguard within her peripheral vision. They stepped toward each other and exchanged whispers. As Elise approached the kitchenette, fresh voices could be heard coming from the direction of the front lobby.

Zaid had arrived, Elise thought. She didn't have much time.

Elise held her breath as she approached the entrance to the kitchenette, fantasizing that Valerie would be there with her back to her just as before. But although the window was cracked open, the room was empty.

Elise poured herself a glass of water and stood close to the doorway where she could hear voices if they approached but remain out of sight. The water did little to settle her. Such was her plight, she thought. She wouldn't know peace until she acquired the alleged treasure from the man in the wheelchair for Christendom and extracted her sister from Eurabia.

A rustling noise sounded outside the window.

Elise slipped behind the water cooler to prevent Valerie from seeing her. Valerie descended through the window, back to the room, one leg at a time. Her feet barely kissed the table between a pile of napkins and a pastry knife before she vaulted onto the floor with a perfect dismount.

"Back for another smoke?" Elise said.

Valerie glanced at her, let out a muted gasp, and brought her hand to her lips to seal them. "You're really here," she said.

"And so are you," Elise said.

Valerie glanced at the cabinet where the teas were stored, and then turned back to Elise, who shrugged with indifference. Then Valerie sealed her lips and burst into action. She whipped the cabinet open, pulled out three cigarettes, and quickly put everything back in place.

Eyes brimming with excitement, Valerie reached out and offered Elise one of the cigarettes.

"What, only one for me, and two for you?" Elise said.

Valerie swallowed, put a second cigarette in the palm of her right hand, and offered them both to Elise.

"I'm just kidding, Miss Safa," Elise said. "You keep all three."

"Are you sure?"

Elise remained expressionless.

Valerie put the cigarettes in her pocket.

"Why do you smoke?" Elise said.

Valerie shrugged. Then a light flickered in her eyes. "Why does the morality police smoke?"

"Because the morality police—like everyone else—is immoral every once in a while. Because it makes me feel good. Do you not feel good when you're not smoking?"

Valerie shrugged.

"Do you not like it at Imam Salim's school?"

Valerie's expression brightened. "I like it a lot." Then just as quickly, she cast her eyes downward. "For as long as I'm here, I guess."

"Have you been told you'll be leaving soon?" Elise wondered if someone had bought Valerie.

"I've been taking special lessons lately," Valerie said.

"What kind of lessons?"

At first Valerie hesitated and blushed. But then she became animated.

"Men are the protectors of women," she said like a machine, "because Allah has given one more strength than the other, and because they support them from their means. The world is just temporary consciousness and the best comfort in the world is a righteous woman. Do you ever … do you ever get scared, Miss Kawlah?"

"Only when I'm awake," Elise said.

Valerie pursed her lips with determination. "I'm not scared," she said.

"What are you not scared of?"

Valerie shook her head.

"You can trust me," Elise said. "What are you not scared of, Miss Safa?"

"I want to be free."

"Of what?"

"The future."

"What if I told you I can help you?"

Valerie's eyes flickered before fear settled in. "I don't think so …" She stepped toward the window. "I have to go. They'll be looking for me."

"I'll protect you," Elise said.

Valerie stopped. "Why?"

"Because …"

A man's voice bellowed outside the kitchenette. It sounded like Zaid. The sound of rushing footsteps followed.

"Because it's my mission," Elise said. She darted toward the window. "Quick. We need to get out. Now."

Valerie scooted up and out the window and Elise followed. They raced down an alley that looped around an adjacent building. When the street came into sight, Elise told her to stop. She wished she could whisk Valerie away right now but she had nowhere to hide her. The hotels where the delegations from the foreign kingdoms stayed were under constant surveillance for the delegates' protection. Until she made arrangements with Darby, Elise was powerless.

And this realization perpetrated an eerie premonition that this was her only opportunity and she was blowing it, that not only would she never be alone with Valerie again, but she might never lay eyes on her little sister again, either ...

Elise wanted to scream, tear the guts out of Eurabia, get two first-class tickets on that fucking time machine Darby had mentioned as a joke, do something ...

A random car honked its horn.

Elise recovered her senses. "Can you meet me tomorrow?" she said.

Valerie hesitated. "Where?"

"By the statue of the little princess by the Danube."

"Why?"

"Do you want to be free of the future?"

Valerie didn't answer.

"Can you sneak away tomorrow? Can you get away without getting caught?"

This time she nodded.

"Good," Elise said. "What time?"

"Hmm." Valerie maintained enough composure to actually contemplate the time. "Afternoon is better. Before dinner would be best. The guards get tired and the staff is preparing food. Four o'clock?"

"Four it is."

Valerie ran to the street and took a left. Elise let her run ahead, then followed. When she got to the corner, Elise stole a glance and saw an angry man—probably one of the schoolmasters—chewing out Valerie in front of the door to a minibus with tinted windows.

Elise took a right and continued walking in the opposite direction, oblivious to her surroundings, vaguely aware that she'd have to double-back at some point to retrieve her bicycle, knowing that the extraction of Valerie from Eurabia remained a long shot, yet euphoric that she now had a legitimate chance of succeeding.

CHAPTER 17

Ali saw the minibus in front of the entrance to the Persian School of Dressmaking and double-parked next to the least valuable car near the curb, a canary yellow Fiat shaped like a coffin on wheels. He tried to see who was aboard the minibus but the blackened windows prevented him from getting a glimpse inside. He paid no attention to the alley on the nearside of the building where the dressmaking school was located. At first he thought he could see teenage faces gathered at the rear window looking back at him. But the closer he got the darker the tint became and the less he could see.

A clattering noise registered behind him. It sounded vaguely familiar but he paid no attention to it because he was so focused on the window. By the time he realized it was the sound of footsteps rushing toward him, it was too late.

The soldiers burst out of the alley aiming rifles at him. There were more of them than he could count and they were upon him immediately.

"Hands up, kneel down. Hands up, kneel down."

"I'm a cop," Ali said. "I'm a cop."

"We know who you are, Dhimmi Lover. Hands up, kneel down. Now."

Ali caught a glimpse of the patch on the sleeve of a soldier's green uniform before the man slipped a black sheath over Ali's head and rendered him blind. The patch featured the ever-present white crescent moon against a red circular background. It identified the soldiers to be members of the Caliphate's Republican Guard, the most elite fighting unit in all of Eurabia.

The sheath let Ali know the Guard were unlikely to kill him, otherwise they wouldn't be worried about what he might see. Still, none of the soldiers told him he was under arrest, explained why he was being handcuffed and deemed unworthy of walking the same streets he protected, or revealed where they were taking him. They pushed him forward nineteen steps and then another dozen around a corner where the air smelled of diesel. An engine idled nearby. When the smell became overpowering, they told Ali to stop. Two sets of hands grasped him by his upper arms and dragged him a few feet diagonally as though they wanted him to stand at a precise spot on the road.

"Step up," a gruff voice said.

When Ali hesitated, the soldier wasted no time repeating himself.

"Lift your leg like the dog you are," he said.

Ali did as commanded, realized he was climbing steps, and repeated the process until one of the men shoved him in the back. Ali tumbled into what he guessed was the back of a military transport truck. Soon he was sitting, guided onto a bench by one of the soldiers.

How quickly fortunes changed in Eurabia, Ali thought.

One minute he was above the law, interrogating a Knights Templar spy before the terrorist was impaled on a spike, and the next minute someone higher up was making him suffer. One moment he was applying the handcuffs, the next moment he was wearing them.

Ali heard another soldier shuffle into the truck and felt the bench sag as two men sat down and flanked him. He heard and sensed at least two more—possibly three—soldiers take seats on the other side of the truck directly opposite him. Ali guessed that two benches lined the sides of the truck while the middle was a bare space for weapons and equipment.

The transmission groaned, the engine rumbled, and the truck took off. Ali doubted that he was in real danger. The General wouldn't make his daughter a widow and the Caliph's guards were renowned for their integrity.

Invisible arms hauled him to his feet. Ali heard boots stepping toward him, sensed the presence of the soldiers that had been seated opposite him ...

"Every dog needs training," the gruff one said.

Ali took a blow to the gut. It almost knocked the wind out of him. He reacted without thinking, raised his right knee, thrust his foot forward, and followed through.

The sole of his foot connected with something hard.

Whatever he hit gave way. A muted groan followed.

Ali bent his knees and drove backward. He pictured the two soldiers holding him by his shoulders slamming into the wall behind them. He would kick each of them and hurl himself at the door hoping it gave way ...

Toward what end? Ali thought. Even if he managed to jar the door open, he risked falling onto the asphalt and getting run over by a car ...

Ali rammed the two soldiers who were holding him into the wall of the truck as planned. At the same time, he realized there was no escape, not with his hands cuffed and his eyes covered. By fighting back, all he would do was antagonize the men intent on giving him a beating. Someone had given them the order and Ali guessed he knew who. His only recourse was to let them do their job and take solace that his earlier conclusion had been correct.

If they wanted to kill him, they wouldn't be beating him.

After bouncing off the wall, Ali stood straight and pressed his legs together to protect his testicles. They pummeled him, with fists, knees and elbows, he imagined. All of their shots were directed to soft tissue, none to the face where the damage would be visible. When Ali fell to the ground, they didn't kick him. Instead, they hauled him back to his feet so they could deliver their blows with precision. The last thing Ali remembered before passing out was the taste of blood in his mouth and wondering whether that came from kidney or stomach damage, and how bad it would hurt when he took his next piss.

He woke up some time later. His insides burned and his core was so sore he wasn't sure he could stand up. He detected the scent of bukhoor—bricks infused with musk and sandalwood, and soaked in oil. The incense was commonly used at weddings, to welcome guests to one's home, and during relaxing times. Like everything else in Eurabia, this made perfect sense, Ali thought.

What a lovely welcome, he thought. Such relaxing times.

Ali saw coffered boxes made of Indian rosewood, realized he was lying prone on a familiar sofa, and that the rosewood was the substance from which the ceiling had been made. And he recognized that particular scent of bukhoor. It inspired privilege, confidence and guilt because the man who burned it controlled the Central Eurabian police departments and was his wife's father.

"You happy now, Dhimmi Lover?"

The voice, however, didn't belong to the General. It belonged to the man Ali suspected to have orchestrated the beatings, the boss whom he'd disobeyed on several recent occasions. Though exactly what Zaman was doing in his father-in-law's house was beyond his understanding.

Ali sat up. The ordeal took a full five seconds and he winced through every one of them.

"Thanks for telling them not to hit me in the face," Ali said.

"I have no idea what you're talking about, but that's not the first time, is it?" Zaman said. "Here's what I do know. You're out of control. Investigating a case you should have closed the same day it was given to you, tapping Arabiapol to look into other crimes that aren't relevant to our city at all, and disobeying a direct order to come speak to me in my office. You're finished, Ali."

"Who's finished?" a third man said.

Ali turned and saw the General moving slowly into the room. He didn't walk or march so much as gradually shift his weight forward. The humungous stomach that hung over his belt preceded him whenever he entered a room by a few seconds. Ali knew that the General had prospered from impoverished origins and considered his midsection a source of pride, a constant reminder that his family's shelves were not bare.

The General stopped in his tracks and gave Zaman his desert-sun death-glare, the ever-present line of sweat glistening above his eyebrows. "How dare you speak to my son-in-law that way?"

The creases in Zaman's forehead deepened.

"I've been looking forward to berating him for days," the General said, "and you dare to steal my pleasure and my joy by using up my insults?"

Zaman revealed the hint of a smile. "I'm afraid there's no hope for me, General."

"Finally," the General said. "Something all three of us can agree on." He waved his hand for Zaman to leave.

Zaman marched out of the room.

Once he was gone, the General rolled his eyes. "What an asshole."

"I guess I had this coming," Ali said.

"You think?" the General said.

Ali sighed.

"Zaman called the chief of police to let him know that he needed to take disciplinary action against you for your latest insubordination. I got a call as a matter of courtesy. Naturally, because I'm a loving father, I interceded and had the Caliph guards bring you here to buy some time and see if I can save your career. And I had to get Zaman involved so that I could make him certain promises in exchange for him giving you another chance."

Ali groaned.

"Yes," the General said. "That's the mess you've made and that's the mess you've forced me to clean up." He deposited himself into a lavishly upholstered chair. "Get us a glass of port, will you?"

Ali walked over to a wall featuring three framed maps of the continent. One was from the fifteenth century when the Ottoman Empire ruled, the second was from the twentieth century after the fall of the Soviet Union and when the nations of Europe ruled, and the third was current, when Arabia ruled. Ali pressed his lips close to the invisible receiver built into the top of the frame that contained the map of the original Ottoman Empire.

"Open Sesame," he said.

The painting swiveled upward and a small pantry rolled out of the wall. Bottles of scotch, cognac, and port wine, and a collection of glasses filled a tray. Any Eurabian caught imbibing one of the liquids would have been punished with eighty lashes for his first transgression and the death penalty for his fourth.

Ali pulled out the vintage port. He poured two glasses and handed one to the General. The General stuck his nose into the glass and inhaled. The he swirled the port, repeated the process, and drank. He sucked the liquid in through his teeth and made a disgusting slurping noise that almost killed Ali's appetite for the nectar harvested in the country formerly known as Portugal.

Ali took a quiet sip.

"Philistine," the General said. "You're not drinking it properly, the way the old Europeans used to do back when they had a continent."

"Apparently I haven't been doing much of anything properly lately."

"Humility in the face of the end of one's career," the General said. "I'll drink to that."

He raised his glass and took in another mouthful. This time Ali didn't hear the drinking noises that ensued. His heart was pounding too loudly in his ears. If his career was over, what would he do? Suddenly, Ali couldn't bear the thought of a life without real police work. The concept of a completely joyless existence produced a vision of himself hanging from a tree.

"Did Zaman tell you to close the dhimmi girl's murder quickly?" the General said.

"Yes, sir."

"And did you?"

Ali looked at the floor.

"What's gotten into you, son?"

Ali shrugged. "I just want to do my job. The way it's supposed to be done."

"You want to be accountable? In Eurabia? That's like saying you want to be whipped to death because you're bored. What do you think of this port?"

Ali took another sip. Despite his complete lack of appetite, he couldn't help but savor the mouthful of fruit.

"Tell me about your investigation of the church murders," the General said. "Tell me everything, spare me no detail, and we'll see if I can salvage my favorite son-in-law's career."

The General's words of comfort provided little solace. He had only one child, and she, by law, had only one husband.

Ali gave him a full account of everything that had transpired from the moment he'd arrived at Matthias Church until the Caliph guards snatched him off the street a block away from the Persian School of Dressmaking.

The General hoisted himself to his feet and refilled his glass while Ali told his story. He didn't interrupt or ask questions. Even when he was tilting the bottle, Ali knew that the General was measuring every word he heard for truth and authenticity. Despite the risk of being branded a liar, Ali left out the beating he'd endured at the hands of the Caliph guards lest he appeared to be a spineless rat. And he didn't reveal the identities of Chef Florence or Petra Noel. They were informants who deserved to be protected on sheer principle, or so he told himself. The truth was he liked them, too, and didn't want any harm to come to either of them.

The General, of course, zeroed in on them immediately.

"The informant who told you where to find the Catholic priest and the Catholic priest himself. What are these men's names?"

Ali looked away from the General. When the General repeated his question, Ali remained mute.

The General sighed. "I see. You want to be accountable and idealistic. Congratulations. This renders you radioactive in Eurabia. All human beings that touch you are destined to become social pariahs. You know this, yes? Your wife, your child, everyone close to you ..."

The General closed his eyes and took a breath. Then he drained the rest of his port with an extra-long version of his nauseatingly audible intake. When he had sucked every droplet from the crevices between his teeth, he licked his lips and cast his weary eyes at Ali.

"You were never the smartest man, Ali," the General said. "I wanted better for my daughter but she fell in love with you. She said you were sweet and devoted. Those are feminine terms for a simpleton. But I accepted you because I knew you'd be reliable. Reliable and predictable. But now ... now you're trying to be smart."

"Not smart," Ali said under his breath. "Professional."

"What?" the General said, his voice rising. "What is it you say?"

Ali sipped his wine.

"Do you really think you can pull it off? Do you really think you're capable of finding this killer? The killer that no one wants to acknowledge exists because he can't exist because it's not politically expedient? Are you even smart enough to follow my logic?"

Ali shrugged. "Persistence is more important than brains. I'm smart enough to follow the clues."

"Are you now?" The General let out a snort. "Then let's see how well you've followed them so far. Why do I need the identities of the priest and your informant?"

Ali thought about the question in light of their discussion. "Because you've given out favors to keep me from losing my job. And you need some information that you can use to earn some favors back."

"Huh." The General narrowed his eyes. "Maybe I've been underestimating you. Maybe you're not the dumbest detective on the planet after all. Do you want to keep your job?"

"Yes."

"Will you give me the names of the priest and the informant?"

"No."

The General grunted. "I really have been underestimating you."

"Is there something else I can do to show my appreciation?" Ali said.

"Funny you should say that."

The General grimaced and pushed himself to his feet. Ali immediately stood up, too.

"How is my daughter?" the General said.

"She adapts."

"And my granddaughter?"

"She takes after her mother."

"Thank Allah for that. Go home to them. Await my call. There may be something you can do for me imminently. Something that will even the score and put you back in the good graces of your department."

The General reached out as though he was going to pat Ali on the shoulder, but at the last second lowered his aim and jabbed him in the stomach instead.

Ali winced and doubled over.

"Sore there, is it?" the General said.

Ali straightened up. "A bit."

"Well, it's a good thing I told them not to touch your face."

The General turned and left his office.

CHAPTER 18

After the minibus disappeared, Elise circled back, climbed atop her bicycle and raced to Darby's dental offices. She had to wait only five minutes before a dental assistant called her name and escorted her to a bay in the back. A few patients in the waiting area muttered their disapproval that she'd been called in so quickly.

Elise reclined in a dentist's chair and was confused to see the assistant prepare a tray that contained drill bits and—to her dismay—a needle. The sound of intermittent cleaning and drilling from surrounding bays was interrupted by a patient's yelp. Just what she needed to hear at that precise moment, Elise thought. She reached over and flipped a switch that dispensed water into the plastic cup beside her chair. Instead of rinsing, however, she drank the entire cup, unable to keep from glancing at the drill bits one more time when she was done.

Darby marched into the room with more enthusiasm than Elise remembered and greeted her with a smile that consisted of teeth that were way too perfect. They exchanged pleasantries, and then Darby lowered her chair, attached a light to his head, and began to poke around in her mouth.

"How is the pain?" he said in Arabic, with the assistant still in the room.

Elise made up a reasonable answer. "It comes and goes, worse at night when I'm not as distracted by my work."

"Ah, yes. Sweet distraction."

After a quick exam, Darby turned off the light shining in her eyes and put a reassuring hand on her shoulder.

"Don't you worry," he said. "We'll take care of you. When we're done with your root canal and you leave here in an hour, there'll be no more pain. That I promise."

The dental assistant added a second needle to the tray and left the room.

"Root canal?" Elise said in English, once they were alone.

Darby's lips parted in surprise. "You're the one that said she wanted an extraction. I'm offering to save the tooth."

Elise feared he'd gone mad. She'd asked for an extraction of her sister, not her tooth. But then he chuckled and shrugged.

"Forgive me," he said. "Dental humor. We have the highest suicide rate of any profession. We need all the comic relief we can get."

Elise still had her eyes on the needle. "Don't let my appearance fool you then. I'm laughing really hard on the inside. Is this really necessary? Couldn't we've just met for a consultation?"

"Afraid not. You came in complaining of pain. I made a diagnosis that calls for a root canal. That justified your return for a procedure today. I have to obsess over appearances, now more than ever. I think there might be a community infiltrator among my staff."

"A what?"

"An infiltrator," Darby said. "From the Caliph's special branch. Whenever a dhimmi files taxes that show rising income, it's a red flag. Not exactly what Eurabia is hoping for given the purpose of the dhimmi tax in the first place."

"What's the infiltrator's goal?"

"Well, it's not to improve productivity or form friendships, is it? 'Believers, take not Christians and Jews as your friends, they are but friends and protectors of each other.'"

Elise recognized the words. Like Darby's previous quotations, they weren't from the Bible.

"How did you spot him?" she said.

"Experience. The young fellow who offered to help with your X-ray vest yesterday? Recent hire. He's a bit too solicitous, always there when I need help. You can't trust a man who tries too hard. He's always hiding his true motive."

"What will you do?"

"Go about my business. Other than the rare meeting with someone such as yourself, this is, in fact, a dentist's office. There's no black marketeering going on here, no illegal shenanigans with scavengers from the other theocracies. Speaking of scavengers, how was the man in the wheelchair?"

"Handsome as ever," Elise said.

Darby nodded. Elise's description confirmed that she'd met with the right man. This let Darby know that he'd completed his mission on behalf of Christendom. The acquisition of the location of the supposed proof of God was entirely Elise's responsibility.

"And the dressmaking school?" Darby said.

"Has exceeded all expectations," Elise said. "I owe you a debt of gratitude there. Which makes it all the more difficult to ask for help with that extraction—"

"Stop." Darby raised his hand. A look of contentment spread across his face. "Anything . . . Anything I can do to help a young Christian avoid a life of servitude to these soulless savages . . . 'No food for them save bitter thorn-fruit.'"

"I expect the asset to be compliant."

"When do you want this to happen?"

Elise told him when and where she was meeting Valerie.

"There'll be two cars," Darby said. "Four men. All Christians of Arabian descent. All soldiers, all reliable. I trust them with my soul. They'll take her off road over the border to the countries formerly known as Slovakia and Germany and to a ship along the Dutch coastline. Once she's out of BP, she should be safe. The Eurabian authorities are not nearly as concerned about cars leaving Eurabia as they are about the ones coming in."

"How will I connect with the asset once she's safe?"

"The ship is a bulk container vessel returning home to the country formerly known as Argentina. The captain is our connection. He'll have your contact information and you'll have his before you leave here today."

"Then I think we're good."

As Elise started to rise, she heard a vaguely familiar male voice behind her.

"Blanca got called in to help with an emergency," the man said. "I can stand in for her, Doctor Darby."

The voice belonged to the young man whom Darby suspected of being a community infiltrator. In the time it took for Elise to recognize it, Darby was already pressing her shoulders back down into the dental chair.

"Excellent," Darby said. "You're becoming indispensable to me."

Elise tried to rise again and this time Darby pushed her down more forcefully. *Appearances*, he mouthed, without making a noise.

"I'm very optimistic, Miss Kawlah," Darby said. "Very optimistic about the outcome of this procedure."

A minute later the needle was in her gums.

Twenty minutes later the drilling began. Elise's horror yielded to her priorities.

A tooth for a sister, she thought. Seemed like a bargain.

She had thirty-one others if that one wasn't enough.

CHAPTER 19

Two of the Caliph's guards drove Ali home from the General's house. To Ali's surprise, Sabida was waiting for him in the doorway with a sympathetic look on her face. At first her expression buoyed his spirits, but when she sniffed his breath and glanced at his stomach he knew that her father had called her again. Sabida looked like she knew that the General and Ali had shared a glass of port, and that Ali had been beaten, though probably not who had given the order.

"Oh, my beloved," she said. "What have they done to you?"

"And how do you know anyone's done anything?"

"A wife knows."

Ali was too sore and tired to complain that she'd spoken to her father about him again. So he washed, changed clothes and returned to the kitchen where Sabida had cooked up some Arabic home remedies.

"I mixed a teaspoon of black seed with honey," she said. Black seed came from fennel flower and had been found in Tutankhamen's tomb. "Good for abdominal pain and depression."

"Who said I'm depressed?"

"I did. A wife always knows. Eat it and drink some of this tea. I simmered it with a teaspoon of aniseed."

Ali frowned. "I thought anise is used to force gas out of the system."

"It is. I want you to drink the entire cup, and then when you're done, I have a surprise for you."

"I've had enough surprises for the day."

"This one will do you good. Trust me, my beloved."

Ali groaned as he sat down. His stomach felt like a giant bruise. He remembered his instructors in the police academy preaching that the soreness they experienced the day after physical training was "good pain." And they'd been right. It really had felt good. His muscles had been properly stimulated and were in the process of becoming stronger. But if that was good pain, what Ali was experiencing now was most definitely bad pain. He was hurting inside. Still, he didn't dare lose face and ask to see a doctor.

Sabida worked on a grocery list while he ate his black seed and honey, and drank his tea. The liquid warmed his insides while the herbs settled his mind a bit, or at least so he imagined.

"Better?" she said.

"A bit. Thank you."

"Don't be ridiculous. I live for you, husband. You know that." She touched his shoulder. "Now, it's time for your surprise."

After she left the room, Ali sipped more tea and wondered what she could have possibly bought him. He had no material vices to speak of except for cannabis and an occasional swim, and he doubted a gift certificate to the hookah bar or the gymnasium was on the way. Perhaps she'd acquired a copy of one of those old cowboy films they'd made in the country formerly known as Italy more than a century ago. They were *haram*, of course, but he loved to watch them with a plate of pasta.

But Sabida returned with empty hands.

"Your daughter would like to speak with you," she said.

Kinza stepped out from behind her mother. As soon as he saw her, Ali's heart fell. He remembered Sabida's brother reminding him last night to be sure to pick up their girls after school. But he'd forgotten. In fact, not only had he forgotten, he hadn't thought of his own daughter all day.

"I'm so sorry, angel," Ali said. "I got all caught up in work ... How are you? Come give me a hug."

But Kinza would have none of him. She stood defiantly with a look of suppressed rage on her face. Sabida was off to the side, arms folded over her chest.

"No hug?" Ali said.

His daughter shook her head.

"Okay," he said. "I guess I don't deserve one. Tell me a story instead. Tell me what you learned today."

"Today I learned that my father loves dhimmis more than his own family."

Ali cast a look of shock at Sabida, whose eyes were watering.

"And that my father loves a dead dhimmi girl more than me."

Kinza ran out of the kitchen back to her bedroom.

Her words knocked the wind out of Ali. He turned back to Sabida.

"Happy?" he said.

Sabida looked likely to explode any second. All of a sudden, the herbs Ali had ingested didn't seem nearly potent enough.

"When did you learn to be so cruel?" Ali said. "Or have you always been this way, and I've simply been a fool for not noticing?"

"You think I put those ideas into her head?" Sabida said. "I can't control what my father says to her."

Ali shouldn't have been surprised that the General was using his granddaughter to help manage him. The General was a manipulative bastard. That's how he'd become a general in the first place.

"Maybe you didn't put those ideas in her head," Ali said, "but you set this all up. 'I have a surprise for you?' Do you have any idea how much I loathe you at this very moment?"

"You, you, you," Sabida said. "It's always about you."

"No, it just seems that way. Because I'm the man of the house. Because I'm the one who provides."

"Are you sure about that? Are you sure you're the man of the house?"

Ali rose to his feet.

Sabida stood tall.

"Say that to me again," Ali said.

Sabida continued staring at him, lips trembling.

"Say that to me one more time."

Ali knew that his wife understood his threat. He simply refused to be emasculated any further. Neither of them had ever uttered a word about divorce during their nine-year marriage. And yet here they were, at that juncture. Ali marveled at how quickly they'd reached that point, and realized this was further evidence of just how large a shit storm he'd caused by investigating one poor dhimmi girl's death.

Sabida looked away.

Ali sat back down.

They remained quiet for a while. Ali sipped his tea while Sabida polished an already clean countertop. Ali was grateful for the silence. But what he wanted above all was the numbness that only the hookah and the cannabis could bring.

After Sabida had wiped the entire kitchen clean, she sat opposite him with her own cup of tea.

"I hope you put a good dose of those herbs in your own brew," Ali said.

"The black seed is good for all but death."

"Oh, really? It's good to know there's something you and your father can't control."

Sabida glared at him. "What's happening to us?"

"Nothing is happening to us. I'm having some trouble at work. That's all. It happens." Even as he spoke, Ali hoped his phone would ring with the General on the other end of the line. "It'll work itself out."

"You're not being honest with me. You're making your problem at work sound trivial and it's not. And it affects all of. Immediately, in the most dramatic way."

"Everything will be fine. Until I stop providing for you, you have no right to complain."

"If it weren't for Father, you would have stopped providing for us when you came home today. He saved your job. What's gotten into you? I thought you were having a crisis of conscience because this girl reminded you of your daughter, but it's obviously something more."

Ali said nothing. Even if he tried to explain, she would never understand him.

"Do you want a new slave?" Sabida said. "Is that was this is? Because Father said he would buy ours at a premium and subsidize a new one."

Ali pressed his eyes shut. It was bad enough that she'd spoken to her father about his career. *Now this?*

"Talk to me," Sabida said. "I beg of you."

Ali took a deep breath. An excruciating moment of desperation washed over him and then a shocking thought occurred to him. What if he were simply honest with her?

"I'm a cop," he said. "I want to take my job seriously. I want it to mean something. And I want everyone to take me seriously."

"You've always been taken seriously—"

"Don't," Ali said. "You know what I mean. You know that I've never been taken seriously. Why do you think they call me the Dhimmi Lover? It's a joke, don't you understand? I'm a joke."

Embarrassment shone in Sabida's eyes.

"No more," Ali said. "I don't want to be a joke anymore. I want to make a difference. I want my job to matter. I want to matter."

"You want to be creative? Maybe you don't want to be a cop. Maybe you want to be creative through business. Father has some ventures. Maybe there's an opportunity in one of them—"

"I spit on his opportunities," Ali said. "I hate all business that is conducted for the sake of money. I want to be a cop. Why is that so hard to understand that? Why can you not see the joy in that?"

"I thought our joy came from Islam."

"It does. Being the detective on this case and being a Muslim—they're one and the same. Finding this girl's killer—that is the essence of Islam. Islam is about justice. Don't you see that? Doesn't anyone see that? Has all of Eurabia gone mad?"

"No, my beloved. All of Eurabia has not gone mad. This is life. Here as it probably is in the lands of Hindu and Buddha and Christendom, too. Nobility takes a back seat to survival. Men do what they need to do so that their families have a standard of living. So that their families survive."

Ali considered her comments. "That's it then, eyes to my soul. You've nailed it. I don't want to just survive. I want to live. I want my life—I want our lives—to really matter."

"And are they going to matter if you end up being chief of the neighborhood watch in some Transylvanian ghetto trying to figure out who stole the butter?"

"That's not going to happen," Ali said.

He was too proud to admit to his wife that he'd been arrogant, that he'd assumed the General would protect his son-in-law. Ali had forged ahead with his murder investigation without worrying that he'd eventually force Zaman to defend his authority. Going forward, Ali vowed to slow down and consider his moves first.

That assumed he could redeem himself as the General had suggested. For that to happen, Ali needed to be given a second chance.

He sat in the kitchen staring at the phone, willing the General to call.

CHAPTER 20

Elise dropped the kickstand and parked her bicycle beside the front door to the house where the man in the wheelchair lived. The curtains were drawn but light spilled around their edges. She wasn't entirely focused on her mission even though she was carrying a satchel full of investment grade diamonds, enough to buy black market passage to Australia and a comfortable retirement in Sydney. Her thoughts kept drifting to an imaginary scenario that began near the Little Princess statue on the Danube, and ended with her embracing Valerie on non-Arabian soil, where her sister wouldn't be considered the spoil of war or relegated to a life as a slave.

All that changed when Elise reached out to ring the door-bell to announce her arrival.

All that changed when Elise saw that the front door was ajar.

She respected the man in the wheelchair but that didn't mean she believed he was in possession of the exact location of some sort of proof of God. She would have regarded it as complete hogwash were it not for his reputation. The conflict between the man's reputed integrity and the outrageousness of his claim had left Elise ambivalent.

But she was ambivalent no more.

If there were evidence that the dead were rising and that they all belonged to one and only one religion, she needed to acquire it for Christendom to use as it saw fit. Proof of God would change mankind, for better or worse. It was a theocratic weapon, to be shared or revealed, as the possessor desired.

Elise had even experienced a fleeting thought that she needed to get her hands on this proof for personal reasons. If the dead who were rising belonged to a different religion, perhaps she and Valerie would need to reconsider what and whom they worshipped. The notion had revolted and fascinated her almost as much as it had made her laugh—it was still so preposterous.

The door was ajar but still touching the jam. Perhaps the housekeeper was about to step outside for some reason, and had doubled back because she'd forgotten something, Elise thought. Or, maybe she'd just returned from an emergency run to the store to get some medicine for her employer. And in a hurry to deliver the prescription—or Belgian chocolate—she'd failed to press the door shut.

All of these possibilities seemed more likely to Elise than the commission of a crime by a serious criminal. A kid ransacking the house might have been so stupid as to leave the door open to attract attention, but not a professional thief. If a skilled operator had robbed the man in the wheelchair of some his valuable possessions, or heaven forbid, the location of the alleged proof of God she'd come to purchase, he would have closed the door behind him.

The possibilities were endless.

Elise rapped on the door lightly with her knuckles. The door inched open enough for her voice to carry inside.

"Hello? Is anyone home?" Elise said.

She waited three beats, glanced to both sides and to the rear to make certain she was alone and repeated her actions.

No one answered.

Elise rapped the door two more times, increasing the force behind her second knock such that that door swung open. She announced herself one last time, but still there was no answer.

She cursed her luck. This was supposed to be a simple transaction. Extracting Valerie was the much more difficult task. And now she had no choice but to enter the house illegally. She could argue she had an appointment, that she'd met the housekeeper and the man in the wheelchair the day before and that she was concerned for their welfare. And if someone asked her why she didn't call the police, she could tell them the truth. What if one or both of them were in need of immediate medical attention? What if the housekeeper couldn't summon the necessary help because she was mute?

Elise glanced over her shoulder one more time, saw an empty street, and slipped inside the house.

The light she'd seen outside came from the first room on the left. It had been dark when Elise had visited last night. Now illuminated by a collection of antique desk lamps atop various tables, it appeared more warehouse and less living space. The Tiffany shades told Elise that simple robbery either hadn't been a motive, or the thieves could only get away with what they could carry.

A sliver of light beckoned from a familiar location further down the corridor—the room where she'd met with the man in the wheelchair, where he'd made her hot chocolate and told her the nature of the treasure that he was selling. Elise slipped down the hallway. The sconces in the walls were dark this time and the absence of light along the way sharpened her other senses.

She detected a foreign smell. At first she thought there was a floral whiff to it, but then she realized it was more like poppy infused with vanilla. It wasn't a perfume, she thought, but more an incense that reminded her of a Buddhist temple. Funny, Elise thought, because she hadn't seen an incense burner in the main room and the two residents of the home were definitely not Buddhists.

Elise arrived at the door to the main room. It was also pressed shut but not closed, which accounted for the strip of light that shone from inside.

Elise knocked as gently on this door as she had on the exterior one initially.

"Hello, hello. Anyone home?" she said. When no one answered, she rapped on it two more times.

The door swung open.

The man in the wheelchair sat in the middle of the room facing Elise, but he looked markedly different than when she'd seen him yesterday.

He had no head.

The tip of his vertebrae protruded from the cavity that had been his neck. Buckets of blood had showered his clothes and his means of transportation, and pooled around the wheels on the floor. In the man's lap rested his head. It looked more like a stage prop than a body part, eyes shut, tumors purple and blue.

Elise averted her eyes, fought back an urge to vomit and took three slow breaths to calm herself. Once she recovered, she scanned the rest of the room quickly. There was no sign of the housekeeper. Elise wondered if she'd escaped, had been taken prisoner, or was lying dead in another room. The maps and paintings were still hanging on the wall. None of the valuables appeared to have been taken or even disturbed. This wasn't a robbery, Elise thought, unless the object stolen was a simple porcelain cat, a forgery of a classic Herend.

She looked around for the cat but didn't see one. Instead, a black notebook caught her attention. It was bound in rich

Italian-looking leather with a toggle clasp, just the sort of a notebook where a man might jot down a certain set of numbers he claimed to have never seen. The notebook rested beside the pot from which the man in the wheelchair had poured the hot chocolate.

Elise sneaked into the room and glided toward the notebook, eyes on a swivel. She stuck her finger in the pot of hot chocolate—it was cool. Then she lifted the cover of the notebook. She flipped to a few random pages but found nothing written inside. That piqued her curiosity sufficiently to lift the notebook with both hands and fan through the entire book.

Nothing.

Only when she glanced at the back cover and saw the year "1431" stamped on the back did she realize why nothing was written inside.

It was an antique. The notebook itself was the object of value.

Elise put the leather-bound journal back where she'd found it. When she looked up, an object on a table in a corner of the room caught her attention.

It was a porcelain Herend cat. Or more likely, a forgery of one, Elise thought.

Elise stepped around the table and moved toward the cat, or rather, *cats*. There were three of them. Each one had been decapitated just like its owner, as though someone wanted to see if there was a hermitically sealed plastic bag inside containing a piece of paper with three numbers on it—

The floor creaked.

Elise froze. She wanted to examine the insides of each of the cats, praying there might be a fourth in the room somewhere, knowing deep down that she should run but unable to leave before making sure the location of the alleged proof of God was not within her grasp—

A rumbling noise filled the air. The floor began to creak relentlessly even though Elise wasn't moving.

Policemen burst into the room bearing weapons. Elise raised her hands. Two of them secured Elise's hands behind her back and cuffed her, while two others pointed their handguns at her chest at point blank range. A fifth and sixth policeman stood beside the door.

None of them paid any attention to the decapitated man in the wheelchair, which meant they'd seen him before.

The shock of their arrival and the sight of their guns taking aim at her rendered Elise helpless and momentarily mute. A wave of depression washed over her as she realized she'd failed in her mission for Christendom. And an even greater sense of despair gripped her as she remembered her premonition that she'd seen Valerie for the last time outside the Persian School of Dressmaking.

A seventh cop marched into the room and headed straight toward her. He looked strangely familiar, Elise thought, which was impossible because she didn't know any cops. Hell, other than Qattan, Faraz, and Zaid, Elise didn't know any men in BP. She thought of all the security personnel she'd encountered at the Intertheocratic Conference and tried to picture this man's face among them but couldn't place him.

He must have experienced the same sensation because as soon as he saw her he frowned. A light didn't go off in his eyes, though, suggesting he too couldn't remember where they'd met. He stole glances at her while one of the other cops removed her diplomatic passport from her bag and handed it to him.

"Miss … Elise … De Jong?" he said, in decent English. "You're under arrest for home invasion and unlawful trespassing.

You have the right to a fair and speedy trial. You have the right to counsel, the right to be silent, and the right not to be a witness against yourself. Do you understand these rights?"

And then she remembered.

The hookah bar.

"Yes," Elise answered in Arabic. "I understand my rights. A woman should at least know the name of her arresting office. Who are you?"

That's when the light went off in the man's eyes. Elise could tell by his stunned expression that he'd realized where he'd seen her before, too.

"My name is Ali," he said, with breathless surprise. "Major Sami Ali."

CHAPTER 21

Ali sat on the upholstered chair opposite the General and Zaman in the latter's office. The coffee table in front of them was laden with shawurma—shavings of lamb, chicken and beef that had been grilled on a spit for a day. Taboon bread—a Middle Eastern pita—tahini, hummus and pickled turnips accompanied the meats.

"What is this cook's name again?" the General said, mouth stuffed.

"Florence." Ali failed to add that he was the informant who'd led him to the Catholic priest, the one whose identity the General desperately wanted.

"You're sure he takes his hygiene seriously?" the General said. "If the ulamas at the Caliph's office saw me eating food prepared by a dhimmi ..."

The ulamas were the scholars and imams who interpreted the sacred Islamic texts as they related to Sharia.

"He doesn't cook with pork," Ali lied. "Says it's a filthy animal."

"The man's a genius," the General said. "If only he'd submit, I'd steal him away for the Caliph's personal staff."

"We wouldn't let him go without a fight," Zaman said, grinning like the rat-shit ass-kisser he was.

Ali chuckled to himself, wondering what the two hetero-sexual masters of the world would think if they knew they were fighting over a gay man.

After receiving the phone call from the General, Ali had changed back into work clothes, strapped on his gun and practically flown to the station. There he'd received instructions from the General and Zaman. A prominent antique dealer had been murdered, they said. He and a team of men were to position themselves inside the man's home. The General said he strongly suspected that a customer would come calling. If the customer were to enter the home illegally and search it, he and his team were to arrest him. That was all he was told, and Ali didn't ask any questions. His only objective was to get back in Zaman's and the General's good graces. And when he arrested the female translator from Christendom, he did just that.

But now during lunch, Ali began to ask himself the kind of questions he'd failed to consider when he'd rushed headlong into the investigation of Greta Gaspar's murder. He began to wonder why the General had chosen him to arrest the translator from Christendom, and why Zaman had agreed to let him do so. The arrest was a prestigious coup—a member of the diplomatic corps from a rival theocracy had committed a criminal offense, and in the home where a murder had been committed, to boot. Wouldn't Zaman have wanted the arrest for himself?

Only if their trap worked perfectly, Ali realized. And there was obviously something else going on. The man in the wheel-chair had been decapitated. Perhaps the motive for the murder was related to the translator's intended business. No one appeared to understand the players and their motives and that meant there was risk to the arrest. What if she'd had a weapon and she'd been shot? Would that have been a disaster for the Caliph in light of the Conference? Or, what if there were a later development that cast doubt on the police's actions? In light of such risks, a prudent man might have chosen to use a patsy, someone indifferent, blind or desperate enough to be the potential scapegoat without even realizing it.

That's why he'd been given the opportunity to restore his good name, Ali thought. They'd chosen him because he was desperate. They'd chosen him because they knew he wouldn't hesitate to be their patsy if circumstances required one. Fortunately, he'd gotten lucky, or at least he had so far, Ali thought.

"She's a spy from Christendom," the General said. "Of that we're certain."

"How can you be sure?" Zaman said.

"The man she went to visit tonight," the General said, "the man who was murdered … he was a dealer in arts and antiquities in Central Eurabia. Had been for two decades, solid reputation. One of his scavengers had recently found a potentially priceless treasure. Something that could be beneficial or detrimental to the Kingdom of Islam. He'd offered to sell its location to Christendom."

"Its location?" Zaman said.

The General nodded. "The Christians agreed to buy it and sent the translator to complete the deal. She's a legitimate translator, here from Christendom for the Conference. That's a fact. But the small fortune in diamonds she was carrying on her person when we arrested her proves she was a spy sent to acquire the location of the treasure."

"How do you know the man in the wheelchair offered to sell the location of this treasure to Christendom?" Ali said.

"Because he offered to sell it to us, too," the General said. "And to the Hindus and the Buddhists."

"I thought he had a solid reputation," Zaman said.

"He did," the General said. "As far as reputations in the arts and antiquities world go. The truth is all those dealers are liars and thieves. It seems this man built a name for himself more carefully than most, then reached a point where he simply wanted to cash it in. Either that or he thought this treasure had such serious implications for the world that he felt morally obliged to make sure all the theocracies had equal opportunity to acquire it. My guess is it was the latter."

"What exactly is this treasure?" Ali said.

The General gave Ali his desert death-glare. "That's not your concern."

"Why do you think it was the latter?" Zaman said. "What makes you think he was a man of conscience?"

"He told the Buddhists it was a Buddhist nurse who cared for him in the hospital when he was first treated for leprosy. He told the Hindus that it was a Hindu doctor who cured him of his disease. And I'm guessing he told the Christians that it was an old Christian hospital where he received his treatment. He told each buyer he owed them a debt and implied that debt was owed to the buyer's religion, which is to say, its government."

"What did he tell us?" Ali said.

"Yeah," Zaman said. "What did he say about Islam?"

The General chuckled. "He told us that there's no one on this Earth at a greater disadvantage than a leper, that Islam is the religion of disadvantaged, and that he'd only sell the treasure to us."

"So what happened?" Zaman said.

The General tore off a piece of taboon bread, dipped it in hummus, and stuffed it into his mouth. He continued speaking even though some of his words came out garbled as he chewed.

"Someone had other plans," the General said. "At the time, we really thought he was selling it only to us. I'm sure the others thought the same. Our stroke of luck was that he was selling it to us first. Our man had an early afternoon appointment. When he got there, the door was locked from the outside and it looked like no one was home. So he broke in and found the scene exactly the way you found it."

"One decapitated man," Ali said. "Three decapitated cats."

The General continued chewing. "We were suspicious right away because he told our man that the treasure would be hidden in the belly of a small beast. Based on that, when our man found three cats, we assumed that he was selling the treasure to at least three of the kingdoms. So we staked out the house and arrested the Hindu and the Buddhist spies, and then the translator from Christendom."

"Why didn't we have surveillance on his house the entire time?" Ali said. "From the moment some priceless treasure was discussed?"

"We did," the General said. "There are dealers and buyers walking in and out of that place all day every day. Except today. Last night we saw him through his bedroom window pulling the shades tight before he went to sleep. Next day, first person to arrive was our man. And when he walked in, the man in the wheelchair was dead."

"There's a housekeeper," Zaman said. "She didn't live with him. She left the night before at her usual time. She's deaf, mute and old but we're looking for her."

The General and Zaman looked at Ali, giving him the impression that they now needed him to know everything that was happening. That raised yet another alarm within Ali—he wondered what dirty job they wanted him to do now.

"One thing I don't understand at all," Ali said.

The General smirked. "Only one?"

"If the man in the wheelchair was selling to each religion," Ali said, "then there should have been four cats. Four religions, four copies of the treasure, hidden inside four cats. Where's the fourth cat?"

The General took an audible breath, as though Ali had asked the most important question of all.

"Like I said," Zaman said. "There's a housekeeper. We're hoping she can shed some light."

"On the murder or the fourth cat?" Ali said.

The General sighed with irritation. "Just when you think he deserves a seat at the table …"

Ali understood. They suspected the housekeeper might have been involved in the murder and stolen all the copies of the treasure, including the one hidden in the fourth porcelain cat.

"Who led the operation to arrest the Buddhist and Hindu spies?" Ali said.

"We used three different teams with three different officers in charge," Zaman said. "Told the first two to keep their mouths shut about what they saw or it's their jobs."

They'd used three fall guys, Ali thought. "Why?" he said.

"Because we don't want anyone else to know the entire story," the General said. "We don't want it to become common knowledge that spies are walking our streets buying secrets and that antique dealers are getting decapitated in the process."

"But you just told *me* everything," Ali said. "Why?"

The General and Zaman shared a conspiratorial glance. Ali experienced a sinking feeling in his gut.

"Given she's a spy," the General said, "she must know local contacts."

"Maybe if you talked to her," Zaman said, "you might learn something about them."

"If I talked to her?" Ali said. "But why would she talk to me?"

"We don't know," Zaman said. "But we're really curious to find out."

"I don't understand," Ali said.

"Neither do we," the General said. "You see, the spy from Christendom has been asking to speak to you. She's been asking for you by name."

CHAPTER 22

Elise sat alone in the interrogation room with her feet shackled and her hands chained to the cement table. Fluorescent ceiling lights illuminated white cinderblock walls. An eerie silence foreshadowed screaming. No world was this white, Elise thought, and no place where a cop and an accused criminal gathered remained this quiet for long.

It was nine-fifteen at night.

In less than nineteen hours, Valerie would be waiting for her by the Danube at the Little Princess statue. Darby's men would be parked a block away, prepared for Elise to appear with her. If Elise failed to show, Valerie would never trust her again. Even worse, once Elise returned to Christendom she couldn't count on ever getting another assignment in Eurabia. She simply had to be released from prison by tomorrow afternoon, and she would do whatever it took to make sure that happened.

After asking the arresting officer his name at the murder scene, she'd invoked her right to have an attorney present and requested Major Sami Ali to call the delegation from Christendom on her behalf. Ali hadn't said a word in response. Instead, he took her to the police station and processed her through Central Intake. The cops made an inventory and confiscated her possessions, including the diamonds. A team of five female guards strip-searched her. They laughed as she took her clothes off, then gasped when they saw that her pubic hair revealed that she was, in fact, a blond. They repeated the word *mashallah* constantly, in reference to their cumulative joy that a terrible criminal had been captured.

They locked Elise in a holding cell with thirty to forty other women. Based on the snippets of conversation she overheard, Elise inferred that all of her fellow inmates had been arrested by the morality police, most of them for clothing, language or behavioral violations. A group of six teens had committed the most egregious offense. They'd been caught drinking and dancing at a beach party with six male friends. A dozen or more of the other prisoners tried to console the girls, who knew they were facing hundreds of lashes and at least two years in prison each. Women were simply not allowed to mingle with men, let alone dance and drink alcohol.

When Ali arrested her, Elise asked him his name so that she could use him to her advantage. She doubted his career would benefit from his superiors' learning that he indulged in illegal tobacco products in the same place as a spy from Christendom. In a paranoid place like Eurabia, such a discovery might taint a man for life, she thought.

Her immediate problem was that to exercise her leverage over him, she needed him to join her in the interrogation room. And that wasn't happening. It didn't happen for the first fifteen minutes after she was brought to the room or the fifteen minutes that followed. Elise didn't have a watch so she estimated the time as best as she could.

A half hour later, Ali finally entered the room with a thick manila folder under his arm. He fired a blank look in her direction and then marched purposefully toward his seat. He looked like an intense man focused on the job before him, the kind who

OREST STELMACH

paid less attention to what might appear in his peripheral vision. He was a straight-shooter, not a player, she inferred, strong of mind and body but nevertheless unsettled—contented people didn't self-medicate with the dregs of society at the hookah bar.

"I'm told you want to speak," Ali said in Arabic. "So speak."

Elise didn't appreciate his choice of words. He sounded like an owner   addressing a dog with human capabilities. That shouldn't have surprised her, she thought. After all, he was an authority figure and she was a woman.

"I didn't say I wanted to speak," Elise said. "I said I wanted to speak with *you*."

"Fine. I stand corrected. What is it you want to speak to me about?"

"When you arrested me, you informed me of my rights. I told you that I wanted to exercise my right to counsel. Where's my attorney?"

Ali remained mute.

"Have you called the delegation from Christendom to let them know I've been arrested?"

Ali waited for a beat. "Is this what you wanted to talk to me about?

Elise stared at him.

"You could have asked Captain Zaman the same question when he tried to interview you. Or any of the officers working at the holding cell."

Elise glanced at the camera mounted near the ceiling in the corner of the room before looking back at Ali.

"You looked like a man who might be more understanding," she said. "A woman gets a feeling about a man sometimes. Especially the first time she sees him."

Elise had first seen him at the hookah bar. If he didn't understand that she was threatening him before, she thought, he surely did now.

"The first time you saw me?" he said. "You mean at the hookah bar?"

Elise couldn't believe it . He'd just admitted to indulging in haram tobacco products on camera and most likely in front of his superiors.

"A police officer," Ali said, "has to assume various disguises and visit all sorts of unsavory places when he's investigating crimes in Eurabia. And to lure a criminal, sometimes he has to pose as one."

Elise felt the walls close in on her.

"What was your excuse for being there?" Ali said. "What would the delegation from Christendom think if they knew that one of their translators was a drug user?"

Elise didn't answer. She was too busy deflecting images of a forty-five year-old Valerie being sold at a secondary slave market for pennies on her original dollar.

"You have no leverage over me," Ali said. "None whatsoever. And you're in very serious trouble, the kind of trouble that can land you in Heroes Square."

"I have no idea what you're talking about."

"You know exactly what I'm talking about, Miss Elise De Jong. Why did you enter a private residence illegally?"

"I had an appointment to see the owner. I was in his home last night. We set a time for my return tonight."

"And what was the nature of your business with him?"

"I was there to discuss the acquisition of a painting for the Kingdom of Christendom. The agreed-upon currency was diamonds. If you call the delegation at their hotel, they'll verify this to be the truth."

"Don't you understand what's happening here?" Ali said. "No one's calling anyone on your behalf. A man was murdered in a home that you broke into illegally. And you weren't there to buy any painting. You were there conducting espionage activity and thereby propagating against the government of Eurabia."

"How exactly was I propagating against Eurabia?"

"By seeking to acquire an item that could be detrimental to the Kingdom of Islam."

True but inaccurate, Elise thought. It was an item that might bring glory instead.

"More precisely," Ali said, "you were seeking to purchase the location of an item that might discredit Islam."

They knew, Elise thought. They knew about the supposed proof of God.

Elise sat stunned for a moment, and then she understood. The man in the wheelchair must have promised to sell the treasure to Arabia, too. That's how they knew that the treasure was the location of an item. Then Elise remembered that she'd seen three cats in the room. There were four major theocracies. Perhaps the man in the wheelchair had promised to sell the location of the proof of God to all four theocracies. And maybe whoever killed the man in the wheelchair had broken three porcelain figurines to remove the coordinates from inside. And if there was a fourth, perhaps he'd taken that one with him. If so, Elise wondered, why?

"So you see," Ali said. "No one's going to be contacted on your behalf. No lawyer, no official from Christendom is coming to your rescue. You're going nowhere."

"That's not acceptable," Elise said.

"You're more likely to permanently disappear than you are to get a phone call or a lawyer. Unless, of course, you cooperate."

Elise knew what was coming. She knew what they really wanted.

"Tell us the truth about your mission. Tell us what your real business was with the man in the wheelchair. Tell us anything and everything you know about his murder."

"I don't know anything about his murder."

"And your contact here in Budapest."

There it was.

That she would never give them, which implied her situation was hopeless. They'd never let her go by tomorrow afternoon. But Elise refused to accept that reality. There was a solution to every problem. She lived and breathed that philosophy. The prerequisite for finding the solution was to find her opponent's weak spot. She'd thought Ali would be vulnerable to having his drug use exposed. She'd been wrong about that, but there had to be something else.

"I'm traveling on a diplomatic passport," Elise said. "I demand the phone call to which I'm entitled by intertheocratic law. I demand the attorney to whom I'm entitled by intertheocratic law, a law that all four Kingdoms have signed an oath to uphold, including the Kingdom of Islam."

"Tell me the truth, submit to a polygraph test to verify it's the truth, and you'll get your phone call and your attorney immediately."

"Is Eurabia a complete fraud?" Elise said. "Is the Kingdom of Islam a fraud? Do your laws mean nothing? Does your word mean nothing?"

"Of course, it does. I give you my word, as an officer and a gentleman. Tell me your contact's name, submit to a polygraph, and I'll deliver everything you want."

Elise tried to extract a point of leverage against Ali based on what he was saying and how he was saying it, and based on what he wasn't saying. She applied all her skills as a translator to read between his lines but came up with nothing. But then, just as all hope seemed lost, it was the thought of translation—her profession—that made her discover his weak spot. And by him she was not referring to the man but rather the cop. Elise may have had no leverage over Sami Ali, but she had a powerful bargaining chip with the Eurabian Police Department, if not the Caliph as well.

"No," Elise said. "I don't think I'll agree to your terms. In fact, I'm done talking to you. Get someone with real power in here."

"Why?" Ali frowned. He didn't seem so much insulted as he was confused by her request. "That would just be a waste of time. What would you say to one of my superiors that you can't say to me?"

"Actually, I'd be saving you time. It's not that I can't say what I have to say to you, it's that you're just a major so you might not fully understand the magnitude of what I'm about to say."

To Elise's surprise, Ali didn't smirk or act patronizing in any way. Instead he shrugged as though agreeing with her. "That may very well be the case. But to get someone with real power in here, I'm going to have to give him a reason. So, please, tell me anyways."

Elise straightened in her seat and cleared her throat. "I'd like to file a complaint and inform the General of the Eurabian Police Department that I'm going to be filing a lawsuit against the Police Department, the Caliph, and the Kingdom of Islam in intertheocratic court."

Ali remained stoic.

"I doubt your superiors plan on bringing me to court on a silly charge or making me disappear during a time of great intertheocratic harmony. I doubt they want their massively successful intertheocratic conference marred by an international incident like that, or by one where one of their translators files a grievance against a moral crime of the worst kind."

"Moral crime?" Ali said. "What moral crime?"

"You're denying me my basic rights as a member of a diplomatic corps because of the inherent bias of your religion."

Shock flashed in Ali's eyes. "What?"

"I'm filing a lawsuit claiming discrimination."

"That's ridiculous. Why do you think we've discriminated against you?"

Elise straightened her posture. Doing so reminded her of the girl with the perfect posture. It reminded her of Valerie. Then Elise set her jaw firmly and leveled her gaze at Ali.

"Because I'm a woman."

CHAPTER 23

Ali wanted to laugh. Who'd care if some translator filed a lawsuit in intertheocratic court? The latter was a joke. No one took it seriously. Each kingdom had its own religion. None of them were interested in compromising with the others.

But then Ali thought of the murders of Greta Gaspar, Hanna Kalmar and the others girls in Eurabia, and his superiors' desire to bury the crimes. And suddenly he didn't want to laugh anymore. The translator might be right, he thought. Appearances mattered, at least for now, with the feel-good from the conference dominating news headlines. Ali decided to tread carefully and respectfully. He told himself to imagine what a smart detective would do under the circumstances, and imitate that man. And maybe he could still extract something valuable from her in the process.

"No one has discriminated against you because you're a woman," Ali said. "If a man were sitting in your seat, everything would be the same."

"On the contrary," she said. "Everything would be different"

Ali was genuinely curious about her reasoning. He had no idea what she could be thinking. "How so?" he said.

"You've been systematically programmed to treat men better than women since birth. It's part of your DNA. You're not even aware of it."

What nonsense, Ali thought. He doted on his daughter at every turn and cared about his wife more than himself. Despite his outrage at the translator's misinformed claim, Ali managed to stay cool. In fact, in some strange and unexpected way, her statement fascinated him.

"I don't understand," he said.

"Then let me explain it to you," she said. "Muslim men treat women like breeders and personal possessions."

"What are you talking about?"

"I'm talking about the laws of Islam."

Ali glowered at her. "Which laws?"

"A female inherits half of what a male heir does. The testimony of a female witness is worth half a man's testimony in court. A woman is not supposed to hold a man's job. The penalty for killing a woman is half of what it is for killing a man. The child of a Christian mother and a Muslim father must be Muslim or be put to death. A husband can have four wives but a wife can have only one husband. See what I mean?"

"That's the way Allah intended life to be. To say that these laws mean that men treat women like breeders and possessions—"

"For their own benefit," she said, "and for the benefit of the Islamic political movement."

Ali couldn't believe his ears. "What?"

"Islam spreads because Muslim men exploit women to advance their own wealth and power. Islam doesn't grow through religious awakening. It grows through mathematics. A man with four wives tends to have more children than a man with one wife. The European countries that began allowing Sharia in certain neighborhoods eventually lost grip of their own legislatures when the Muslim population grew. It took time but it was inevitable. Like mathematics."

Ali didn't understand her point. "What does any of that have to do with you being discriminated against here because you're a woman?"

"Simple. If I were a man, I would have been given dramatically more respect than I've been given as a woman because in all the laws I mentioned, a man is treated at least twice as well. So it's logical for me to think that If I were a man, I would have gotten a phone call. If I were a man, the delegation from Christendom would have been called on my behalf."

"And this is what you're going to file a lawsuit about?"

"Yes," the translator said. "I'm going to put Islam's treatment of women on trial. How's that going to play with your leaders?"

Ali thought about the question, and then saw an opening to strike a bargain. "I'm not sure. That's beyond my pay grade. But if I had to guess, I'd say, not that well. But how's it going to look when the woman filing the lawsuit is made out to be a drug addict and a spy who was arrested for breaking into a home where a murder had just taken place? What if some journalist decides to suggest you're a suspect in that murder, based on anonymous sources? How's that going to play with your leaders?"

The translator gave him a condescending smile. It was the same kind of look the other detectives used to remind him he was inferior to them. The mere sight of it raised Ali's blood pressure. It always had, Ali thought, and it always would.

"I think we're at a stalemate here," Ali said. "Neither of our kingdoms needs any bad publicity. Give me some information I can use to satisfy my bosses. Give me something. Give me anything. And I'll get you your phone call."

"You haven't been listening," the translator said. "I have nothing to give you but the comeuppance that your backward religion deserves."

Ali exploded from his chair, knocking his manila folder off the desk in the process. He grabbed the translator by her prison uniform, pulled her across the table with his left hand and slapped her face with his right.

When he shoved her back into her seat, she wobbled but quickly regained her composure. Blood trickled from her lip and a sense of remorse washed over Ali. Rather than crying or complaining, however, the translator chuckled and licked the blood with her tongue.

"Still think we're at a stalemate?" she said.

Ali backed away, awash with loathing for this wretched woman and himself, wishing the General had found some other way—any other way—for him to get back in his and Zaman's good graces.

A moment later the door behind him opened. The General and Zaman marched inside. Ali marched over to them and Zaman slapped him on the shoulder.

"Don't worry," he whispered. "You never touched her. It's our word against hers."

The General, meanwhile, didn't betray his emotions. "Only one slap. Such restraint."

The General and Zaman moved to the side and spoke to each other in hushed tones as a guard came in and unchained the prisoner's hands so he could take her back to her cell.

Ali returned to his office. He considered the interview a failure because he hadn't extracted any valuable information from the translator. She deserved to have been slapped, he thought, but a smarter detective would have restrained himself and continued trying to get something out of her. Ali walked in circles around his desk for a minute, and then realized all was not lost. As long as she was a guest in their jail, he still had an opportunity to try again.

Ali grabbed his phone and called the kitchen. When one of the assistant cooks picked up and greeted him, Ali asked him to put Florence on the line.

"Yes, Major?" Florence said.

"I brought in a translator from Christendom a few hours ago. A woman."

"I heard."

"She hasn't had anything to eat. Fix her a dhimmi tray. And bring her an ice pack."

"An ice pack?"

"To reduce the swelling of her Christian head."

"On it."

"And Florence?"

"Yes, boss?"

"Make her some of that spaghetti your famous for, and try to maximize those anti-depressant qualities you told me about."

"I cook to serve."

Ali ended the call.

Only after he hung up did he realize he was craving some of that pasta himself.

CHAPTER 24

Elise savored the stinging sensation on her lip. Now she had an episode of tangible physical abuse that strengthened her threat of a lawsuit. Ali's superiors probably had seen it on a live monitor. Even if they denied it happened and erased the surveillance tape, Elise would pass a polygraph that would strongly suggest she was telling the truth.

Not that it would ever come to that. She had no intention of filing a lawsuit. She merely wanted to become such a nuisance that they let her go sooner rather than later. The satisfaction she experienced from manipulating Ali into hitting her by insulting his religion didn't embarrass her at all. In Eurabia and beyond, a woman had to take her pleasures where she could. In Eurabia and beyond, a woman had to enjoy those pleasures without remorse.

And then she saw the pictures.

They'd slipped out of Ali's manila folder when he'd jumped up to slap her, and she'd stolen a glimpse when he'd bent down to collect them. The first one was a picture of a dead blond girl who appeared to be Valerie's age. The second was a print advertisement for the Persian School of Dressmaking.

At first Elise's head swirled, still hazy from being hit. Then she recalled Valerie's strange behavior and palpable fear. Her sister had chanted that she was not scared in an eerie manner that suggested she was frightened of something more than becoming a slave. Later, she'd said that the truth could get a person killed in Eurabia. Now, seeing the dead girl and knowing that a cop was looking into the Persian School of Dressmaking—the same place where Salim was training his slaves—Elise was struck by the coincidence.

Elise feared Valerie was in even greater peril than she'd suspected.

In the time it took for Ali to gather his material and leave the room, Elise regained her senses from the beating he'd administered. She cursed herself for alienating him, then realized that if she hadn't infuriated him, he wouldn't have reached over to slap her, and the contents of the folder wouldn't have spilled onto the floor.

Ali had left the interrogation room. The man she'd refused to speak with earlier, the one Ali had referred to as Captain Zaman, was eyeing her with hate. Beside him stood the fattest Arabian she'd ever seen. She inferred he was Zaman's superior, most likely the chief of police or a government bureaucrat. He wasn't even looking at her, he was looking through her. To him she was a non-entity, a means to some political end who didn't even register as a human being. Elise could tell by the way he disregarded her that, in his eyes, she was little more than an animal.

Nevertheless, Elise thought, she had no time for pride. The two men stood whispering to each other near the doorway. The guard who'd brought her in was making his way to uncuff her hands.

"I'll talk," she said to Zaman and the fat man. "Tell Major Ali to come back, please. I want to talk to him one more time."

The fat man paid no attention to her and continued talking. Zaman's head shifted slightly in her direction but he continued nodding and looking directly at his boss. After the guard ambled in, the two men left.

The guard, an apathetic middle-aged man with a mustard stain on his uniform, led her back to the holding cell. Elise asked politely, pleaded and then tried to cajole him into calling Ali on her behalf.

"Tell him I saw the pictures that fell out of his manila folder," she said. "Tell him I have information about the dead blond girl. The one with ties to the Persian School of Dressmaking."

The guard ignored her, stopped short of the holding pen, and unlocked the door to a private cell. He ordered her to step inside and place her hands on two metal rings attached to the door. After cuffing her wrists to the rings, he removed the shackles from around her ankles, uncuffed her, and locked her inside.

Before slamming the door shut, the guard uttered three and only three words in response to what Elise thought was a plea with a shocking amount of detail to it, sufficient to prove she really did know something.

"Shut up, bitch."

CHAPTER 25

Ali returned home from work with a renewed sense of hope. Sabida, of course, knew that he'd done his job and pleased the General even before Ali stepped foot in the house. He could smell the baklava she was baking for him as soon as he walked into the kitchen. He enjoyed a long shower, a hot cup of tea, and an in-depth debriefing of what his daughter had learned in school today. When he awoke the next morning, he felt as though his life was back on track.

Despite these developments, Ali didn't hesitate when he got in his car after breakfast. Zaman wanted Elise De Jong to stew in her cell for twenty-four hours before further questioning, so Ali wasn't scheduled to interview her until the end of the day. Thus, instead of driving directly to the station, he took a detour to the place he longed to visit more than any in the world, even more than the glorious city of Florence in the country formerly known as Italy.

He drove to the Persian School of Dressmaking.

A light shone on the second floor of the building where the school was located. Ali spied a silhouette moving about from street level, which left no doubt that either class was in session or someone was preparing the school for opening. He buzzed the intercom and a surly-sounding woman let him in. As he climbed the stairs, Ali remembered the young woman at the Curry House, who'd described the killer's dinner companion as a woman with fat, old eyes.

A sleepy receptionist sat drinking coffee at the front desk. Ali asked if the owner was present, and a minute later a second woman joined them from a door in the wall behind the receptionist. One look at the pronounced folds of fat and wrinkles under the woman's eyes and Ali knew he'd found her.

"Arabic chicken curry with noodle rice?" Ali said.

The woman frowned. "Excuse me?"

Ali showed her his ID and introduced himself. She told him her name was Miss Mona. He asked if they could speak somewhere privately, and she escorted him into a massive room with chairs and tables arranged by work stations. Ali suspected that the dead dhimmi girl, Greta Gaspar, had sat in one of these chairs as she learned how to sew a dress as part of the curriculum of Imam Salim's slave training school.

"I'm conducting an investigation," Ali said, "and a garment bag from your school is an important piece of evidence."

"A garment bag?" Miss Mona's face lit up with fascination. "From this school?"

"Is it a common item?"

"Common?"

"Have you had many of them made? Are there many of them around?"

Miss Mona shrugged. "I don't know. It's a relative question, isn't it? I've probably had a hundred of them made since my husband and I started our business nine years ago. That sounds like many, but compared to our retail store across the hall—Reza Couture—it's a small amount."

"Who gets these garment bags? The teachers? The students?"

"Just the older students, the full timers. When it comes time for them to work on their final thesis—their masterpiece dress—they're given one to carry their work to and from class. And the teachers get them too, but there are only three teachers."

"And what about you? Do you use one of these? Do you carry one around with you often?"

Miss Mona appeared to consider the question seriously for a moment, then narrowed her eyes. "Why does that matter?"

"Please answer the question."

"Not until you tell me exactly what this is all about."

Ali reached into his manila folder and pulled out a picture of Greta Gaspar's corpse. "Do you recognize this girl?" he said.

Miss Mona glanced at the picture of the strangled girl. "Greta," she said, without a hint of emotion. "I was told she was ill…"

"Greta Gaspar," Ali said, images of the look-alike he'd known as a child dancing in his eyes. "She's what this is all about."

"She looks… I mean, obviously she's… how did she die?"

"Answer my question. Do you use your own garment bags?"

Miss Mona drew a line with her lips. "I still don't understand why you're asking me such a question. What does this dhimmi girl… what do garment bags… what does any of this have to do with me?"

"Do you like curry?"

"What?"

"Did you go to the Curry House for lunch a week ago?" Ali informed her of the specific day in question.

Miss Mona took a step back. "I don't like your questions or your tone of voice."

"You have me confused with someone who cares what you like," Ali said. "Answer the question, please."

Miss Mona arched her chin. "No. I don't think I will. Do you know who I am? Do you know who I'm in business with?" She glanced at Ali's folder with disdain. "You dare to suggest I had anything to do with some dhimmi girl's death?"

"I haven't suggested anything—"

"Isn't there enough crime in our community to keep you busy? Why are you wasting time on a dead dhimmi girl?"

Ali took a step forward. Fear clouded Miss Mona's face and then vanished. She stood nose-to-nose with him refusing to yield.

"I'm investigating the murder of Greta Gaspar because she was a citizen of Budapest," Ali said. "A citizen of Eurabia. Her parents pay a dhimmi tax that earns them—that entitles them—to the protection of the police."

"In theory—"

"I *am* the police. That's the only thing you need to be concerned about. And you will answer my questions or I'll arrest you right now as a suspected accessory to murder. I'll haul you into the police station. I'll lock you in a holding cell and make you sit there for twenty four hours before you even see an attorney. I'll make it my life ambition to ruin your business. Yes, I know who you are. You're in business with Imam Salim. I don't give a shit. Now, do you want to answer my questions, or do you want to go to jail?"

Ali watched and waited for her answer. If she were involved in some scheme relevant to Greta's murder, she'd refuse to submit to him and would seek Salim's protection. But if she were merely conducting business and innocent of wrongdoing, she'd answer his questions. Salim was a cleric and a businessman. He accumulated power and money by selling people a sense of purpose. Like all ambitious men, he didn't want to waste time or be associated with scandal. Neither did the parents of her other students.

"Arabic chicken curry with noodle rice," she said. "I had it at the Hindu place. The Curry House."

"You had one of your garment bags with you," Ali said.

"I'm working on a dress for Imam Salim. Something personal."

"Who was the man in black that you were having lunch with?"

"The Gentleman from Prague."

"Real name?" Ali said.

Miss Mona shook her head. "I only know him as the Gentleman from Prague."

Ali remembered Elise De Jong's dissertation on Muslim gentlemen. She'd love this bastard, he thought

"Who is he?" Ali said.

"A broker," Miss Mona said. "He scouts and acquires specimens on behalf of distinguished clientele."

"A private slave broker?"

"A buyer's broker."

"But you don't know his name," Ali said. "What was the nature of your business?"

Miss Mona shrugged. "Just as you'd guess. He scouts the best and the brightest across Eurabia."

"And how did he find you?"

She glared at him. "All the top training schools have reputations. Those who are looking for the finest specimens know who they are. Dressmaking is a core curriculum. I'm more accessible than the Imam, so it was only natural for him to come to me."

"If you don't know the man's name, how could you be sure who he is? How could you be sure you could trust him?"

"The first time we met—about a month ago—he showed up with an incredible list of references. A who's who of power brokers in Budapest, Prague—"

"Vienna, Copenhagen, Bern…"

Miss Mona stared at him with amazement. "How did you know that?"

"Did you check those references?" Ali said.

"I did."

"How many?

"Enough to make me comfortable."

Ali returned her glare. "How many?"

"Three. One person called me back."

"Only one?"

"But he had glowing things to say," Miss Mona said.

Ali reflected on Miss Mona's willingness to do business with a man whose references she'd barely confirmed.

"Did any money change hands?" Ali said. "Did the Gentleman from Prague pay you an introductory fee of some sorts?"

"He paid in gold, as he did when I shared our class rankings with him."

"Was Imam Salim aware you were meeting with him?"

"Of course," Miss Mona said. "He has a team in charge of placing all his specimens—his pupils, he calls them. When I get inquiries, such as this one, I keep them informed."

"And did the Gentleman from Prague make any bids?"

"Not yet."

"How many times have you met?" Ali said.

"Just twice."

"How were the meetings set?"

"By e-mail. We ended up meeting at the same location. I guess he likes the food there."

"Did you get a good look at his face?" Ali said.

"No. He was completely covered up except for his eyes both times. They were brown. Warm, friendly. Like he sounds. He has a nice voice."

Ali asked questions about the man's height and weight, and the answers were consistent with what the priestess had told him. He looked like a common man.

"Anything else you noticed about him?" Ali said. "Anything peculiar?"

Miss Mona shook her head as she thought about it. "No, not that I remember … Oh. There was one thing. He massaged his right wrist every once in a while, as though it was bothering him."

"If the first visit was an introduction," Ali said. "What did you talk about the second time?"

"The specimens. I shared the class rankings with him."

"The girls of yellow."

"Yes," Miss Mona said. "That list, too."

"You mean there's more than one?"

Miss Mona shrugged. "There's an overall class rank. And the girls of yellow."

"You mean there's a separate list of girls with blond hair?"

Miss Mona nodded. "The girls of yellow. They're rarer, and over time they've become a bit of status symbol, so they cost more."

"Was Greta Gaspar on the list of girls of yellow?"

"Yes, but what does that have to …. You're not suggesting the Gentleman from Prague …"

"If there's a change to the list," Ali said, "say there's a new girl that's worth seeing, how do you get in touch with him?"

"E-mail, and then wait for a reply."

"I'll take that e-mail address and all his references," Ali said, "including the one that you checked. And I'd like copies of both lists. The most recent ones, and the ones when Greta Gaspar was still alive."

"If I give them to you, will that conclude our business?"

"Almost. The last thing I need you to do for me is to call the Gentleman from Prague and tell him you have three new specimens to show him, that they're climbing the class rankings and that buyers are circling already."

"Is that … is that really necessary?"

"Tell him you'd be happy to meet with him at his favorite location."

Miss Mona's face fell.

"Look at the upside," Ali said.

"I'm trying to but I can't see it," Miss Mona said.

"Arabic chicken curry with noodle rice. Sounds delicious to me."

CHAPTER 26

Elise's cell contained a bed, a sink, a toilet and a closed circuit camera hanging near the ceiling in the corner of the room. Her first order of business was to wash her face and let the cold water remove some of the sting that lingered from Ali's slap. Her second goal was to calm her mind. Images of the dead girl in Ali's crime scene photo kept morphing into pictures of Valerie's corpse in an identical setting. Only the faces changed.

In the absence of narcotics, legal or illegal, Elise prescribed physical exhaustion and meditation for herself. She began with ten burpees, falling to the floor to execute a push-up only to thrust herself back to her feet and repeat. Then she sat with her back pressed against the wall at a ninety-degree angle for a count of sixty, using only the muscles in her thighs to support herself. She repeated the cycle ten times, after which her legs wobbled when she tried to stand. She drank water and paced in her room until her heartbeat slowed to ninety beats per minute. Then she began her practice of yoga, nothing strenuous, focusing more on breathing and the visualization of stress leaving her body.

All the while she reminded herself that her situation wasn't hopeless. Once she didn't return to the hotel by midnight, Christendom would go looking for her. The Eurabian police might lie and deny that she'd been found and placed under arrest. Later, if discovered, they could feign confusion. Or, they could just as easily tell her colleagues that they did, indeed, have her in custody. The purpose for the Intertheocratic Conference was to facilitate dialogue and prevent the theocracies from destroying the planet. Her arrest was just the sort of trivial event that could escalate tensions and ignite a war, Elise thought. It was in everyone's best interest for her to be treated in accordance with intertheocratic diplomatic guidelines.

Still, such a rescue would likely take time. She couldn't assume that Christendom would be informed of her arrest, send a lawyer and secure her release before her scheduled meeting with Valerie tomorrow. That meant her most promising path to release remained Ali. He wanted to solve a murder. The pictures that fell from his manila folder proved as much. Why else would he be carrying them around? She had something to offer, namely inside information from the Persian School of Dressmaking via her sister.

Ali and his superiors would take another run at her, of that there was no doubt. The question was, how long would they wait?

After she finished her yoga, Elise meditated in a cross-legged position for half an hour and then went to bed. Her prescribed medication worked, and she fell asleep from sheer exhaustion.

A tremendous racket woke her up the next morning. At first she thought a guard was preparing to enter her cell. Then she saw that he'd merely opened an aperture in the door above a ledge that rested on the inside. A tray of food appeared, and beside it a half-bottle of water.

Elise bounded toward the door to grab the tray and water for fear the guard might pull it away if she didn't take it. When she glanced at the tray, she saw that it contained half a pita and a cup of some sort of soup. Steam wasn't rising from the cup. Elise hadn't expected anything better. In fact, she'd been prepared to fast indefinitely in case they didn't feed her at all.

But as she reached out for the tray, a pair of hands pulled it back. Elise caught a glimpse of the shirt sleeves above those hands. They were black.

Two men began to argue. Elise recognized one voice. It belonged to the guard who'd taken her to the interrogation room and back. He was a man of few words and less intelligence, and wasn't very fond of Major Sami Ali. Elise had deduced this based on how he'd ignored her when she'd told him she had insight into the Persian School of Dressmaking that Ali would covet. The other voice spoke lovely Arabic but there was something about its precision that struck a chord with Elise. There was just a hint of a foreign accent now and then, too. Both of these observations reminded her of her own Arabic. This man was a foreigner, she thought, though only the trained ear might realize this based on his voice alone.

A moment of silence passed between the two men, and then Elise heard the guard ask the other man a question. The guard raised his voice so Elise could hear his words clearly.

"What's in it for me?" he said.

Elise couldn't hear the other man's answer, but she could have sworn it included a reference to some sort of sandwich whose recipe had originated in the country formerly known as Cuba. A further exchange on the topic of beverages ensued, followed by a loud grunt and a warning by the guard that the other man had five and only five minutes.

The sound of metal sliding onto metal repeated itself, and then the man in black sleeves reappeared bearing a second tray. This one contained a ladle of pomodoro sauce nestled on a mound of steaming linguine, topped with fresh parsley. *What's the difference between parsley and pussy? No one eats parsley*, a

Cardinal had once joked, after a security briefing in Christendom and two bottles of wine. A tossed salad with roasted red peppers and kalamata olives, a roll with a pat of butter, and a small dish containing tiramisu accompanied the dinner. Sealed in a bag beside the plastic utensils lay an icepack.

"Your breakfast, madam," the man in the black sleeves said. "It was supposed to be dinner but some things in Eurabia … they take time."

Elise snatched the tray.

The man lowered his voice. "Courtesy of Major Ali," he said.

Elise realized she had reason to hope. Ali was an asshole. He probably didn't care if she starved to death. He was obviously treating her to a delicious meal to soften her up for his second interview, which was exactly what she wanted. That had to be his motive, Elise thought. He certainly couldn't have been motivated by compassion.

"I'd like to thank Major Ali in person," she said.

"I'm sure you'll get that opportunity soon."

"That might not be soon enough."

The man didn't say anything but his black sleeves remained visible, arms folded over his chest.

"Are you someone who can get a message to Major Ali?" Elise said.

"I tend to be on the receiving end of requests from Major Ali, not vice versa."

"Tell him this concerns the dead girl whose picture he's carrying in his folder. Tell him this concerns the Persian School of Dressmaking."

The man stood still, listening.

"But tell him I must see him alone immediately," Elise said. "If he doesn't speak to me by noon, I can't help him."

The man in the black sleeves didn't answer.

"A girl's life depends on it," Elise said.

"I'll do my best to get him the message," he said.

"And please thank the chef."

"That won't be necessary."

"Why not?"

The man's arms fell to his sides. "You just did."

CHAPTER 27

The killer walked into the Curry House just as Ali had hoped he would, against all odds, in a plan Ali had orchestrated straight out of the Eurabian police manual on exactly how not to conduct an operation.

Allahu akbar.

God is greatest.

The Gentleman from Prague had answered Miss Mona's e-mail in less than an hour and agreed to meet her for lunch the next day at his favorite restaurant.

This brought into question whether the Gentleman from Prague was really from Prague, Ali thought, given how quickly he was able to meet her. A plane trip from Prague to Budapest took only ninety minutes, but the circumstances still struck Ali as being too coincidental. Once his meeting with Miss Mona was set so quickly, Ali began to operate under the assumption that the Gentleman from Prague lived in Budapest, or a town within driving distance of the Central Eurabian Caliphate's capital.

The references he'd supplied Miss Mona had been of no help. All the men were real and powerful but the phone numbers supplied were no longer in service. Even the one belonging to the chief executive of a water purifying company who'd supposedly spoken to Miss Mona had been disconnected. Ali doubted she'd spoken to the man in question, but rather to someone who'd been paid by the Gentleman from Prague to impersonate him. Ali didn't dare dig deeper and contact the references through another means for fear Zaman would somehow discover that he was still pursuing the case.

Securing tactical support for his noon operation was beyond problematic. Ali was effectively operating as a rogue cop without Zaman's consent or approval, so he was almost on his own. Fortunately, he had Ismael. Eurabian crime scene investigators were also sworn police officers, which meant they carried firearms and retained the authority to stop and arrest. Ali had known Ismael long enough to know that he could trust and rely on his friend.

"My kingdom that this bastard turns out to be a dhimmi in disguise," Ismael said, when he climbed into Ali's car across the street from the Curry House, two hours before lunch. "If ever there was a case where you could get two for the price of one..."

Ali thought about what Ismael had just said and shook his head. "Do you really want to get rid of all of them, Ish? All of them?"

"What?"

"I said, do you really want to get rid of all the dhimmis?"

"Why, do you want to start a collection? Think it might appreciate over time?"

Ali managed a chuckle.

"First comes Saturday," Ismael said. "Then comes Sunday."

"And then what? You think Monday will be better if there's no one left but us?"

"Much."

"You won't miss Dhimmi Town?" Ali said.

"Sure. Like the virus I had last year."

"You don't think life is more boring when everybody and everything's all the same?"

Ismael scoffed. "You think it was more exciting when the dhimmis were invading our lands and waging war at will?"

"The dhimmis didn't tax us at an increasing rate to force us to submit to their religion or leave our own country. You think the Pact of Umar is reasonable?"

"Who cares if it's reasonable? Some dhimmi agreed to it a thousand years ago. Now they have to live with it. What's up, A? Are we going to take this bastard down or what?"

Ali sighed. "Yeah." He fixed his gaze on the restaurant. "That we can agree on."

The hunchbacked woman Ali had met yesterday was working at the Curry House today. In her husband's absence, she served as the restaurant's manager. When she came out from the kitchen to talk to him, Ali didn't mention that he'd forced Miss Mona to set up the lunch, merely that she and the man for whom Ali was looking were going to arrive at noon.

"I want no part of this," the hunchbacked woman said.

"Neither would I if I were in your shoes," Ali said. "But look at it this way. You don't have a choice. Two people are coming to have lunch at your restaurant. If it weren't for me, you wouldn't even know they were coming. They would have just arrived."

"Obviously because you set it up," she said. "You think because I serve food for a living I'm a fool?"

"I think if you fail to cooperate with a policeman who's trying to apprehend a killer of dhimmi girls—younger versions of your own daughter—you're much worse than a fool."

"I don't want any violence in my restaurant."

"You think you're more likely to have more violence if the police are there, or less?"

"If there's any damage to my restaurant, you're paying."

"Of course I am." Ali had been paying in one form or another since he'd taken an interest in the case. Why should this operation be any different?

"What do you need me to do?" the hunchbacked woman said.

"Exactly what you always do. Take the customers' orders and get out of their way."

They discussed logistics, including the selection of the table where she was to seat Miss Mona. Afterwards, Ismael volunteered to walk a one-block radius around the restaurant as a general precaution. When he returned through the rear entrance into the kitchen, he gave Ali the thumbs up. Then he planted himself at the furthest table in the back of the restaurant with a newspaper, a cup of tea, and a menu. His mobile phone rested on the table in front of him, obscured from the entrance and any customers by his paper. From his vantage point, Ismael could text Ali freely about what he was seeing without arousing suspicion.

Meanwhile, Ali exited via the rear door and returned to his car. He was parked between two sedans with a clear view of both sides of the street and the sidewalks leading to the Curry House. His unmarked vehicle appeared indistinguishable from those surrounding it. Ali watched the pedestrians walking along the sidewalk, scanning from left to right in an attempt to catch a glimpse of the killer before he got close to the restaurant. Five minutes before noon, Ali couldn't spy anyone resembling the killer's description on the streets.

Then a man in a hooded robe made a sharp turn toward the Curry House, whipped the door open, and powered inside. Ali had dismissed him on first sight because he appeared slightly bow-legged with a stocky build, which conflicted with the description of the average Eurabian man. But now that he'd vanished inside, Ali feared he'd been premature in his conclusion.

Perhaps the man was wearing padding and feigning a limp to disguise himself.

Ali texted Ismael. *Customer.*

Ali's mobile phone confirmed the text message's delivery, and he waited for a reply.

Eyes and ears, Ismael said, meaning he could see and hear the customer.

Ali texted, *table*?

The mobile phone flashed speech bubbles to indicate that a response was en route, but none came. Ali waited for fifteen excruciating seconds for five words to finally come across.

Chicken curry. Extra rice. Takeout.

Ali sat back, relieved his judgment hadn't proved faulty with the restaurant's first customer of the day. He resumed scanning the streets, and at precisely noon, Miss Mona from the Persian School of Dressmaking came into his peripheral vision. She strolled at a slower pace than she did when she flitted around the confines of her school suggesting she was reluctant. Ali couldn't blame her. She had no idea what would transpire once her date arrived. Neither did Ali or Ismael.

But then her eyes inadvertently found Ali sitting in his car and she froze.

Ali cursed under his breath and nodded toward the Curry House. He willed her to keep moving and keep her eyes on the street and not on him. The second nod of his head delivered the necessary message. She nodded once in return and resumed walking. This time she marched purposefully, as though seeing Ali had injected some confidence into her, or reminded her that she didn't want a rumor floating around that she'd been jailed as a suspected accessory to murder.

She disappeared into the restaurant.

Ali quickly exchanged messages with Ismael, who verified that the hunchbacked woman had seated Miss Mona at the agreed-upon table against the wall. This location restricted the killer's paths of escape, and left Ali and Ismael with overwhelming odds that they'd be able to corral the suspect if he tried to run.

Five minutes followed. No one else entered the Curry House. The Gentleman from Prague was late. Ali had expected him to be punctual. Any killer that took such care with his victims' corpses had to be an exacting individual. His tardiness caused Ali concern, made him question whether Miss Mona might have deceived him.

And then he appeared. A man of average height and build, head and face covered by his black robe, marched toward the restaurant. When he turned toward the entrance, Ali texted Ismael.

Customer.

Three seconds later, Ismael's response arrived. *Eyes only,* meaning he could see the new customer but he hadn't heard him speak yet.

Ali got out of the car and hustled across the street, alternating glances from the phone to the traffic pattern to make sure he didn't get killed as he crossed the road.

Halfway across the street his phone jingled. Another message from Ismael.

Suspect seated. Go.

Ali let a car go by, raced across the rest of the street, pulled his gun from its holster and burst into the Curry House.

The killer sat at the table with Miss Mona, his back to Ali. The co-owner of the Persian School of Dressmaking sat wide-eyed, forehead glistening.

"Police," Ali shouted. "Hands in the air. Don't move."

In the far corner, Ismael drew his gun, pointed it at the killer and exploded toward the table with shocking speed and agility. He shouted the same instructions as Ali and had the killer covered before Ali arrived at the table.

Ali pulled the hood off the killer's head from behind. He was dark-skinned with salt and pepper hair. Ali held his breath as he stepped to the side to glimpse the face of the man who murdered children. Although this killer had nothing to do with the death of the girl that persecuted him, it was her that Ali pictured at this very moment, alive with his lips pressed to hers, and dead with a rope around her neck. Arresting this man and securing his conviction might finally bring him some peace, Ali thought. Regardless of whether it soothed his conscience, his arrest would be the most satisfying achievement of Ali's life excluding the birth of his daughter. Of that he was certain

There was just one problem, Ali realized, when he saw the man's face.

This man was not the killer.

He was a retired cab driver from the country formerly known as Libya who wandered the streets looking for handouts during the day. He was well-known to the police, a whiner and an agitator but utterly harmless.

"Hello Dhimmi Lover," he said, crushing the consonants to mock Ali's nickname. "Are you buying?"

"Who sent you here?" Ali said.

The old cabbie cackled.

Ali grabbed him by the scruff of his collar and lifted him off his chair. "Tell me who sent you here, or as Allah is my witness, I'll lock you in a cell and have one of the female officers go to work on you with a car battery and a pruning knife."

"A man with binoculars sent me here."

"What man?" Ali said.

"He gave me a gold dinar to put on these clothes, come to this place, and sit down with the woman who would be waiting." The old cabbie nodded at Miss Mona. "The tired old hag who dresses like a man and doesn't know her proper place."

"He gave you his clothes to wear?" Ali said. "That means he took them off—"

"Did you see his face?" Ismael said. "What did he look like?"

"I didn't see nothing," the old cabbie said. "He made me stand in an alley, gave me my money and told me to look away. Told me to wait ten minutes and then come here."

"Where?" Ali said, shaking him. "Where was this?"

"A block away, near the coffee shop on the corner where they give out stale pastries for free when they close."

Ali bolted outside and ran toward the only coffee shop in sight. It occupied the corner just as the old cabbie had described. The Gentleman from Prague must have had binoculars and seen Miss Mona stop, exchange signals with a man in a car, and continue onward. There was no logical reason for Miss Mona to have purposefully drawn attention to herself and Ali. If she wanted to prevent the killer's capture, she could have warned him in an e-mail that a trap awaited him.

The only other possibility was that the Gentleman from Prague was familiar with police personnel. If that were the case, the moment he saw Ali's face through his binoculars he would have recognized the trap. In such a scenario, he could have simply left and not shown up for the rendezvous. The only reasons for him to send the old cabbie in his place were to confirm the sting, mock Ali, or distract him while he comfortably made his escape.

Some criminals liked to hang around and watch the police try to solve the crime they'd committed, whether it was burglary, arson or murder. Such was not the case this time, Ali decided.

There was no sign of a man who fit the killer's description milling about in the restaurant's vicinity.

The killer now knew that Ali was looking for him. This would render him ultra-cautious, Ali thought, as he trudged back to the restaurant. His chances of finding the Gentleman from Prague had just plummeted.

When Ali's phone jingled, he assumed it was a text message from Ismael, who was eager for a status report. Ali was surprised when he saw that it was Florence who'd sent him the message and even more stunned by its means of transmission and content. Florence had sent the e-mail from his personal account to Ali's non-work related address. His friend only did that when he wanted to make sure there was no trace of his message on a police department computer server.

His message read:

> *Dhimmi tray delivered, prisoner wishes to discuss Persian School of Dressmaking.*
> *Urgent.*
> *Florence.*

CHAPTER 28

After savoring her delicious dinner-turned-breakfast, Elise washed her face and brushed her teeth with the toothbrush and toothpaste she'd been provided. She repeated the same exercise regimen she'd performed the night before, this time with more vigor, grunting and groaning through her final repetitions of each set, guards be damned. When she was finished and exhausted, she tried to meditate for twenty minutes without success. Once again, images of the dead girl in Ali's photo haunted her, and she thought of Valerie.

Hours passed. Lunch wasn't provided. Perhaps the jail only served two meals a day, Elise thought. Her dream that Ali would arrive to interrogate her by noon gradually disintegrated. She fought off moments of hopelessness as she imagined Valerie arriving at their rendezvous point and discovering Elise was a no-show. The meeting wasn't until four o'clock, Elise kept reminding herself. Her dream wasn't dead until then.

Some time between one and two o'clock, or so she guessed, her door clanged. Lying in her bed, Elise peered at the slot through which her food was delivered, expecting it to slide open. But this time the jangle of keys followed, and the door to the cell swung out instead.

Elise jumped to her feet.

The guard who'd extorted a bribe to allow the cook to deliver her a special meal walked into her cell.

Elise retreated to a corner, never turning her back on him.

The guard glared at a spot on the floor directly in front of her feet as though she were too putrid a sight for him to take in. He had no tray in his hands, nor did he say anything. He just stood there, two meters away from her.

A wave of fear washed over Elise as she wondered why the guard was in her cell. But the door was open behind him, she reminded herself. As long as the door to the cell was open, Elise thought, the guard wouldn't dare –

Major Sami Ali marched into her cell. The sight of the man who'd slapped her face conjured fantasies of violent payback, but that's all they were—fantasies. They lasted no more than a nanosecond. Her exercise sessions, the meditation and the fine meal supplied by the asshole himself had restored her perspective.

The guard left and closed the door behind him. Elise could see Ali's eyes drift toward her cheeks, and she knew that he was checking how much damage he'd done when he'd struck her. She was curious herself because there was no mirror in the cell or any other substance upon which she could see her reflection. She'd iced the tender spots three times this morning. Ali showed no sign of emotion, nor did he come bearing any additional treats from the country formerly known as Italy.

They stood facing each other. Elise realized her hands were folded over chest, though she didn't remember placing them there.

"You wanted to speak to me again?" Ali said.

"Thank you for dinner last night. And the icepack."

Ali's lips parted but no sound came out. He appeared stunned by her tone and choice of words, just as she'd hoped.

She was no longer the bitch from Christendom. Oh, no, Elise thought. She was sweet syrup, raisins and coconut flakes.

"I heard they had some extra pasta left over from the guards' dinner," Ali said, shrugging. "So I told the cook to send you some. You wanted to discuss something?"

"Have you called the delegation from Christendom on my behalf?"

"Did you give me a reason to call them yesterday?" Ali said.

"What if I give you a reason to do something for me today?"

Ali considered her proposition. "That depends on the reason you give me, doesn't it?"

Elise didn't respond.

"I'd give you my word as a gentleman that if you help me you'll be rewarded. But then, I'm no gentleman, am I? So you're going to have to trust me, or not. It's up to you. But I'm giving you no guarantees about anything except to tell you that Christendom has not called worrying about your whereabouts, and it doesn't look like anyone cares about you at all."

"I need to get out of here and the only way that happens is if I have a lawyer from Christendom here within the hour."

"That will never happen."

"Forget it then," she said. Elise retreated to the corner of her cell. "If you don't want any insight into the Persian School of Dressmaking, the woman who runs the place, or Imam Salim's slave training school … If you don't want information that might help you solve that girl's murder, then I'll just rest until Christendom comes looking for me. And they will come looking for me."

Ali looked at her stone-faced but Elise guessed that he had to be dying with curiosity. To her shock, he wouldn't agree to her terms.

"Fine," he said. "So be it. Enjoy your exercise."

He banged on the door. The guard came and opened it, and Ali left.

Elise swore at herself. Perhaps she'd overestimated his professionalism and commitment to his job. Maybe solving the girl's murder didn't matter that much to him. Had her instincts failed her? Elise wondered. Had her obsession with Valerie clouded her judgment?

She got her answer less than a minute later.

Ali returned, face red and carriage stiff, carrying a small folding ladder. He stood still for a moment, alternately staring at Elise and the floor. Then he shouted to the guard to turn off the camera. When the light on the camera stopped blinking and turned solid red, Ali pulled a black muslin cloth from his pocket, stepped on the ladder, and draped it over the lens.

"Belt and suspenders," he said. "The camera's off but just in case you don't believe me, it's covered up. And the camera controls the recording of sound, too. If you don't believe me, then don't. But I'm going to proceed as though there are only two people involved in this conversation. If you want to strike a bargain, I suggest you do the same. This is our one and only chance. "

Elise took three steps toward him until she was only a meter away. She had no choice but to trust him and if she was going to do so she needed to project confidence. Worst case, she'd remain stuck in jail. Best case, she'd actually get a chance to see Valerie. There was no advantage, however, in speaking first.

"You wanted to see me," she said.

Ali studied her. "What is it you think you know?"

"I don't think I know anything. I know what I know."

"And what is that?" Ali said.

"I know there's something suspicious going on with the girls in Imam Salim's slave training school, and I know it has something to do with the Persian School of Dressmaking."

Ali sounded incredulous. "How can a translator from Christendom in town for two weeks possibly know things like this?"

"I have my ways and my reasons for knowing."

"You've got to give me more than that. You saw the picture of a girl who was murdered and another one of the school building. I understand that. But for you to be aware that she was enrolled with Imam Salim and taking classes at the Persian School of Dressmaking..."

"Actually," Elise said. "I didn't know that..."

"... makes your knowledge of all this highly suspicious."

"Like I said, I didn't know the dead girl was part of the slave training school, though the thought had crossed my mind when you dropped her picture on the floor."

"Why? Why did that thought cross your mind?"

Elise realized they'd arrived at the crossroads of trust, risk, and the possibility of reward. There could be none of the latter without a disturbingly large quotient of the former.

"I want you to let me out of jail tonight," Elise said. "Just for an hour. Then I'll come right back and the Eurabian justice system can do with me as it pleases."

Ali stared at her for a beat. "Did we just really hit a language barrier this time?"

"I don't think so. I'm a translator, remember?"

"That is ridiculous and you know it."

"This is personal," Elise said. "Not business."

"Ridiculous."

"I know something, and I know someone who knows a lot more. I have a meeting set with this person for four o'clock. You can come with me. You can ask her some questions. Whatever you like. Then I get to speak with her for a minute. After that, you can bring me right back here yourself."

"Who is this woman?" Ali said.

"I don't need a phone call. I don't need to speak with anyone from Christendom. All I want is one minute alone with my sister."

"Your *sister*?"

Elise took a deep breath. She was being honest. Well, almost honest. She wasn't going to tell him that Darby's men would be waiting to snatch Valerie off the street after their meeting and whisk her out of Eurabia.

"We were separated," Elise said. "Her mother sold her to the Office of Slave Procurement right after her birth. I traced her here. Met her at the dressmaking school. That's where she told me she's frightened. And I mean, very frightened."

"Maybe she's just scared of what it means to become a slave," Ali said.

"No. It's something more than that. She's known she was going to be a slave since birth. She was owned by a different family before. Her reality isn't a new concept to her. I don't think it's any kind of abuse."

"I agree. There's no chance of that. None. There are grooming schools for sexual exploitation—horrible places. I'm sure every theocracy has to deal with such scum. And then there are Arabian training schools for slaves. And then there's Imam Salim's training school, which would be held to the absolute highest ethical standards."

Elise nodded. "So I've heard. I didn't get a chance to ask her why she's so scared, but now that you tell me another girl was killed … it's like my sister knew all the girls were in danger … or something like that."

"How did you find out she was with Salim?"

Elise shrugged.

"And how did you find out he sends his pupils to that school in the first place? You didn't just waltz in there one day and find her."

"I did some research."

"I'm sure you did. Does she know you're related?"

Elise shook her head.

"Was it your plan to tell her that tonight, before you tried to sneak her out of Budapest?'

Elise kept a straight face to hide her dismay. It was a logical conclusion, but she'd hoped it would somehow evade him.

"Will you have men there?" Ali said. "Because I can't be party to an extraction. It wouldn't be the first time it happened in Eurabia, that someone came to retrieve a long lost relative. A father tried something similar last year. It didn't end well for him or his son."

"I don't have any men. Like I said. This is personal. I'm on my own."

An admission that Darby's men would be there would put them at risk of capture and eliminate Elise's chance of having Valerie extracted, a hope that was becoming more fleeting with each minute.

"So," Elise said. "Do we have a deal?"

Ali looked her over one more time. "I'll let you know."

He removed the muslin cloth from the camera, took his ladder, and left.

CHAPTER 29

Ali tried to imagine sneaking Elise De Jong out of jail for an hour, surviving the rendezvous with her sister without some sort of duplicity on their part, and returning her to prison without experiencing an unpleasant surprise in the interim, the kind that could permanently ruin his career and prevent him from solving Greta Gaspar's murder.

It really was a crazy idea, no matter how desperately he wanted to believe otherwise. At least that's what he thought until Zaman called him into his office with urgent news.

"Christendom is demanding to see her," Zaman said. "Their officials arrived at the Caliph's offices an hour ago. They're demanding to see her and they're demanding her immediate release."

"How do they even know we have her?" Ali said.

"Who knows? Our own people may have confirmed their suspicions. It's among the diplomats, beyond our pay grade. All that matters is that we're going to have to let her go tonight."

"Tonight?"

"Look, we're not savages here. We're a nation of laws. If there were any evidence she was spying ... if she were a suspect in the murder of the man in the wheelchair ... but there isn't and she isn't."

At first Ali was crestfallen. The moment she learned of her impending release, Elise De Jong wouldn't need him anymore. Any hope of gaining a lead from her sister would vanish. But then Ali told himself to think harder, even pretend to be Zaman. What might a devious man do in this situation?

And then Ali saw an opportunity.

You're right," Ali said. "We have to follow the law, especially given the purpose of the Intertheocratic Conference."

Zaman nodded. "Religions need to co-exist or eventually there won't be a world left for them to go to war in. And that starts with diplomacy. The Caliph has made it clear to the General, and the General has made it clear to me. We can hold the woman for twenty-four hours in accordance with intertheocratic law because she committed a crime at the scene of a murder. But after twenty-four hours…"

"She gets counsel—"

"She's gone," Zaman said.

"The opportunity in all this," Ali said, pretending the thought was just dawning on him, "is that she doesn't know that, does she?"

Zaman raised his eyebrows. "No. She doesn't, does she?"

Ali sat quietly.

"What do you have in mind?"

"I'm thinking that until those twenty-four hours are up," Ali said, "we're still entitled to try to squeeze out the name of her local contact. There must be one. Someone had to be on hand to help her get the lay of our land."

"And how would you go about doing that? Take another run at her? You can't try anything rough. Not with the stakes what they are and the order coming down from the Caliph. So what good would it do?"

"We'll get nothing out of her in an interview," Ali said. "No, no. I was thinking of something more intimate. After all, an interrogator has a better chance of learning something from his prisoner by forging a bond with her as opposed to hitting her."

"Relationships take time to build."

"It depends on the people involved."

Zaman chuckled. "What are you saying, Ali? You're going to seduce her with your charm?"

Ali remembered what Elise De Jong had called a Muslim gentleman. "That's an oxymoron, isn't it? Ali's great charm?"

Zaman laughed out loud. "What then?"

"When a man has little charm and even less time, he needs to humble himself and seek assistance."

"What kind of assistance?"

"Narcotics."

"A chemical inducement to speak? After I told you what the Caliph has decided, are you insane?"

"Not torture." Ali said. "Pleasure. There's no telling what a person will reveal when he or she is under the influence of the golden weed."

"Ah," Zaman said, brightening. Then he frowned just as quickly. "You can't bring cannabis into our jails."

"Of course not. And the ambience would be all wrong. But I can bring her to the hookah bar."

Zaman narrowed his eyes, but then he eased back in his seat and turned reflective.

"We have to let her go anyways," Ali said. "I'm certain I can get her to go with me voluntarily."

"Voluntarily?"

"Yes."

"Why on Earth would she go with you voluntarily?" Zaman said.

"Leave it to me. It may be better for you if you don't know everything. That way I'll be accountable if anything goes wrong."

"Ali, the politician. I may have to watch out for you yet. Get her clothes out of storage. Take them to Tech and have them sew a GPS unit into her *jihab*. They've done it before. She'll never find it. If anyone asks, tell them she's due to be released. Under no circumstances does anyone know about your plan."

"Understood," Ali said. The operative phrase was *your plan*.

"That means if you run into any trouble out there, you're on your own. No calls for back-up, no calls to me for help. Because what you'll be doing is the kind of thing that can't be done. So it won't really be happening."

"No, sir. It won't."

"Good. I'm glad we understand each other." Zaman studied Ali with a blank face. "You know, Ali, there's no such thing as a brilliant detective. That's a myth created by the entertainment business. Unless there's a witness and an obvious solution within twenty-four hours, murders are rarely solved. But when they are solved, it's not because some new clue was discovered by the guy with the big brain. No, it's almost always a function of persistence and luck. The guy that never gives up ends up being at the right place at the right time. That's why I'll take the persistent guy over the smart guy any day of the week."

Ali wasn't sure but he thought he detected a compliment in there. "Thank you, sir," he said, face flushing.

"Carry on," Zaman said.

Ali spent the early part of the afternoon filing overdue reports and contemplating his strategy for later. He was completely on his own. Circumstances had created a chance for him to find out what Elise De Jong's sister knew. He had no intention of trying to convince the translator from Christendom to go to the hookah bar where they'd first seen each other. That was just misdirection to keep Zaman from meddling.

Ali took a break at three o'clock and drove home to tell Sabida that he'd be working through the evening on an undercover mission for Zaman. She would love that, he knew, as such an assignment confirmed that he was back in the police hierarchy's good graces. In addition, the General had seen him go nose-to-nose with a defiant diplomat. The General was probably pleased that Ali had stood his ground, and not displeased that he'd had the audacity to strike her. Ali wouldn't have been surprised to step into his house and get some extra love from his wife.

Instead he found two suitcases waiting for him in the foyer. They knocked the wind and all the joy out of him.

"Are you going somewhere?" Ali said.

"No," Sabida said. Her eyes looked puffy, as though she'd been crying. "You are."

Ali stood speechless.

"Did you meet a Christian woman at your hookah bar?"

Ali assumed she'd learned about tonight's plan. "No—"

Sabida screamed. "Don't lie to me. I smell that disgusting smoke on you when you come home late and I don't say anything because I understand. I understand that a man needs a release of some kind. But today Father told me that you frequent the same place as some Christian translator who turns out to be a criminal and is now in your jail. Who is this woman to you?"

Now Ali understood. Sabida was talking about the revelation he'd made during the interrogation about his chance sighting of Elise De Jong. The General had witnessed the interrogation, heard Ali admit that he'd seen her at the hookah bar before her arrest, and called his daughter today. Even though Ali had explained his presence at the hookah bar as a function of police work, the General could have chosen to believe it was complete bullshit, which it was. The irony was that his run-in with Elise was completely innocent. It was momentary and accidental. He really had been there only for the weed.

"You've been misinformed," Ali said. "I never met the woman before I arrested her. It's true that I saw her face at the hookah bar, but I didn't *meet* her. I don't *know* her."

"Oh, no? Then why are you having your Christian friend in the kitchen cook gourmet dinners for her?"

Ali wondered how the General could have possibly learned about that. Then he realized that Jabil—the pork-loving sergeant he'd threatened to find the dhimmi witness—had probably delivered the meal and told Zaman all about it. Zaman, in turn, had probably informed the General. Ali also realized that his ordering Elise a special meal might have encouraged Zaman to approve the plan to lure her to the hookah bar this evening. Zaman might have deduced that Ali was working to gain her trust.

"I had an ice pack delivered to her," Ali said. "Because I hit her. I hit her because she insulted Islam. Did your father tell you about that, too?"

Approval flashed on Sabida's face, but her contempt quickly returned. "Who is this woman to you?"

Ali had just about had enough of her.

"You've lost your mind, wife," he said, letting his voice rise. "She's no one to me. She's a prisoner. She's a potential source of information for Eurabia. I didn't know her before she wandered into my jail. I don't know her now. And I have no interest in knowing her."

Sabida stared at him for a few seconds, and then her tone softened. "What about the dead dhimmi girl? Are you all through with that?"

Ali didn't want to lie to her. He hadn't lied to her since he'd seen the suitcases and he wanted to preserve the purity of his responses. So instead of saying a word, he looked away.

"No," she said. "I didn't think so. My father gave you a way to get back into Zaman's good graces, and still you want to risk everything we have on a dead dhimmi."

"She has no one else but me. Her parents have no one else but me. It's my duty as a policeman. It's my duty as a Muslim. Islam is about justice. I must bring them justice."

Sabida erupted. She launched into a tirade about his obligations as a husband, father, and subordinate to his bosses in the police department.

Ali stopped listening. He stared at the suitcases instead, the conflict of what to do with them stirring inside him. On the one hand, he wanted to pick them up and leave. On the other hand, he was the man of the house. This was *his* house. His daughter lived in it. If anyone were leaving the home, the wife should be the one leaving, not the husband. The thought of word spreading that he'd allowed Sabida to kick him out of his own home made his face burn.

Eventually she calmed down and a glorious moment of peace passed between them.

"Whatever this thing is inside you that's compelling you to choose a dead dhimmi girl and her parents over your own family," Sabida said, "it's obvious that there's no stopping you. So go, do what you have to do, and when you're done, we'll have a discussion and see if we can start all over."

"Eyes to my soul—"

"Get out."

Ali picked up the suitcases and left.

CHAPTER 30

Elise stood on the promenade along the Danube River beside the Little Princess Statue, scanning her surroundings, praying Valerie would appear. Foot traffic was light. Cars sped over the Chain Bridge to the right. When Ali had arrived in her prison cell at three o'clock and told her to be ready to leave in fifteen minutes, she couldn't believe her luck. His agreement to let her out to meet Valerie meant he had an ulterior motive, but they were doused by sheer joy.

Soon she would see her sister again.

Elise had suspected they'd imbedded a tracking device somewhere in her clothing. It only made sense given Ali might fear she would try to escape. She found it as she was putting on her *jihab* in her prison cell. It was sewn into the hem at the bottom of her robe, barely distinguishable from the material around it. She located it without drawing attention to herself, certain that a guard was watching her on a remote camera monitor. But she remembered where it was, and when Ali lit a cigarette and turned away from her to enjoy the majesty of the Chain Bridge, she bent her left knee to let her *jihab* touch the ground and crushed it with her right foot. Now, if she needed to escape, with or without Valerie, no one would be able to follow her.

Elise knew that Darby's men were probably close. They may have even seen her. But if they'd seen her, then they'd seen Ali, too. He was leaning against the railing on the opposite side of the statue. By now Darby's men would be appropriately suspicious. If they thought one cop was present, they'd fear more might be lurking in the shadows.

There was no sign of Valerie yet, but it was only three forty-five. They were fifteen minutes early.

Ali ambled over to her.

"Do you know the story about this statue?" he said.

Elise shook her head.

"A Hungarian sculptor named Marton had a daughter who played the princess. She pretended her bathrobes were gowns and made crowns out of newspapers. So he made a statue in her honor. After it became a symbol of Budapest, he made a copy and gave it to a museum in Tokyo. No big deal back then, but now it's a symbol of intertheocratic harmony, Buddhist and Islamic cooperation."

"You and your oxymora," Elise said.

"You and your darkness. There's beauty all around you but you're too busy judging people to stop and see it. Look at the Chain Bridge behind you. You know why the Caliph lights it green in the night? Because green is the color of Islam. It's the middle of the color spectrum and the Prophet Muhammad preaches moderation."

"Is that why you slapped me instead of punching me? Moderation, is it?"

"You're here with me now, against all odds, aren't you? And look around. There's not another cop to be found. On the streets or in the buildings."

Elise couldn't deny the improbability of the event but it would be a cold and frigid day on the equator before she apologized to the bastard.

Ali didn't say anything more. They leaned against the railing beside the Little Princess and remained silent for a minute.

Daytime running lights flashed from the street perpendicular to the promenade. A car headed directly toward them. It descended down the hill and turned right. As the vehicle drove by, Elise spied a man's face in the passenger seat.

Four men, Darby had said. *Two cars. All Christians of Arabian descent. All soldiers, all reliable. I trust them with my soul.*

The sequence of the man's expressions informed Elise that he was one of those four men. First he glanced at her, then he appraised Ali, and then he looked back at Elise, seemingly without emotion.

Ali's mere presence was enough reason for them to abort. She was supposed to be alone. In addition, they could probably sense he was a cop. Experienced agents and cops were the same that way. They recognized their own kind.

"Who were those men?" Ali said, as they drove out of sight.

"How would I know?"

"Because you arranged for them to be here."

"You're paranoid," Elise said. "I'm here alone."

"Those men were here for you. I could see it in their eyes. What have you not told me?"

"No more than you haven't told me, I'm sure."

They stood beside the statue quietly. There was nothing more for either of them to say, because neither was prepared to divulge any more information, Elise thought.

She resumed scanning the promenade and beyond for any sign of Valerie. The scheduled rendezvous time of four o'clock came and went. A second vehicle, this one a small van, descended down the hill and retraced the route the car had covered. A different passenger matching the description of Darby's men glanced at Elise and Ali nonchalantly. Then he looked away and the driver continued onward.

They would not return, Elise thought. As she suspected would be the case given Ali was with her, she was on her own.

Over the next fifteen minutes, Elise grew increasingly despondent. She'd been so worried about her incarceration and finding a means to be released that she hadn't stopped to consider the risk that Valerie would not show up. But as the minutes passed, she grew increasingly certain that her smallest fear had turned out to be her greatest risk.

She had no doubt that Ali could sense her apprehension.

"Do you have a way to get in touch with her?" he said.

Elise shook her head.

They waited, and waited, and waited. To Ali's credit, he paced back and forth along the Danube to stretch his legs and pass the time, but didn't complain or pressure Elise to give up, even though she was to be out of jail for only one hour. In fact, he appeared to be waiting for her to admit the rendezvous had failed. Meanwhile, Elise's imagination began to run wild with ugly possibilities, most notably that the killer whom Ali was trying to apprehend had struck again. She had absolutely no foundation for such a fear, yet her mind kept returning to that scenario.

At five-thirty, an hour and a half after their agreed-upon meet time, Ali spoke again.

"If she were going to show," he said.

"She would have showed by now," Elise said.

"She might have been caught trying to get out of her house, or something might have happened that kept her from even trying. A man like Salim is going to run a tight ship. A girl isn't going to be able to just wander off that easily."

"Yeah. You're probably right."

"I don't think there's any way I can get to her through police channels," Ali said. "This case isn't exactly the department's top priority. But I'm going to give it some thought tonight and see if there isn't a way."

Elise couldn't hide her surprise. "A way?"

"A way for me to get access to your sister, whether as a rumored witness to a crime or something entirely unrelated. Like I said, I doubt it's possible but if it was … If I managed to … would you like me to pass on a message to her?"

Elise was so shocked at his offer that she couldn't contemplate an answer.

"Think about it," he said.

They returned to the car and Ali drove away. Elise was crafting a message for Ali to deliver to Valerie when she realized that they weren't heading toward the police station.

"Where are you taking me?" she said.

"To our favorite place in the world."

"Excuse me?"

"I've been given orders to take you to the hookah bar and see if the cannabis loosens your tongue."

"You're joking," she said.

"The most successful interrogations are based on trust," Ali said, "not violence. Trust is based on a human bond, and the hookah is our bond, is it not?"

"You're not kidding."

"No, I am not."

"I'm just a translator. I don't know anything about anything else."

"I'm not going to ask you about anything. I'm not going to ask you about anything other than what you want me to tell your sister if I happen to get through to her tomorrow. You have my word on that. I know that doesn't mean much to you but you have it."

"So what do you want?" Elise said.

"To tell my boss that I did what he told me to do so that I stay in his good graces. This business with the man in the wheel-chair is more important to Eurabia than the murder of a bunch of dead dhimmi girls."

"A bunch? There's been more than one murder?"

Ali hesitated, but then he sighed and said, "There've been eight other murders."

"Oh my God." Elise's stomach turned over. "Is it one man? Do you have any leads?

"That I can't discuss with you."

"Please."

Ali sighed again. "He's of average height and build, dresses in black robes, speaks perfect Arabic, and loves curry. And something's wrong with his wrist."

Elise waited for more description but none came. "That's not much to go on ..."

"If you prefer not to go to the hookah bar, I can take you back to jail, but it might cost me some political capital, which might make it impossible for me to try to reach out to your sister."

The truth was that Elise could already taste the smoke, feel the cloud swirling in her brain, and savor the sweet relief that would follow.

"I don't want to cost you any political capital," she said.

Ali drove to the hookah bar and parked on the street nearby. When they entered the establishment together, the attendant at the front desk did a double take.

"Two bowls, buttered rum," Ali said. "With cannabis. We'll be here three hours. No longer."

"Men and women cannot smoke together," the manager said. "That is strictly forbidden. Strictly forbidden."

Ali flashed his police ID. "Official business."

"I'm the manager here," the attendant said. "And I don't care if the future of the planet depends it. Not in this bar."

"Of course not," Ali said. "Who said anything about us smoking in the bar?"

The attendant frowned. "Where then?"

"Where there are no men or women that could be offended."

"There is no such place."

"Of course there is," Ali said.

The attendant shook his head.

"Your office."

The attendant stood dumbstruck.

"I'm going to give you my business card," Ali said. "And with it will come a favor, from me to you. One and only one favor, to be paid on demand. Now a man who runs an establishment like this ... surely a business card like that is of value to him."

Five minutes later Elise and Ali were seated in a cramped basement office that smelled vaguely of dead mice. Ali told Elise to sit behind the manager's desk while he took a seat in a folding chair facing her. His reason for doing so was immediately apparent. By seating her in the manager's chair, he was placing himself directly between her and the exit. The most noticeable result of this arrangement was that Elise sat two heads higher than Ali, whose chair was built low to the ground.

The manager brought the hookah and the cannabis. The hookah contained two mouthpieces. They passed it back and forth, alternating taking slow, deep inhalations. The smoke poured into Elise's chest and she held it there—cool and soothing—until she exhaled and pushed it out her nose and mouth. Forcing the smoke out her nose maximized the hookah's flavor and left Elise with a dazzling rum sensation from her sinuses to the tip of her tongue.

Soon the sweet taste of rum-flavored pot rendered all other sensations except for one irrelevant. The shock of having been arrested, incarcerated, and thrust into uncertainty dissipated. But the fear that something had gone terribly wrong with Valerie remained.

"When did you start using cannabis?" Ali said.

"In my teens." Elise took a long hit and blew the smoke out her mouth slowly. "What about you?" she asked, her speech garbled from smoke.

"A year after I got married."

"You needed relief from marriage?"

"No," Ali said. "From the past."

"Your marriage brought up baggage from your past?"

Ali didn't answer.

"How did that happen?" Elise said.

"I had a daughter."

"Ah."

"What about you? What did you need relief from?"

Elise thought of something that might sound like the truth. "The dhimmi tax, loss of religious freedom, persecution, the usual Christian maladies in Arabian controlled lands."

"Where exactly are you from?"

"East of Budapest, or west depending on your perspective."

"The more cannabis you consume, the more you sound like a spy than a translator. Aren't you going to ask me where I'm from?"

Elise thought about the question. "I'm more concerned with where you're going tomorrow…"

"When I see if I can find your daughter and get a message to her. I'm sure you are. It's very noble of you to care so much about a person you never met before, whether she's family or not."

"It's not a matter of nobility," Elise said. "It's a matter of forgiveness."

"Forgiveness. I've heard of this word. It's a Christian concept, isn't it?"

"I think it transcends religion. Just like guilt. You're a cop. You know—"

"Yes. I know all about guilt." Ali's face tightened. He appeared to be contemplating something that had brought him great anguish. "Whom are you trying to forgive?"

"The same person you are."

They exchanged a look of understanding. Then Ali took a long drag from the hookah, Elise did the same, and they sat reflecting privately for about ten minutes. The cannabis calmed Elise's nerves and slowed down her thought process. With each passing minute the silence became more comfortable and less awkward, until the reality that she was a prisoner and he was her captor became a secondary consideration, background noise that neither of them was going to allow to infringe on their disengagement from the world outside.

After they passed the hookah again, Ali slouched in his seat so low that Elise feared he was going to slide off the chair and under her desk. She had to remind herself that it wasn't really her desk, although her chair was quite comfy and the cheap metal furniture was starting to look like retro, industrial chic.

Elise eyed Ali. "Why did you really bring me here?" she said.

"I told you. And about this I wasn't lying. I'm just trying to stay in my boss's good graces."

"If you didn't lie about that, what have you been lying about?"

Ali didn't answer. He merely stared into space, deep in thought.

Elise recalled his previous admission that he used the hookah to get relief from something shameful in his past. Her memory was a bit foggy now, and she couldn't quite remember the source of his shame. Ah yes, she realized three beats later. It was a girl.

"The first step to forgiving oneself is to confess one's sins," Elise said.

Ali remained mute for a moment, then seemed to realize that he wasn't alone. "Why? A confession won't change the past."

"No, but it can help put it behind you."

"How?" said Ali. "If you've committed one of the most heinous acts imaginable by a human being, how can you ever put it behind you?"

"By accepting that you're human and, by definition, fully capable of doing something heinous under the wrong circumstances."

Ali studied her. "And this confession, it works for you?"

"Sometimes yes, other times no. In my experience, it helps the least when you need it the most."

"Why is that?"

"Sometimes, when we've done something that stains our soul, we can't forgive ourselves without some sort of act of contrition. Sometimes we have to *do* something instead of just talking. But the confession is still a good start because we're overcoming our pride and ego, and that's essential if we're going to purge our-selves of shame."

Ali reflected on her words for a moment. "Okay, you first."

"Excuse me?"

"You first. Confess, and then I'll do the same."

The first and last time she'd seen Valerie flashed before Elise's eyes. Her confession would be effortless because she replayed the sequence constantly. She wasn't ashamed to admit that in the final scene she'd watched her sister taken away for money. She was ashamed of having done nothing to prevent this from hap-pening, but not of admitting it to a stranger. She had no pride or ego left to defend. She'd purged them over time, or at least that's what she wanted to believe.

She told Ali how a nurse came and took Valerie away after her mother gave birth to her, in accordance with the bill of sale she'd agreed to with the Office of Slave Procurement.

"And you blame yourself for this?" Ali said.

"I blame myself for not defending my sister. For not sav-ing my flesh and blood from becoming someone else's property and losing the rights she's entitled to in the eyes of all reasonable men."

"The shame is the mother's, not the sister's. If that's the rea-son for your unhappiness, you must want to be unhappy. Because you were too young at the time—"

"I was eighteen …"

"And didn't have the resources—financial or political—to do anything to change your mother's decision."

"I could have tried," Elise said. "I could have fought for her. I could have stolen her in the night and run away. That's the thing. It doesn't matter what my odds of success were. What matters is that I made no effort. I didn't want to put myself in danger. I failed my sister, and in so doing failed myself."

Ali shook his head. "Are you one of these people that's only happy if she's miserable? Because there's no reason for you to be so hard on yourself. Absolutely none. And I can prove it to you. Have you ever met a man so loathsome that you couldn't stomach the thought of being in the same kingdom as him, let alone the same room?"

Elise actually felt a twinge of anxiety at the prospect of what he might tell her.

"I'll take your silence as a no. Well, there's a first for everything. My wife thinks the reason I want justice for the dead dhimmi girl is because she reminds me of our daughter. I didn't tell her this isn't true. I've told some of the people who've helped me with this case that my first love was a dhimmi girl that looked just like the dead girl, and that this is the reason I keep at it. But that's a lie, too. I could never tell them the truth, which is that I won't let go of this case because I'm trying to make myself feel better about what I did to the girl I knew long ago, which is basically something that makes me sub-human."

"Tell me what you did," Elise said, "and I predict right now that I'm going to tell you the same thing that you told me, that you're punishing yourself way too much."

Ali shook his head with self-loathing. "Listen and weep." He took a long, deep breath. "When I was a teenager, my parents were upper-class professionals in the country formerly known as Jordan. My father was a family lawyer and my mother was a psychologist for women. They secretly yearned for a modern version of Islam—the kind you were thinking about when we had our conversation in the prison—one that condemned all violence and treated women with equal respect. But they could never come out against a fellow Muslim, especially not when the mullahs were blessing their actions, no matter how much they disagreed with them. Once in a while they'd even provide shelter to boys who were in hiding before a suicide mission.

"When I was sixteen, a group of boys like that stayed in our basement for a month or so. They were uneducated, arrogant, and filthy. Back then I was a shy kid—I was such a disappointment to my parents because I wasn't a good student. I just didn't take to school or anything else, for that matter. All I ever wanted was to fit in. So I tried to be friends with these guys, but they hated me from first sight. When I look back, it's no surprise. I had parents, we had money, to them I was super-rich. They made my life miserable when my parents weren't home. They teased me, beat me up, told me to keep my mouth shut or they'd kill me. I knew what they had in those rucksacks they kept by their sides all the time. I knew they were different. They had nothing to lose and that gave them the upper hand over me.

"There was a European girl in the neighborhood. Her father worked in the oil business and he'd married a Jordanian woman. I don't know how old she was. Thirteen, fourteen, fifteen? I have no idea. But she was very pretty and I always had a crush on her, but of course, she wouldn't even acknowledge my existence. I always imagined she was a nice girl but it turned out she was the exact opposite. The boys that were staying with us had cannabis and hashish—I have no idea where they got it from but they had a constant supply. Well it turns out that the girl that I was in love with loved to party. She was a wild child.

"So they became friendly with her. They would invite her over to share their drugs and watch *haram* movies and listen to *haram* music when she came home from school. Once they were all headed for the stairs to the basement, and one of the boys saw me down the hallway in the kitchen and said something. They all started laughing, including the girl. That's when I knew she thought I was a joke. From then on I avoided all of them. I just wanted them to leave.

"About two weeks after she started coming around, my parents went to some banquet on a Saturday night. They were going to be out all night. I was in my room doing whatever, paying no attention to those boys downstairs, until one of them came into my room and told me they had a surprise for me, that I was to go downstairs with him right away. I didn't want to go with him but I didn't want to get in a fight, either.

"When I got downstairs, one of the boys was having sex with the girl while the other two were cheering him on. I tried to leave but the kid who brought me punched me in the stomach and told me he'd do worse if I didn't do as I was told. The girl seemed a bit out of it. She was conscious but not all there. I had to sit and watch as they took turns with her. And then when they were done they said it was my turn."

He stopped talking. Previously unnoticeable cracks and crevices deepened on Ali's face. A long silence passed between them.

"You had no choice," Elise said. "They forced you. Your life was in danger. There's no telling what they would have done to you if you hadn't done as they said."

"You don't understand."

"What don't I understand?"

Ali fortified himself with a breath. "They didn't force me. I was aroused. Some vile primal urge got hold of me. My blood was so hot, I tell you, I didn't even feel in possession of my own body. No one forced me. Whatever I did to her I wanted to do it. And when I was done with her, they dragged her upstairs and threw her out the front door. Then she went home and hung herself from a drainpipe in her cellar."

Elise watched as Ali rocked back and forth in the chair and chanted something under his breath—a prayer, she guessed. She understood his anguish now, just as she knew her own. And as opposed to reviling him for having committed a horrible crime, she sympathized with his plight.

"You're wrong," Elise said. "I do understand..."

"How can you possibly—"

"I understand why you brought me here."

When Ali looked up, Elise could see the longing in his eyes. He wanted contrition, atonement, and forgiveness. She knew the feeling all too well.

"You brought me here because you needed someone to listen, and it couldn't be a Eurabian. It had to be someone who'd leave the country soon, someone who could never use the information against you, someone you'd never see again in your life."

Ali straightened in his seat. "I'm just trying to stay in my boss's good graces."

"But if you think your act is so heinous, think again. In fact, take a ticket and get in line behind me."

"You cannot possibly think that what you did is in any way as horrible as what I did..."

"I can and I do," Elise said. "In fact, it's not even close."

"What am I missing?"

"The truth."

Ali frowned. "I don't understand."

"Everything I told you?" Elise's heart pounded in her ears. "It's all a lie."

CHAPTER 31

Ali was still savoring the unexpectedly blissful sensation of having finally admitted his sin to another human being. His skin tingled and he felt strangely lighter. And then Elise told him that everything she'd confessed to him was a lie and he felt even better. He'd been able to follow her advice while she herself had been unable to do so. Maybe that meant she was right. Maybe he really had helped himself by confessing.

He was also shocked by the magnitude of his empathy toward the Christian spy. What had she really done? Ali didn't even know how to start answering that question because her admission cast everything that he knew about her into doubt.

For the first time, Ali spied desperation in her eyes. She looked as though she needed to confess her sins to someone. To his surprise, Ali wanted to offer her words of encouragement to do so. Whom better to confess to than a man whom she'd met only in passing?

Then his phone rang.

Ali answered it.

"Are you alone?" Zaman said.

Ali answered. "No."

"Get some privacy. Now."

Ali stood up and promptly almost fell. He steadied himself by grabbing the edge of the table, motioned to Elise that he was leaving, and stumbled out of the office. He pressed the door closed behind himself, his brain engulfed in a fog.

"What's up, boss?"

"Any progress?" Zaman said. He sounded suspiciously cheerful.

Ali suffered a pang of guilt. He hadn't even tried to extract the name of a local contact in the Christian spy network from her, and for obvious reasons. Any attempt would have been folly. But he was a professional and should have made an effort.

"Not yet," Ali said. "And to be honest, we're forging a bond but I doubt I'm going to be able to pull it off in one night."

"Don't feel bad about. It was a long shot. I want you to bring her back to the station immediately."

"Why? We're not … I'm not in the best of shape."

"Drink some coffee, chew on some khat, dunk your head in ice water if you have to. Do whatever you have to do, but I need you at the Matthias Church within the hour."

Matthias was the church where the killer had brought Greta Gaspar's corpse. It was the place where it all had begun.

"Why Matthias?" Ali said.

"Because I have a tremendous gift waiting for you there."

Ali remained skeptical. The last time he'd been told a great gift awaited him, Sabida had trouped out their daughter, who proceeded to tell her father that she hated him.

"What kind of gift?" Ali said.

"Another dead dhimmi girl."

"What?"

"But this time," Zaman said, sounding downright ebullient, "we caught the killer red-handed—or, dead-handed—I should say." Zaman laughed. "We caught the bastard carrying the dead girl into the church with his bare hands."

"Who?' Ali said. "Who is he?"

"I want you and only you to wrap this up for us, Ali. The reason I want you to do it is because I know the case has become a bit of an obsession for you. Well, this will put your mind to rest. And the other reason I want you to close this case is because the killer has asked for you."

"Asked for me?"

"That's right," Zaman said.

"Why would he ask for me?"

"Because you know him."

Zaman told him the name of the killer.

Ali lost his breath, train of thought, and equilibrium. He had to reach for the wall to keep from falling. His brain swirled. He hung up on Zaman before the conversation was finished, not out of malice but because he needed to get to Matthias as quickly as possible to understand the circumstances, see the alleged killer with his own eyes, and most of all, speak with the person himself.

Ali returned to the office and told Elise they were leaving immediately. The wind whipped their faces when they stepped outside the bar. The air felt moist as though a storm were imminent.

"It's another body, isn't it?" she said, as they walked along the sidewalk.

Ali wondered how she could have possibly known.

"I've had this feeling," she said. "I've had it since last night. God help me, I hope I'm wrong."

Ali realized the obvious, that her sister hadn't shown up at the rendezvous. He'd been so focused on the alleged killer's identity that he hadn't thought about the implications for Elise at all.

A gust of wind sobered him up just enough for him to realize that he wasn't entirely sober at all, and as they approached his car, Ali tried to remember if there was a bodega on the way to the station where he could buy a large cup of coffee so he didn't show up looking like a —

He heard a thump between his ears. Pain wracked his head. His knees gave out from under him and his vision blurred.

Ali fell to the ground. He saw the arc of a man's boot headed toward the side of his head and told himself to move but his reactions were too slow. Another sharp sting in the head was accompanied by the sound of a foot connecting with his cranium.

As Ali's eyes pressed shut, the last thing he saw was two men descending on Elise and two more emerging from behind him. One of the men wrapped duct tape around her mouth while the other three corralled and lifted her up. Ali watched as the four masked men hustled past him, further away from the hookah bar, where life had seemed tranquil and manageable, and then everything turned black.

CHAPTER 32

Elise recognized Darby's men as they snuck up toward Ali. She assumed they were coming to free her, until she saw one of them raise a blackjack over his head. Even before the man hammered Ali's skull, the other two men grabbed Elise from behind and a third taped her mouth shut. They were trained, confident and physically fit. She had no chance of escape. Before she knew it, Elise found herself bound and gagged in the trunk of the sedan she'd seen circling by the promenade.

If they were sure they wanted to kill her, she'd probably already be dead, Elise thought. They didn't need the risks associated with keeping her alive and conscious in the trunk of a car, such as being discovered during a traffic stop or an accident. They could have injected her with a lethal substance or broken her neck. They still might kill her later, she realized, depending on what they learned from her about the rendezvous.

She could predict their questions. *Why didn't the girl show up? Why did a cop accompany her? Why didn't she warn Darby that the cops were onto her?* Ali carried himself with a cocky sense of entitlement that most cops possessed without even knowing. Darby's men might have guessed who he was instinctively, or they might have snapped his picture and run it through a database they'd hacked and identified him. These were all questions she'd soon be asked and her answers might dictate whether she lived or died. For no matter how much Christendom valued its personnel, no individual was more valuable than a local network that had taken years to assemble.

En route to whatever destination her captors had in mind, Elise gathered her senses and prepared to fight for her life. Until she was certain that Valerie was dead, her personal mission was incomplete, and she'd do whatever was necessary to stay alive to see it through to the end.

Ironically, she wished she hadn't destroyed the GPS device. If it were still operational, Ali could have tracked her and caught up to her captors. But now, thanks to the precautions she'd taken to prevent him from following her if she needed to escape for whatever reason, he'd never come to her rescue.

Elise knew she was on her own.

CHAPTER 33

Ali woke up to find a pair of twenty-somethings in hiking gear and backpacks leaning over him and shaking his shoulders. They asked him if he was okay and if he needed an ambulance. He responded by standing up, albeit with their assistance. Ali thanked the good Samaritans—anarchists, he thought, because people who slept in the forest, by definition, loathed society—and climbed into his car. The blow to his head had knocked the cannabis high out of him and replaced it with a concussion of unknown severity. Ali tested himself by trying to remember his name, address, occupation and current personal and professional circumstances. The answers came quickly and with depressing clarity.

He drove directly to Matthias Church, the ache in his head exceeded by the tenderness in the place where he'd been hit. He steered with his left hand and turned on his GPS tracking device with his right. The device wouldn't come to life—it seemed frozen. Ali swore out loud, then realized that for the moment, this was irrelevant. Even if it were working, he couldn't do anything to help Elise. Zaman had given him explicit instructions that should anything go wrong he was on his own. He couldn't call for help. No one would come to his assistance. Thus, hard as it was, he pushed aside his concern about her life for now, and thought only of his impending meeting with the accused killer.

When he arrived at Matthias, it was clear that this time, news of the murder had not been effectively suppressed. Twenty or more dhimmis stood gathered near the police tape, and vehicles representing the state-controlled media outlets were omnipresent. Two dhimmis were seated in the back of a police cruiser, hands folded in the their laps. Material witnesses, Ali thought, waiting to be driven to the station so that their statements could be taken.

Ali flashed his ID and stormed into the church with a disturbing sense of déjà vu. Every wall sconce and overhead light shone but the church was still dim. Three uniformed cops stood chatting beside the altar while two CSI technicians knelt before it examining something. Ali assumed it was the body, no doubt wrapped in a blanket.

Ali looked around for Ismael. He found him sitting alone in a pew. His friend was leaning forward, head hanging in the pew in front of him, hands cuffed behind his back. Sitting with one's hands cuffed behind one's back—metal digging into bone, shoulders straining and back aching—was one of life's truly miserable experiences. But for a man's who'd finally been revealed to be a serial murderer, perhaps it was less excruciating, Ali thought. Perhaps there was a measure of relief that came from the type of confession Ali had just made himself.

Except, in this case, Ali didn't believe it. Not for a minute. Ismael was a decorated crime fighter, among the most respected in all of Eurabia. And he was a Muslim. He believed in righting the wrong, not creating it.

Ali started toward Ismael when he heard his boss' voice.

"Where have you been?" Zaman said.

Ali's hand went to his wound of its own accord. "I was delayed."

"Where's the Christian woman? Did you drop her off at the station?"

"We can talk about her later. What's the evidence against Ismael?"

"The evidence is he's a murdering piece of shit," Zaman said. "That's the evidence. He took his hatred of the dhimmi a bit too far."

"Ish isn't a killer," Ali said.

"How do you know?"

"Because he loves his job. And it's his job to solve crimes, not commit them. How could a man who investigates crime scenes to solve murders also commit them?"

"Easy," Zaman said. "He's called a crooked cop."

Ali shook his head. "I don't believe it."

"Well then, believe this. The dhimmis that guard this place—the neighborhood patrol—they caught him carrying the dead girl's body into the church. It was wrapped in a blanket. And the body had been washed and anointed with oil just like the other ones. How much you want to bet that the girl's still a virgin like the other nine, too?"

"They said they saw Ismael bringing the body into the church?" Ali said.

"No, Ali. They said 'watch this video' of the man bringing the body into the church."

"They made a video?"

"They're the neighborhood dhimmi church patrol. They can't carry weapons so they carry cameras instead. Got to give them credit, no?"

"And what does Ismael have to say?"

"Nothing," Zaman said. "An innocent man would have jumped up and down and said he didn't do it."

"He said nothing?"

"He asked for you."

Ali started toward Ismael, less certain about his friend's innocence. There was no logical reason for Ismael to have been at the church if not for the purpose demonstrated in the alleged video—to deliver the body of the girl he'd murdered. He couldn't have been investigating the crime scene as it related to Greta Gaspar's murder—the church had been re-opened to its faithful. And Ismael certainly couldn't have had personal business in the church. That was even more preposterous. His perverse and relentless sense of humor constantly demonstrated how much he loathed dhimmis.

Ali remembered how he'd hid the truth about the sins of his past from his wife, and how Elise had told him she'd been lying to herself her entire adult life. He wondered how well anyone knew anybody else.

"The Christian woman," Zaman said from behind. "She's at the station. She's healthy and in one piece, right?"

Ali continued onward, lifting the index finger of his right hand to signal that he'd be right back. When he got to the pew in question, Ismael turned and saw him.

"It's over for me," Ismael said.

Ali slid into the pew beside his friend. "What's over for you?"

Ismael stared at the body lying on the floor in front of the altar. "Now everyone's going to know what I am."

For the first time since Zaman had called him at the hookah bar, Ali began to think like a cop instead of a friend. Ismael fit the killer's limited physical description—he was of average height and build. He travelled all over Eurabia training crime scene investigators—he could have easily been visiting the various cities when the murders of the other seven girls had taken place. Also, Ismael had scouted the perimeter of the Curry House before the noon rendezvous between the Gentleman from Prague and the owner of the Persian School of Dressmaking, Miss Mona. There'd been ample time for him to slip into a robe and bribe the retired cab driver to show up at the Curry House pretending to be the killer. And then there was the most damning evidence of all—why the hell else would he be photographed carrying a dead child at the dhimmi church? For the first time since Zaman had called, Ali began to accept the high probability that Ismael must have loathed the dhimmis far more than he'd ever imagined.

"And what are you, Ish?" Ali said.

"I'm a dead man."

CHAPTER 34

Elise sat in a comfortable Scandinavian chair before a wood-burning fireplace in the remote cabin, her spirits considerably improved.

They'd driven for half an hour, which meant they were probably fifteen to twenty kilometers outside of Budapest. When Darby's men opened the trunk and let her out, she saw forest all around her. The cabin wasn't the rundown shelter one might have expected Christendom to use as sanctuary for its agents and assets, but rather a slick contemporary structure made from black and mahogany timber panels. Odd-shaped windows—a triangle, circle, and a parallelogram—confirmed that the building looked more like the hunting lodge of an eccentric dentist and less like a safe house.

Darby's men removed the tape from her mouth and apologized for their rough treatment of her. They said they couldn't waste time on the street trying to convince her to go with them, and didn't want her visible in the car just in case they were stopped for an alleged traffic violation or a random search—just as Elise had suspected. She had to agree with them that the most mundane occurrence could wreck even the most carefully crafted plan.

They escorted her into the cabin which was appropriately sleek, with a minimalist décor consisting of glass and light colored wood furnishings. They brought her a carafe of water, some cheese and crackers, and left her alone in a living room in front of the roaring fire.

Elise walked the perimeter of the room and looked out the door and windows to see where the men had positioned themselves. She found two of them sitting in the kitchen and the other two walking around outside. Both of the men inside the house effectively prevented her from leaving. None of the windows in the living room opened and she would have had to cross their line of vision if she decided to make a run for it. Not that she was in a hurry to escape. If they wanted her dead, they wouldn't be feeding her, she thought. Plus, she didn't know what plight awaited her in jail.

Elise waited for almost an hour until the distant sound of a car engine grew louder and was accompanied by a pair of shining headlights. Darby arrived in a late model Mercedes Benz.

He greeted her with a pleasant smile. He was dressed in a blue blazer and charcoal slacks and carried a small black leather bag that doctors might have used in a prior century to store their tools and medicines.

"How is your tooth?" he said.

"What tooth?" Elise ran her tongue over the stump that remained. "I sacrificed it for your cover."

He winced. "I know you did."

"And this is my reward? Bound, gagged, lifted off the street and locked in the trunk of a car?"

"The trunk of a car?" Darby glanced at the door as though he was contemplating berating his men. Then he looked back, saw the carafe and scowled even more. "And all they gave you is water and cheese?"

"What should they have given me?"

"Some fine wine, obviously. But my good fortune they didn't. We'll have a chat, share a glass, and then I'll have them run you back to the hotel where the delegation is staying. One of the emissaries will go with you to the police station, and you'll be out in no time."

"I'll be out in no time?"

Darby snapped his fingers and grinned. "You're being released. Don't you know that?"

"No." It was too good to be true, Elise thought. "How do you know that?"

"Christendom has been working relentlessly to get you released since you didn't return to the hotel after your meeting with the man in the wheelchair."

Elise wanted to kiss a cross. "They have?"

"You didn't know." Darby studied her. "The police didn't tell you."

Elise shook her head.

"Bloody brilliant. They had you believing you'd be disavowed, didn't they?"

"Well…"

Darby put his bag on a table and sat down on a sofa opposite Elise. "Who was the fellow at the statue?"

Elise barely heard him. Relief gave way to ambition. Now that she was to be freed, Elise was already wondering how she could get to Valerie again before departing Eurabia.

She looked at Darby. "The man at the statue? He was the cop that arrested me."

Darby lifted his eyebrows.

"But he was alone. I'm sure of it. It wasn't about the man in the wheelchair or the treasure."

Darby smiled politely. "On the contrary. *Everything* is about that treasure. Now, tell me what you've done with it and we can have that glass of claret. I've been saving it for a special occasion."

"What do you mean 'what have I done with it?'"

"We've learned from our informant—actually, we learned it from our informant in the Kingdom of Hindu who learned it from their informant in the Kingdom of Buddha who have an informant here in Eurabia—that the treasure was sealed in the bellies of four ceramic cats—one to be sold to each of the major theocracies–and that three of those cats were present at the murder scene. But the fourth is missing."

"I don't have it," Elise said. "Why do you think I have it?"

"Because stealing it would have been the smart move. There are treasures, and then there are treasures. We're all human, and as humans when we dream, we dream of money."

"I thought we dreamed of freedom and equality."

"Exactly," Darby said. "You can find those on a faraway island, and those islands are very, very expensive."

"You're being ridiculous. I'm not motivated by money. What about the housekeeper? No one had more opportunity than her."

"An illiterate, invalid leper? I don't think so. She doesn't know how to spell treasure let alone sell it on the black market. You, on the other hand…"

Elise stood up. "I what? I had my tooth drilled to keep up your appearances. My loyalty to Christendom has no price."

"Whenever someone says it's not about money," Darby said, "it's always about money. There's always a price."

Elise stormed toward the door but one of Darby's men appeared and blocked her path.

"You're not going anywhere until you answer my question," Darby said. He stood up, took his jacket off, and reached for his black bag. "And you will answer it one way or another. Now, where is the treasure you stole from the man in the wheelchair?"

CHAPTER 35

Ali touched Ismael's shoulder. There was no substitute for the touch of another human being during a time of despair. No matter what he'd done, Ismael was still his friend.

"Why are you a dead man, Ish?" Ali said.

"Because no one will ever forgive me," Ismael said. "And no one will ever forgive her."

"Forgive who?" Ali glanced from Ismael to the body at the altar and back at his friend. "This girl? Or the other girl, Greta Gaspar? Or all the girls in all the towns?"

Ismael stared straight ahead. "One girl. There's only one girl."

Ali shook his friend's shoulder. "Ish, you're not making sense. You asked for me, remember? Zaman said you wouldn't talk to anyone else. So I'm begging you, speak to me, friend. What girl? How can you say there's only one girl when there were nine? And now ten?"

Ismael nodded, then turned to Ali and frowned. "What are talking about? Are you saying I killed all these dhimmi girls? Your grandmother's vagina, A."

"So you didn't kill them?"

Ismael glared at him.

Ali sat up straighter. "All right, all right. That's more like it. Why didn't you tell Zaman?"

Ismael scanned the room on the sly and lowered his voice further. "Because he wouldn't understand. It would be all over for me as soon as he learned the truth. And all over for her, too."

"All over for who, Ish? Who are you talking about?"

Ismael sighed. "My girlfriend."

"Your girlfriend? What girlfriend? You have a girlfriend?"

"She's a dhimmi. A divorced dhimmi."

Ali stared at his friend in disbelief. Sitting before him was the last person he knew who would ever associate with a non-Muslim in a fraternal let alone a romantic way.

Ismael seemed to deduce what Ali was thinking, because he cast a knowing look at him. "We can't control who we fall in love with, A."

An image of Sabida greeting him in the doorway of his home with his suitcases packed flashed before Ali. The suitcases were still in the trunk of his car.

"How does your girlfriend explain what you were doing here?" Ali said.

"This is her church. She comes to pray here every day. You have to admit, it's a beautiful place. All the gold icons, the statues, the pictures. It's peaceful, man. I was waiting for her outside after work. I didn't see anyone from any neighborhood watch. I was just standing all alone, enjoying the air, when all of a sudden she comes running out, shouting and screaming."

"What was she saying?"

"'Call an ambulance, call an ambulance. I think she's dead, I think she's dead.'"

"She saw the body?" Ali said.

"She was carrying the body. She said she was praying in the pews and saw this bundle near the altar and figured it was something the priest had left. I mean, no one walks up that close to the altar unless you have a reason and curiosity got the better of her."

"And what did you do?"

"What do you think I did? I saw right away that the kid had been dead for hours, checked for a pulse anyways, then took the body back into the church."

Now Ali understood. "To recreate the crime scene."

"I knew what the prior crime scene looked like and there was nothing to it. Just a bundle in front of the altar. Plus I was fighting for our lives at that point. I didn't want anyone to see us."

"And that's when the neighborhood watch shot a video of you."

Ismael nodded. "I told Gabriela to run as soon as I took the body from her so that no one would see us together. She's probably outside right now with all the other dhimmis waiting for me to come out. Man, she's going to be devastated when she sees me in cuffs."

Ali didn't need to ask Ismael why he feared being exposed as a dhimmi woman's lover. His colleagues would look at him differently, and none would ever trust him completely again. After all, he was consorting with the people the government was trying to tax out of the kingdom. And the same could be said for his girlfriend. Once Dhimmi Town learned she was dating a Eurabian cop, she'd be ostracized.

"I'm going to have to tell Zaman the truth," Ali said. "But I think I can do it in a way that keeps your girlfriend out of it."

"Really?"

"You were going for a walk, just happened to be passing by, some woman comes running out carrying a body … You take it from her. You don't know if the girl is alive or dead and you see a storm is brewing, you feel the raindrops, and you want to give her shelter. And you need light to see what's going on. So you hurry back inside the church to get that shelter and get that light…"

Ismael brightened. "Come to think of it, that's not that far from the truth."

"You have a picture of this Gabriela?"

"A picture? What for?"

Ali checked his watch to see how much time had passed since he'd been hit over the head. "So I can find her outside and get our story straight. Come on, Ish. Do you have a picture of her?"

"Wallet. Front right pocket."

Ali fished the wallet out and found the picture of an unremarkable middle-aged woman.

You really can't control who you fall in love with, Ali thought.

He hurried out of the church to find her.

CHAPTER 36

Elise realized that she'd misjudged Darby's concerns from the beginning. She thought he'd be worried that she might expose him as Christendom's man in BP to win her freedom, and that his primary agenda would be to confirm that she hadn't sold him out during questioning. But he told her that he wasn't worried about her discretion. The cops weren't going to subject her to the type of brutality needed to extract her contact's name, he said, not when the world was desperately trying to sustain some measure of harmony.

Now she understood. It really was all about the proof of God. He'd never called it such. He'd only referred to it as "the treasure." But she suspected he knew exactly what it was Christendom had sent her to purchase. Darby didn't strike Elise as one of the blindly allegiant. He behaved more like an informed fanatic.

And she'd had more than enough of him this evening.

"For the umpteenth time," Elise said. "When I left his house the night before, the man in the wheelchair's head was still attached to his body. His housekeeper escorted me in and out. The next day when I showed up, the door was ajar but no one answered. I went inside and found his head detached from his body. And I found three decapitated ceramic cats. Then the cops came flying out of the walls. They were everywhere. They were waiting for me."

"And did you examine the insides of these ceramic cats?"

"They were eye-level on a table. They were hollow inside. There was enough space to store a computer chip or a rolled up piece of paper. But there was nothing inside any of them."

Darby opened his black leather bag. "So you say."

"Yes, so I say. And let me ask you something, Doctor Darby. If I'd acquired the treasure, how could I still have it if the cops arrested me and strip-searched me?"

Darby considered the question as he unzipped the bag. "That thought occurred to me, which is why if you do have the treasure, you had to have acquired it last night, the first time you went to his apartment."

"And how exactly did I do that? Bribe the man in the wheel-chair with a bunch of diamonds I bought with my meager life savings? Because I didn't get the diamonds until today."

Darby shrugged. "You have an answer for every question, which is to be expected. You're a spy. There's only one remaining course of action for a situation like this." He peered into his bag.

The room had become insufferably hot. Elise waited for Darby to pull out a weapon. His dentist's drill would work just fine, she thought, especially in the absence of Novocain.

Instead, he pulled out a bottle of wine.

"Best way to transport a *haram* libation," Darby said, grin-ning. "No one wants to see the inside of a dentist's office, or his black bag." He pulled out a corkscrew. "Sorry about the Span-ish inquisition. Procedure, you know? Obviously I believe you. From the moment I met you I could see you were obsessed with the extraction of that girl, not money. Now let's have some of this claret."

Elise followed him into the kitchen where the two guards sat reading papers at the table. He'd given up his absurd accusation so quickly that she had difficulty accepting his sincerity. But Darby certainly was sounding and behaving as though he believed her.

He pulled out two glasses and uncorked the wine.

"Speaking of extraction, what did happen to the girl?" he said.

"No show," Elise said.

"And the cop? Why was he there?"

Elise told him about the dhimmi murder at Matthias, Ali's investigation, and how Valerie might have helped him with his investigation.

"The girl they found at the church altar," Darby said. "I heard about that. But the Eurabian police ... they don't really care about a dead dhimmi girl, do they? Is this fellow really investigating, or just going through the motions?"

"Given he took me from jail to the statue on his own, I think you can answer that for yourself."

Darby looked at Elise and struck a reflective pose. "Yes, he does seem motivated, doesn't he? I wonder why ..."

The question hung in the air as he turned to his men and told them to gather the others and go home. Darby thanked them and told them he wouldn't need them anymore this evening. The men rose and left.

Meanwhile, Elise stood in the kitchen trying to make certain she wasn't imagining what she'd just heard. It wasn't the dismissal of the four men that were supposed to drive her back to Budapest that had caught her attention. It was the manner in which Darby had delivered the message.

He hadn't spoken in his usual broken Arabic and poor accent. Darby had delivered his order in a fluent and mellifluous manner. She wondered why he'd hid his fluency from her and all his employees. No answer occurred to her immediately, and the question left her unsettled for reasons she couldn't explain.

"The wine would have been wasted on them," he said, "and a man hates to be rude to his staff. Sending them home was the best compromise. More for us, yes?"

He aligned the screw over the cork, gripped the bottle with the vise ring attached to the device, and tried to lift the lever which would force the screw through the cork. But he winced before he could complete the process, dropped the corkscrew on the counter and massaged his wrist vigorously.

"My wrist," he said. "Repetitive motion injury. The perils of dentistry."

Elise glanced at his hand. Then she remembered something Ali had told her earlier tonight. A horrific thought occurred to her and a sense of impending doom seized her.

Outside, a pair of cars started. Headlights shone through the window, and Darby's men drove away.

Elise tried to speak but choked on her first few words. She so dreaded what she might discover that she had to swallow and start her sentence again.

"I don't remember you speaking Arabic so beautifully at your offices," she said.

"It pays to remain inscrutable, in life and in business. Better all the locals—employees and patients alike—underestimate me, don't you think?"

"Makes sense," Elise said. "Where did you learn it?"

"In Maharashtra, on the road between Mumbai and Agra. I was stationed there as a technical consultant for the Kingdom of Hindu in my prior incarnation. Rugged territory, but oh the curry."

"Mmm," Elise said, but her mind was not on food but rather Ali's description of the killer, which he'd shared on the way to the hookah bar.

She'd never measured Darby before but now observed that he was of average height and build. He spoke perfect Arabic, something was wrong with his wrist, and he loved curry. It was impossible, Elise thought. Based on the devotion to Western ideals and Christianity he'd conveyed in his philosophical musings, Darby was among the least likely men she'd ever suspect of being a killer of dhimmi girls.

And yet, much to her shock, he was the killer. She certain of this, not only for the reasons that had just occurred to her but because an insufferable tension had spread through the room. With this realization, Alice's fight or flight instincts kicked-in, and she understood that her own life was in imminent danger.

"I wish you hadn't mentioned curry," she said, drifting around the perimeter of the kitchen to give herself a better chance of getting to the door before he could stop her. "I didn't have dinner and now you've made my mouth water."

Elise fired a glance at the exit. When she looked back at Darby, she realized she'd been unlucky. He'd lifted his eyes from one of the glasses mid-pour and caught her plotting her route of escape. That's all it took for a man so experienced in detecting human emotion—one look.

Darby finished pouring two glasses in silence while Elise's heart pounded in her ears. Then he brought them over and handed her one.

"Cheers," he said, and raised his glass for her to clink it.

Elise answered in kind and obliged. She watched her hand, praying that she'd be able to keep it steady. When she managed to do so, she savored a small measure of victory. But her satisfaction was short lived.

Darby studied her with a wry smile. "You think I'm a monster, don't you?"

The ruse was over, Elise thought. He knew she knew he was the killer.

"What?" she said, doing her best acting job. "No. Why would you say such a thing?"

"Oh, come now. We both know what we're talking about here. Let's not waste time pretending otherwise."

He was going to kill her any minute, Elise thought. He couldn't trust her no matter how much she tried to convince him otherwise. He had to eliminate her out of self-preservation. It was the smart move.

Elise scrambled to come up with a plan. She wasn't trained in self-defense. It was rule number one where Christendom's spycraft was concerned. Self-defense skills compromised a spy's commitment to her cover. It also reduced the odds of a spy's survival behind enemy lines, because the moment the spy fought or ran she was confirming the enemy's suspicions and she was dead. A spy who didn't fight or try to escape, but rather maintained her cover always had a greater chance of surviving than the one who did. This had been the philosophy of the former Soviet Union's notorious secret police, the KGB. Christendom's spymasters had borrowed from the best. Given her current circumstances, however, Elise wished her employer had borrowed from someone else.

When no plan came to her, Elise decided her optimal strategy was to stall.

"Why did you kill those girls?" she said.

Darby raised his eyebrows and sighed as though she'd asked an important or complicated question—she couldn't tell which. But when he took a sip of wine, scrunched his forehead in deep concentration and began speaking, Elise exhaled. She suspected she'd just bought some time. Based on her experiences in his dental chair, Darby loved to hear his own voice as much as the Cardinals.

"The Muslim fascination with blondes goes back to Byzantine days," Darby said, "to the eighth century. It was the last vestige of the Roman Empire, in the city now known as Istanbul, which was the front line against the Islamic assault. Muslims gushed over the Byzantine woman's blond hair, blue and green eyes, and their figures. The Byzantine maiden was the most coveted slave from Muslim conquest.

"Fast forward more than a thousand years and nothing changed. When European countries opened their borders to immigration and decided to become multi-cultural, the countries formerly known as Sweden and Denmark became the rape capitals of the world. Eighty percent of those rapes were committed by Muslim men. Scandinavian women started dying their hair to cut the odds they'd be attacked by a stranger. This was long before Eurabia became reality."

"You can't blame an entire religion for what some men did," Elise said, "unless you have the evidence to back it up. Statistically, those men probably amount to an asterisk. That's racist and bigoted."

"There's nothing vague about what went on there or in England. Rotherham, Rochdale, Derby, Oxford, Bristol, Telford, Banbury, Keighley, Halifax ... and those are just the towns we know about where someone came forward. Where witnesses weren't intimidated. Muslim men trafficking in under-aged English girls—in their case, hair color be damned as long as they're not Muslim. *Thousands* of girls abused and barely a headline around the globe. And the media and the politicians unwilling to make an issue of it for decades. *For decades*, man. Since when is an enlightened man afraid to ask questions, no matter how politically incorrect they may seem?"

"Was the West that enlightened after World War II?" Elise said, "when it carved up Arabia randomly and put its puppets in charge of the countries? It ended up creating a world of slums. Take away their opportunity, and some men lose their way."

"Yes," Darby said, "but they always have their religion, don't they? And therein lies the problem. Their religion is governed by a literal interpretation of eighth century ideals. There's been no enlightenment. They say God created the laws of Islam. Well, God created reason, too, didn't he?"

Elise pressed the point as his devil's advocate, to buy time and extend her life expectancy.

"Were the Crusades in the name of Jesus—the so-called Prince of Peace - reasonable?" she said. "Was the Inquisition reasonable? The rack and the head crusher?"

"Obviously not," Darby said. "But the Crusades were almost a century ago. Again, I ask—where is the reformation of Islam? And for that matter, where the hell are all the moderate Muslims? You know, all those decades of jihadism before Europe became Eurabia, and I never saw a moderate Muslim community protest against the so-called extremists. Well, the time for protests has long passed. I'm interested only in action."

"What kind of action?"

"The definitive kind. Did you know they keep a list at the top slave training schools called Girls of Yellow? I posed as a broker for wealthy individuals looking to acquire a slave—forged some references, even had an asset act as a legitimate one—and got some of those lists in several cities. They came complete with pictures of the girls and thorough personality evaluations. Can you imagine something so vile?"

"I'm confused. If someone's looking to acquire a slave, wouldn't they want to see the candidate's picture?"

"My dear, the Girls of Yellow isn't a list of slave prospects."

"What is it then?"

"It's a list of matrimonial candidates."

Elise shuddered.

"A Muslim man is allowed to have four wives and he's allowed to marry his slave. There's nothing some wealthy and powerful men want more than to have a girl of yellow among them."

Perhaps this explained why Valerie was so scared, Elise thought. All the girls probably knew there was such a list.

"The legal age for marriage in Eurabia is sixteen," Darby said. "You think a sixteen year-old girl is mature enough to decide she's ready for marriage? Of course it doesn't matter—most of the time the decision's been made for her. And that age is often a technicality. Many clerics sanction even younger brides. They have throughout the Islamic world for centuries. After all, the prophet Muhammad was fifty-three when he consummated his marriage to a nine year-old wife."

"And your solution is what, to kill the girls?"

Darby looked aghast. "Heaven forbid. I'm not killing them. I'm liberating them. I'm accelerating their path to heaven and falling on the sword for them. I'm the one who's going to burn in hell for all of eternity. Not them. But it's worth it. Anything to prevent our most precious girls from being defiled by men using an ancient religion to justify their abuse."

Elise could barely keep her voice steady enough to ask her final question. If Darby answered her as she suspected he might, she feared she would come mentally unhinged.

"And what of the girl who was supposed to meet me tonight?" she said. "What of the girl we were going to extract?"

"Oh, you mean your sister?" Darby smiled. "I couldn't help but see the resemblance. Stunning girl. She was ranked number one on BP's list of Girls of Yellow."

Elise took a breath. "Did you liberate her, too?"

Darby's eyes radiated compassion. "The sanctity of her soul … is in God's hands."

Elise kicked Darby in the groin.

He screamed and doubled-over.

She wanted to plunge a kitchen knife through his left eye, stuff his head into the kitchen sink disposal, or beat him to a pulp with her bare hands. But he was merely stunned, not incapacitated, and her fight or flight instincts took charge again. The next thing Elise new she was rushing to the exit and turning the handle, only to find that the front door wouldn't open. She spun the knob the other way and yanked with all her might. Only then did she see the deadbolt securing the door to its frame.

One of the guards had locked it from the outside, she realized.

She couldn't escape without a key.

He was upon her almost as soon as she heard him moving. Darby pulled her back from the door. Only when she started falling did Elise see that he'd thrust his leg out to trip her up, and as she tumbled he fell on top of her. His hands were around her throat and squeezing before she could collect herself.

She tried to roll to one side to no avail. He extended his elbows and kept his neck arched to prevent her from clawing at his eyes. Darby had much longer arms than Elise, and the highest she could reach was his own neck. She wrapped her hands around it but by then she was already fading, alarm registering in her brain that she was going to run out of air.

She squeezed his neck as hard as she could but the muscles surrounding it felt like knots. Panic gripped her. She kicked, punched, and tried to thrust her fingers in his eyes but all for naught. And then as her face began to burn, the sensation that it was going to burst from the blood becoming all too real, an eerie calm fell over her.

An image from primary school flashed before Elise. Her Spanish teacher, Miss Joba, stood in front of the class telling the story of an old man who lifted an automobile when it rolled over his torso and trapped him under one of its tires. People were capable of extraordinary feats of strength, she told the class, and the source of that strength was God.

As that lesson echoed in her ears, Elise squeezed Darby's neck and began to pray. She prayed that God would forgive Valerie for all her sins and welcome her into heaven. She prayed that God would forgive Valerie's mother for all her sins, too. But most of all, Elise prayed that God would give her the strength to kill Darby before he killed her.

When that final thought flitted in and out of her mind, Elise realized the absurdity of the tale her Spanish teacher had spun. Darby was twice her size and strength. She was going to die and there was nothing she or God could do about it.

Her grip slackened. Black splotches filled her vision.

And then she rose, forcing Darby up and onto his back, and tumbled atop him, their hands still wrapped around each other's necks. Elise couldn't understand what was happening. She hadn't experienced any magical surge of strength, and yet she'd clearly overpowered him. Yes, she was not imagining things. She really was on top of him. He was writhing beneath her. She squeezed his neck with all her might, which didn't feel like much—

It was the Holy Ghost, Elise realized. She'd prayed to the Father, the Son and the Holy Ghost, and her prayers had been answered. It was the Holy Ghost who'd assumed control of her body. It was through his mystical ways that she was overpowering a man twice her size and strength, just like the man who'd lifted a car in Miss Joba's story. This meant that if the proof God really existed, it would show that all the dead who were rising were Christian. The Christians could rise to power again!

Air entered her lungs. Elise began to cough. Gulp after gulp, she consumed air frantically. And somewhere along the path to cardiovascular recovery, Elise regained her sense of smell and realized something very strange. The Holy Ghost smelled of musk and man. Not only that, he had hands, too. Big, hairy hands with a vise grip …

Elise saw the second set of hands beneath hers were real and realized that another human being had pinned Darby to the floor. A ferocious glint shone in this man's eyes as he gnashed his teeth and strangled Darby. Elise's prayer had been answered in the form of assistance, she realized, not divine intervention.

She didn't release her grip from Darby's neck until long after he was dead.

Neither did Ali.

CHAPTER 37

Ali lay exhausted on the floor beside the dead man, his right leg stinging from the cut he'd suffered when he'd snuck into the house by breaking a window. Elise lay on the floor beside him, back propped up by her hands, lungs still heaving.

"How did you get in?" she said.

"Bedroom window. Ground level. I assume you know this man."

"How did you find me?"

"GPS unit."

"Impossible," Elise said. She gathered the bottom of her *ibaya* and found the tracking unit that had been sewn into its lining. "This thing? I crushed it with my shoe. There's no way it's working. No way."

"Not that one. I used a back-up just in case the first one malfunctioned."

"Where is it?"

"In your right shoe. The one you used to crush the primary unit. The boys in tech imbedded it in the heel. You'd have to be looking for it to see a trace of the incision."

Elise glanced at her shoe and then back at Ali. "Why didn't you just shoot him?"

"I was afraid I'd shoot you."

"Then why didn't you hit him over the head with your gun?"

Ali considered her question. It was a good one because she was right. He should have used the safest form of lethal force. And yet, instead of hammering the killer with his weapon, Ali had chosen to use his hands.

"Rage," Ali said. "I wasn't entirely in control of my faculties." He staggered to his feet and offered his hand to Elise. "Come. I'll show you."

Elise took his hand and he pulled her to her feet. She followed him down the corridor to a room on the far right.

"Careful of the broken glass," Ali said.

Ali stepped aside, let Elise enter the room first, and followed her in.

The room had an aromatic smell to it—woody, earthy and fruity. A dresser had been transformed into a shrine for the killer's victims. Pictures of each dead girl hung on the mirror. Christian crosses, icons and small jars of oils rested on top of the bureau.

"Why did he cover their bodies in oil?" Ali said.

"It was an ancient custom. To seal in the goodness and prevent dangerous spirits and demons from entering."

"Sounds tribal."

Elise ignored his comment and the shards of glass, and marched right up to the mirror to study the victims' photos.

"I don't see her," she said. "I don't see Valerie."

Ali mumbled obscenities under his breath. "There was another murder tonight."

Elise blanched. That was consistent with Darby's statement that the sanctity of Valerie's soul was in God's hands.

"Where?" she said.

"The body was brought to Matthias."

"Did you see it? Did she look like me?"

"What?"

"Did the dead girl look like me?"

Ali shrugged. "I didn't look."

Elise screamed. "How could you not look? What kind of cop are you?"

To his own surprise, Ali understood her anger and managed to contain his dismay even though a woman—and a Christian at that—was yelling at him.

"I had a different agenda," he said.

"Take me to the crime scene. I have to see the body. I have to see it now."

Ali shook his head. "That's impossible. You can't be seen out of jail because you aren't really out of jail. I'm here alone. Come to think of it, an anonymous informant told me about the shrine in this house and I drove out to investigate by myself." Ali paused. "I'll tell you what I can do. I can make some calls on our way out of here and get someone from the crime scene at Matthias to take a picture and send it to me. Assuming I can get someone to help me, you'll see the picture before you get to the station. And while we drive, you're going to tell me exactly who this man is and how you met him."

Ali made the necessary phone calls to get the picture, and then called in the killer's murder.

"Don't you have to be here," Elise said, "when the other cops get here?"

"Nothing is more important than getting you out of here," Ali said. "I'll make up an excuse for leaving later. Something to do with being needed at the crime scene at Matthias. A cross-up in communication or the like—"

Ali's phone rang. He glanced at the screen and was immediately concerned when he saw who was calling. He picked up the call.

"What is it, Chef?" Ali said.

"You know I don't call unless it's important," Florence said.

"I know. That's what scares me."

"Well, the General was in Zaman's office and I delivered them dinner. I was outside the office getting my tray organized before I went back to the elevator and I overheard something. Not that I was eavesdropping or anything..."

"You've caught me at a bad time, Florence. What did you hear?"

"The housekeeper...the one who worked for the man in the wheelchair? She was spotted at the airport."

Ali pressed the phone closer to his ear. "When?"

"Fifteen minutes ago."

"That's incredible."

"But the thing is," Florence said, "I don't think anyone's interested in apprehending her."

"What? Why not?"

"I heard the General say that sometimes it's best to let things lie. And if that's the case, I'm not sure it's in your best interest to go anywhere near her. But I thought you'd want to know."

Ali considered Florence's warning. If Zaman and the General were letting the housekeeper leave Budapest, they had to have a reason.

"Where was she seen at the airport?" Ali said.

"General Aviation Terminal. Next to Terminal One. It's for private planes."

Ali was about to end the call without another word, but then remembered his last lunch with Florence. If the roles had been reversed and Florence had threatened Ali into revealing something he had preferred to keep confidential, Ali wasn't sure he would have made the phone call tonight.

"Florence?"

"Yes, Major?"

"Thank you, Florence."

A slight pause followed, and Ali could sense that he'd been wrong. Somehow, their friendship was far from broken.

"I cook to serve," Florence said.

Ali ended the call and looked at Elise. He needed to get her out of here, and she needed to know if the dead girl at Matthias was her daughter. And yet there was an even greater urgency than either of theirs, he thought. The man in the wheelchair had been a liar and a con artist, but he'd been a tax-paying dhimmi who deserved the protection of the law. In addition to that protection, he also deserved justice in the event a crime was committed against him, and there was no bigger crime than the man's own murder.

"We have to get you to safety," Ali said, "but we're going to make a quick stop, first."

They drove to the airport. Ali parked in front of the entrance to the departure area and put his special parking permit in the windshield. Two limousines were dropping off a family and a businessman, and airport employees were assisting with their luggage.

Ali burst through the doors and looked around inside. A spacious and plush waiting area flanked a courtesy desk. A man in a suit stood behind it smiling and helping passengers. Ali counted six people waiting to board a plane. None of them resembled a leper.

"Who are we looking for?" Elise said, stepping up beside him.

"You'll know when you see her."

Elise's eyes shot up when Ali implied that she knew the person.

The waiting area extended beyond their line of vision, which was obscured by a wall to the right. The sound of an airplane idling came from the same direction, suggesting the gate itself was located in the same area.

Ali stepped forward to see around the wall. Two huge men in suits who looked like expensive bodyguards lifted four suitcases. As they departed toward a spot further beyond Ali's peripheral vision, something flashed in their wake.

It was the metallic glint of a bionic hand.

CHAPTER 38

Elise stood transfixed by the sleek and elegant prosthetic hand, silver knuckles gleaming amidst the matte black metal hand and fingers, all in sharp contrast to the leper's ancient *hijab* and the sores on her face. Elise recognized the housekeeper immediately, and her first thought was of the man in the wheelchair and his likely expression when the woman he considered a friend lifted her blade into the air to sever his head from his body.

The housekeeper had free access to the house and the greatest opportunity to commit the murder. The only question remained her motive. Why would a woman kill a man who cared about her so much that he'd restored her sense of touch with state-of-the-art myoelectric hands that connected with her brain? What could she value more than such thoughtfulness—if not love?

As these questions flitted in and out of Elise's mind, she followed Ali's eyes beyond the wall that was obscuring their vision, and saw that the fingers on the housekeeper's other bionic hand were curled together as though gripping something. Elise took another step forward and realized that the object in the housekeeper's hand was, in fact, another hand. The fingers were entirely human, however, supple and smaller. Elise strode further and saw that the hand belonged to a girl. As if sensing the presence of a new arrival, the girl turned and looked at Elise.

The girl was Valerie.

Elise stopped breathing for the second time that evening. Valerie's eyes met Elise's for a split second and continued onward to Ali, then darted back with recognition. Elise held the girl's gaze, sealing her lips and reminding herself not to move or say a word because she didn't understand the current circumstances. The same shadows hung in the corners of Valerie's eyes, even darker than before. How easy it was to spot a child's sadness, Elise thought.

When Valerie turned forward again, Elise glanced at her free hand. Elise realized that it wasn't free at all. In her other hand, Valerie held the fourth ceramic cat. The figurine's bottom had also been cut off. Whatever had been hidden inside had been removed. This cat, too, was hollow.

A man further ahead of Valerie and the housekeeper said something indiscernible to Elise, but his voice sounded distinctly familiar. Elise recognized him from the Persian School of Dressmaking. His name was Moncef Zaid. As she remembered her encounter with him, Elise's thoughts turned to the man's boss, whom he'd accompanied to visit Miss Mona's classroom.

Imam Salim emerged from beyond a wall. The housekeeper followed the bodyguards toward him, black metal fingers engulfing Valerie's petite hand. The radical cleric said something and they all stopped to listen. Elise couldn't make out the words but the mere sound of the man's voice commanded attention. It sounded more like music than human speech.

As his entourage listened and Elise watched, Valerie turned around and glanced at Elise one more time. The fourteen year-old elevated her chin and looked Elise straight in the eyes. Gone were the shadows Elise had detected previously. In their place she saw strength and composure, and a commitment to perse-vere no matter what awaited her beyond the departures gate.

They all left the lounge and boarded the airplane. Elise stood still, paralyzed with joy and frustration.

And just like that, the plane took off down the runway, and Valerie was gone.

CHAPTER 39

As the scene gradually unfolded at the airport, the bionic leper went from person of interest, to prime suspect, to being the killer with ninety-nine percent certainty in Ali's mind. As the murder victim's housekeeper, she had free access to his home, and her employer's trust gave her more opportunity than anyone else. Her motive for murder was now clear as the night was dark. Salim had sunken his religious claws into her. He wanted the treasure that all the kingdoms were trying to buy for himself. She'd killed her boss to get it for him and prevent anyone else from ever acquiring it.

Who knew how Salim had met the bionic leper? The man in the wheelchair dealt in all kinds of antiquities and treasures. Maybe Salim had seduced her with a religious calling for the purpose of acquiring the location of this particular treasure, or perhaps she'd joined his cult in search of contentment and proven to be more useful than he could have ever imagined. Either way, the treasure that the entire world wanted was now in Salim's hands. That was the most likely scenario because Valerie De Jong was holding the missing cat in her hand.

The bionic leper had probably taken the contents of the other three cats, and for some reason taken the fourth intact. Why not take all four? Ali wondered. Why not break the fourth?

The bionic leper had held Valerie's hand in an intimate manner, like an aunt or a nanny. Perhaps she'd thought the ceramic cat would make a nice gift for a girl to whom she'd taken a liking. It didn't matter. What she did or didn't do with the ceramic figurines was irrelevant.

Far more relevant was Salim's destination. If he had the location of the treasure that could benefit or discredit Islam, it was safe to assume that he was flying there to find it. Ali assumed that Elise's sister was accompanying him because Salim had decided to graduate her early from his school and had chosen her to be *his* slave.

None of these conclusions and questions superseded Ali's outrage that the bionic leper was going to get away with murder. She needed to be brought to the station and interrogated. Ali contemplated what he'd do if the housekeeper resisted or the bodyguards engaged him. The personal risk to him was of secondary importance. He couldn't stand by and do nothing while dhimmi's murderer left the city.

Ali started toward Salim's entourage. But then Florence's words echoed in his ears. *I heard the General say that sometimes it's best to let things lie.* If the General was letting the bionic leper escape, that meant he'd weighed the cost and benefit of capturing her, and decided that letting her go was in his best personal interest. If Ali acted in a contrary way, he'd once again incur the General's wrath, who'd be unlikely to forgive him a second time, especially so soon. And if that happened, whom could the remaining dhimmis rely on once he was fired from the police force?

Al retreated and watched Salim and his crew depart. Then he noticed that Elise was doing the same. He murmured for her to drop her eyes but she didn't seem to hear him. Ali had seen the two men who'd just entered the lounge, staring down the passengers and the man at the front desk with a palpable sense of moral superiority. The last thing he needed right now was a showdown with the morality police.

Ali stepped in front of Elise and blocked her view of the window so that she had no choice but to look at him.

"Drop your eyes," he said.

She spotted the two men and promptly lowered her gaze to the floor. As Ali led her to the front desk, the morality police glared at him. Ali ignored them, surprising himself yet again, because a week ago he might have given them a piece of his mind.

He pulled out his police ID and flashed it at the man at the courtesy desk.

"I have an urgent matter to discuss with Imam Salim," Ali said. "Is he on that plane?"

"Yes, sir," the man said. He reached for a telephone. "I'll call the cockpit."

"Out of the question," Ali said. "This must be done in person. Can you tell me where that plane is headed?"

"To the nuclear wasteland," the man said. "To the country formerly known as the United States of America. There will be a great celebration at the Amerabian outpost."

"Why is that?" Ali said.

"Because Imam Salim is getting married. He's taking a fourth wife."

Ali remembered what Miss Mona had told him at the Persian School of Dressmaking. *I'm working on a dress for Imam Salim. Something personal.* It hadn't made sense then, but it did now. She'd been working on a wedding dress, Ali realized.

He glanced at Elise and feared she might respond poorly to this news, which could attract the attention of the morality cops, who might ask questions about her identity, the kind Ali and Elise couldn't answer. Ali nodded toward the exit and reached out to guide her but she needed no assistance. She kept her eyes low and remained silent as though strangely contented.

Ali wondered how Elise could be contented, given Valerie's fate, but then he recalled her confession at the hookah bar and the truth hit him. Elise was contented because Valerie was alive, and Valerie's life mattered more to Elise than whom the girl married. In fact, Valerie's life mattered more to Elise than anything else in the world, including her own life.

Back in the hookah bar, Elise had confounded him with the magnitude of her guilt for not saving her sister from a life of slavery, even though such an outcome was effectively impossible. How could she have stopped the execution of a legal transaction sanctioned by the Kingdom of Islam? Ali kept wondering why she was so hard on herself, but what he should have been questioning was whether Valerie was, in fact, her sister.

When they stepped outside the terminal, a cold wind snapped Ali out of his trance. They climbed into the car and Ali drove. He didn't bring up Valerie, and neither did she. Elise told him about the child killer, a local dentist who'd been recommended to her by more experienced diplomats from Christendom. She never revealed that he was her contact in Budapest because there was no reason to state the obvious. Given he was dead, there also was no reason for her to protect him any longer.

"What about this treasure?" Ali said. "If Salim knows it's location and he's headed to Amerabia..."

"That means the dead are rising in the land of Satan."

"Excuse me?"

Elise chuckled. "The kind of treasure he's seeking, people have been looking for it since Adam and Eve, and I suspect they'll be looking for it forever. I think the man in the wheelchair was an even better con artist than anyone realized."

Ali waited, hoping she would reveal more about the treasure but she didn't. It didn't feel right to him to inquire any more about it, so he continued onward the rest of the way in silence. He wanted to drive Elise to her hotel, but he parked in front of a familiar building in Pest instead.

"Your hotel is close by," he said, "but all the places where the delegations are staying are under surveillance for obvious reasons. It's probably best for both of us that we don't get caught on camera together given I was obviously at the dentist's house. Someone might think you were there with me and that can't have happened."

Ali reached into his pocket and pulled out the satchel of diamonds Elise was carrying when he arrested her. He handed her the loot and grabbed a clipboard from the back seat.

"Sign here, please," he said.

Elise signed the acknowledgment that she'd received all her personal possessions. When she handed the clipboard back to him, Ali grasped it with his hand but didn't pull it away. Elise held onto her end lest it fall, and for a moment it hung in the air suspended between them.

"I want you to understand something," Ali said. He channeled as much emotion as he could muster. "Everything I do that is good … Everything I did tonight … Everything I do is for Allah."

Elise appeared to consider what he'd said carefully, and for that he was eternally grateful.

"Don't worry," she said with a straight face. "Jesus still loves you."

She released her grip of the clipboard. Ali couldn't remember when he'd last smiled, even a smile such as this one, which was only an imaginary one to himself. He stowed the clipboard in the back seat and glanced at her one more time.

"Walk three blocks straight, then take a right. You'll see the hotel where the delegation from Christendom is staying another three blocks up ahead. Good-bye, Elise De Jong."

Ali got out and marched across the street, leaving her alone in the car, suppressing the twinge of regret he experienced upon realizing that he would never see her again.

CHAPTER 40

Elise stepped out of the car and breathed the moist air.

Valerie was alive.

Nothing else mattered. Ironically, Valerie was going back to the place where she was born, for the Amerabian outpost was in the state that had been called Massachusetts and in the city that was known as Boston.

Elise watched as Ali rang a doorbell and spoke into an intercom. A minute later the lights went on inside the building and illuminated a row of barber's chairs in front of a mirrored wall. A man and woman appeared at the front door. They seemed to recognize Ali, and after a few words were exchanged, they let him in. The woman led Ali to the barber's chair nearest the window and extended her hand for him to take a seat. But Ali shook his head and motioned to the man beside the woman, as though suggesting that he take the seat instead. The man did so.

As Ali spoke, the woman massaged the man's shoulders. The ease with which the two comported themselves and the familiarity with which the woman handled the man suggested they were husband and wife. Less than a minute later, Elise knew from their reactions to Ali's speech that her suspicions were true. She knew with absolute certainty who these people were and why Ali had stopped here.

Ali stood with his back against a floor-to-ceiling mirror as he faced the couple and held court. When Elise studied the scene in the mirror, Ali's proximity to it gave him the appearance of being a giant among men. He delivered information without hesitation, doubt or emotion. The couple absorbed it with similar composure until they finally couldn't do so anymore.

Outside, rain began to fall. It started out as hail, chunks of ice that bruised Elise's scalp, but quickly turned to sheets of water. Cars slowed. Pedestrians scattered. Elise stood still, soaked in rain, wiping her eyes, unable to tear herself away from the scene before her. Soon, not another soul could be seen on the street.

As for proof of God, it was everywhere. In the thunder that cracked in the sky and the lightning that flashed across it. In the words of the Muslim cop as he closed the case on a dhimmi's murder. In the tears of Christian parents, as they wept for the loss of their child, and out of gratitude for closure. And in the bravery Elise had seen on her daughter's face when she'd boarded the plane with her future husband.

The logistics of Elise's next plan of action were less than vague. They were entirely unknown. But one thing was certain.

Elise would see that face again.